Snow Maiden

Naomi Hudson

Pixel tweaks
PUBLICATIONS

SNOW MAIDEN

NAOMI HUDSON

ISBN: 978-0-9956190-9-8

Book interior & Cover Design by Russell Holden
www.pixeltweakspublications.com

Cover Photo by Russell Holden

The author can be contacted at bluebellnovel1@gmail.com
or on Facebook under Naomi Hudson

*In memory of Valodya, and for Ludmila,
Sergei and all of my friends in Russia*

PART ONE

SEPTEMBER 1996
to
MARCH 1997

CHAPTER ONE

MOSCOW

Thursday, a wet and cloudy late September day, and the busy summer tourist season was drawing to a close. Many Muscovites had returned to the city from their summer dachas, and the large numbers of tourists had dwindled, now that the hot weather was over. There would be more visitors later in the year, of course, including those who preferred the "winter experience" that Moscow and St Petersburg offered and others who desired a different Christmas or New Year.

Red Square, however, was always busy and small groups of tourists dodged the showers as they headed for GUM after queueing to enter Lenin's Mausoleum or visiting the bauble-domed St Basil's Cathedral. The once-dreary Victorian arcades in GUM had been transformed since the collapse of the Soviet Union and were now full of classy shops run by the international names seen everywhere in the world. Up-market cafes and restaurants vied with each other to lure the visitors away from the gift shops for a short while. The late afternoon saw a gradual trickle of couples and groups, many clutching bags with designer names and heading for a rendezvous with their guides or looking for the nearest metro station to make their way back to their hotels. The square grew quiet for a while, until the illuminations on St Basil's Cathedral and the Kremlin would attract a new wave of evening visitors.

Beyond Red Square, the roads were filling with the late-afternoon traffic, which slowly wheeled around Revolution Square to the theatre district, where more tourists were thronging around the Bolshoi Theatre, searching for tickets or looking for somewhere to eat before the evening show. "Swan Lake" was always a popular draw. The lines of cars edged their way into Lubyanka Square, where the Soviets had built Detsky Mir ("Children's World"), Russia's largest toy store, in 1957. The irony was not lost on many of the city's inhabitants: Detsky Mir was situated directly opposite Lubyanka, the headquarters of the Federal Security Service, successor of the KGB, Russia's feared secret police. Six years earlier, the huge statue of Felix Dzerzhinsky, the hated head of Cheka, the forerunner of the KGB, had been toppled in front of cheering crowds following the unsuccessful coup against President Gorbachev in 1991. The Solovetsky Stone, a monument to victims of political oppression, now occupied the centre of the square, but every day dozens of passing motorists or passengers in tourist coaches glanced or pointed at the colossal building and whispered "KGB", before the weight of traffic whisked them away from the city centre.

***

Inside the vast building, beyond the lavish exterior and the parquet flooring and pale green walls of the entrance hall, the labyrinthine corridors meandered their way down to the lower levels where daylight was not seen. A dimly-lit corridor led to a small conference room, where several people were waiting quietly. The reading-lamp on the table at the front of the room cast shadows in the corners, picking out the swirls of cigarette smoke as they drifted towards the doorway. Footsteps could be heard in the corridor, and a heavily-set man entered the room and sat behind the table. He lit a cigarette and, without glancing around the room, he addressed the shadows.

"We have a problem," he muttered gruffly, "in England." One of the figures in the back corner shifted uneasily in his seat, as the speaker continued. "One of our agents, Boris Nikolaiovich Orlov, has gone missing." He lifted his head, and continued. "One of your network, Rudnev, I think?" He glanced around at the shadows.

"Yes, Sir," a voice from the back corner replied, "I was his original handler. Orlov has always been a reliable agent, so when you say missing, what exactly do you mean?"

"We are still making enquiries," the speaker responded, "but it seems that he has gone native, and moved away from London."

"I did hear a rumour," another voice spoke from the shadows, "that he had become involved with a woman from the north of England, or perhaps from Scotland."

"England, Scotland … I'm not interested." The speaker raised his voice. "I'm more concerned with the information that he holds, and with what he might do with it. An agent such as Orlov would be a useful catch for the British Secret Service … agreed?" One or two heads nodded, and a few mutterings could be heard. "I seem to remember that Orlov was useful in removing nuisances. Is that correct, Rudnev?"

"Yes, of course, he's a big man, very physical, very efficient."

"Perhaps he's become involved in some kind of private protection scheme?" another voice chipped in.

"I don't know," Rudnev replied angrily. "As I stated before, agent Orlov has always been very reliable, very loyal. This all seems to be out of character. I find it hard to believe." He shook his head and squinted around the room, looking for a familiar face, then he lowered his head. In situations such as this, it was usually better not to know who else was in the room.

"Enough!" the speaker sat up quickly. "This is not the time for guesswork. We will, of course, find out more information regarding agent Orlov," he glanced around the room, and one or two shadows nodded in agreement. "When we do, Rudnev, you will be given the information and then I expect you to do," he paused, searching for the appropriate words, "what is necessary. I hardly need to stress that we cannot allow this man to fall into the wrong hands." He looked towards Rudnev's corner. "He must be persuaded to return to Moscow," he drew on his cigarette and sat back in his chair, "or eliminated. Is that clear?"

In the darkened corner, Rudnev and the figure sat next to him both nodded slowly.

CHAPTER TWO
SCARBOROUGH

Karl Griffin pushed his way through the throngs of holidaymakers as he headed for his parents' gift shop on Westborough, the main shopping street in Scarborough. It was the October half-term week, traditionally the last busy trading week in Yorkshire's North Sea resorts, and the many visitors were determined to make the most of the unusually-fine autumnal weather, as well as doing some early shopping for Christmas presents.

Karl shaded his eyes from the sun as he approached the shop, opened the door then stepped back as two female shoppers were leaving the shop. They both carried gift bags and Karl smiled at them as they left, then he looked around the shop for his father. A couple were being served by his mother at the far counter, and he smiled and waved, waiting patiently until his mother had wrapped the gift and taken the payment.

"Where's Dad?" he smiled, glancing again around the shop.

"Well, he told me he was going to the wholesaler's in Whitby, Karl," she answered shrilly, "but I have a feeling that he's disappeared for a sneaky round of golf." Karl laughed. "He seems to have taken more of a back seat since you became involved in the family business," she continued to look peeved, "but *I'm* still working, aren't I?"

"You can't blame him, Mam," he said, putting an arm around her shoulder. "It's such a beautiful day. He won't get many more opportunities this year, will he?" His mother shrugged.

"It's not fair, Karl. I could have enjoyed a day out with my friends. Golf isn't the most important thing in the world."

"It's just about the most important thing in his world, Mam," he said, laughing, "apart from you, of course! Anyway, enough about Dad. I've come here to invite you both for a meal on Friday evening. Maggie and I fancy trying that pub on the Whitby road … I can't remember its name, but it's under new management and has had some rave reviews for its food."

"Friday," his mother thought for a moment, "isn't that your birthday?"

"Yeah, twenty-five-years-old, Mam. Look, it's our treat, so are you coming along?"

"Of course, it will be a nice change, and I'll get to know Maggie a little better."

"What if Dad's playing golf?" Karl laughed, as his mother glared back at him.

"We'll be there, don't you worry. Now, if you don't mind, I have a shop to run…on my own!" she snorted, as she moved along the counter to attend to another customer.

***

Karl smiled to himself as he walked along Eastborough, then took the steps down a narrow alley heading for the harbour. *Life's pretty good*, he thought. It was over three years since he had left university, and after months of deliberating which career path to follow, he had reluctantly agreed to help out with the family business until he had made a final career decision. His parents owned a gift shop selling quality goods on Westborough, and another shop selling traditional tourist souvenirs – cheap rubbish! Karl called it - close to the harbour. In addition, his father had inherited two large houses in the old town area on the South Bay, and had had converted them into small flats for leasing to the tourists in the summer. His parents also owned a larger apartment, a more exclusive holiday let, on the North Bay, and lived in a large family house on the outskirts of the town. In agreeing to help out until he decided upon a career, Karl had insisted that he lived in one of the flats on the South Bay, and he selected one on the top floor, where he could enjoy the splendid views of the harbour. After three years of fending for himself at university, he had no wish to share his private life with his parents.

It was now over two years since Karl had become involved in the family business, and he had to admit, he did like it! Every week was different. Sometimes he helped out in one of the shops, serving customers or organising the stockroom; and he also had spells of supervising the cleaning and maintenance of the holiday flats. There was always the occasional break to go to trade fairs or meet wholesalers, and in recent months his father had begun to involve him more in the business accounts. Karl was a good-looking young man, dark-haired and over six feet tall, and he enjoyed the amount of female attention that he received, particularly in the summer months. He had always been a gregarious person, and he enjoyed the contact with "Joe public". There was no pressure to take life seriously, but now he did suspect that his parents were slowly grooming him to take over the running of the business at some point in the future. He had no brothers or sisters, so it was perhaps inevitable that this would happen at some point in time.

Karl stepped out of the darkness into the bright sunlight on the harbour side, and joined the crowds once more. He enjoyed "people-watching", especially at holiday times, and he spent ten minutes sitting on the shallow wall, close to the piles of lobster-pots and fishing nets, just watching the world go by. Behind him were the small boats and yachts, bobbing gently at their moorings in the harbour, and as Karl glanced towards the slipway he saw parents and children boarding the "Hispaniola", a miniature pirate ship, ready to do another trip around the South Bay. To his right was "Luna Park", with its popular fairground rides, and in front of him there was a constant flow of tourists visiting the shops and cafes on Sandside. Karl thought briefly about visiting the other shop, then decided against it and headed back along another alley towards his flat in the old town.

He fished for his keys as he neared the house, and he looked up again at the blue sky. Great! A quick shower, a pint or two with some friends, then he could catch up with Maggie later on. *Life's pretty good!*

***

The waitress came over to the Griffins' table after they had finished their main courses.

"Would you like a pudding ... sorry, dessert?" she asked, smiling at Karl. He flashed a smile back at her, always pleased to attract another female admirer, while Maggie glared at her.

"I feel pretty stuffed, to be honest," Karl said, glancing at the others, "but if the rest of you fancy some more, then fill your boots!" He laughed. "After all, it's my treat, so make the most of it."

"I've eaten too much already," Karl's mother confessed, glancing at her husband. He knew that look. No pudding.

"How about you, Maggie?" Karl turned to ask the question. A pretty girl, with long dark hair, she shook her head. Karl looked at the waitress. "I think we're fine, thank you, but we'll all have coffee." The waitress smirked, and headed for the kitchen, while Karl leant back in his seat. "I've just remembered," he glanced around the table, "some news I haven't given you."

"Oh," remarked his mother, leaning forward. "You've had a busy birthday, I know, so what have you forgotten to tell us?" She looked at Maggie, and grinned. "Let me guess ... is it something to do with you and Maggie?"

"God, no, Mother, calm down." Karl laughed, but stopped when he saw Maggie's face. "No, it's nothing to do with us, just me. You see, I'm going to Russia next month."

"Russia?" they exclaimed, almost simultaneously. "Russia, Karl," his father continued, "whatever for?"

"Well, I'm not sure if you remember. It was back in June, or July, when I went to Oxford. I didn't say too much at the time, but … just a minute." He paused as the waitress returned with a tray of coffee. "Just leave it on the table, please," he instructed her. "We'll sort it out." His mother began filling cups, as Karl carried on with his story. "Yes, Oxford. I went to see some friends for a week or so, and at the weekend we visited some kind of arts and crafts show at a mansion somewhere near Oxford. Hmm … Waterperry, I think it was called. Anyway, there were some Russian artists in one of the marquees and they were producing some fantastic things, you know, traditional Russian crafts, like those nesting dolls, painted trays, and some beautiful hand-painted lacquered boxes. Lovely miniature painting. I thought they might be an interesting line for the shop, so I bought a few things and," he paused, "I'm sure I showed them to you, Dad?" He raised his eyebrows and looked at his father.

"Yes, come to think of it, you did and I've put them in a cupboard somewhere."

"Somewhere safe?" laughed Maggie. Karl's father smiled, as his son shook his head and continued.

"Typical!" he muttered, glaring at his father. "Anyway, a lady called Irina was acting as an interpreter for the artists, as most of them couldn't speak English. Only one of them knew a bit. He was a sculptor called Dmitri, and he came to Scarborough for a couple of days about a week after the show finished." The others looked blank.

"Came to Scarborough?" Maggie looked puzzled. "I never met him."

"No," Karl nodded, "none of you did. I think you were away, Maggie, with friends at York? I didn't bother showing him our shops. He was more interested in sketching the harbour and having a few beers. He stayed in my flat for a couple of nights, then caught the train down to London. He did invite me to stay with him if I ever visited Russia."

"So, has he arranged your visit?" his mother pushed for more information.

"No," Karl replied, sipping his coffee, "Irina faxed me an invitation, so that I can apply for a visa. She can do all of the hotel bookings for me, and I'll probably stay with Dmitri for a few days as well."

"Have I been invited?" Maggie asked optimistically, looking doe-eyed and giving Karl her best smile.

"Sorry, pet, it's just me. You see, I discussed with Irina the possibility of buying a range of Russian traditional crafts and selling them in our shops. I think they'll be a good line, honestly. There's some beautiful stuff, mostly not expensive, and I don't know any other shops or wholesalers who sell Russian crafts. Irina and her husband can arrange all of the customs and shipping if we decide to go for it. I think we could even wholesale some lines over here." He paused. "Well, what do you think?"

"I think there's some real potential there, son," Mr

Griffin said, with an apologetic smile on his face. "I'm sorry that I forgot about the crafts that you showed me. You must have caught me at a busy time. I'll dig them out, and show them to your Mam and the girls who work in the main shop. Let's see what they think, but if Irina and Co turn out to be reliable, it might be worth investing a few grand in a new line. Try to bring back a good selection with you, Karl ... fill your suitcase!" The others laughed.

"OK, that's settled," Karl remarked as he stood up. "I'll see what I can do," he muttered, as he headed for the bar to settle the bill.

***

"Russia!" Maggie barked at Karl, after he had dropped off his parents at their house. "I don't believe it - you're going to piss off for a week on some boozy holiday."

"Ten days, actually, and it is work, after all." He turned and smiled across at her.

"Ten days! Bloody Hell, I'd love to go to Russia. Crisp snow, fur coats, and all that vodka. You must be able to get another invitation for me?"

"Sorry, pet, no can do. Irina said it's quite complicated getting invitations and visas, unless you're on some kind of trip organised by a Russian tourist agency. Perhaps there'll be another opportunity in the future, you know, once I've got things established?" He gently caressed her leg until she brushed him off. "Anyway, we'll go somewhere nice for a few days when I get back."

"I'm not happy, you're a selfish pig!" Maggie rasped, staring out of the side window.

CHAPTER THREE
MOSCOW

Karl stood up as he heard the exit doors open on the Aeroflot plane, and felt a swish of cooler air drifting through the cabin. Pushing against his neighbouring passengers, he opened the overhead locker and grabbed his hand luggage and coat. He had already checked his passport and flight documents as the plane made its final descent to Sheremetyevo Airport, north-west of Moscow, but as he waited for the other passengers to start moving, he unzipped the front pocket and flicked through his documents again. A few minutes later he shuffled along the cabin and smiled at one of the hostesses as he left the plane. *That was an experience!* he thought, *weird food and uncomfortable seats. Now for the Customs.* Irina had already warned him that it could take a long time for the passengers to be processed by the Russian passport and customs officials. He followed the crush, glancing occasionally at the bi-lingual signs overhead, until he reached the windows and had a view of the airport. It was late afternoon and the clouds looked full of snow. He had noticed some white fields and forests as his plane descended towards Moscow. Now he reached the stairs leading down to the passport control, and he jostled his way into one of the queues. It was slow going, and he had plenty of time to gaze around at the dark-looking terminal. Irina had told him that Sheremetyevo was Moscow's most modern airport terminal, built for the 1980 Olympics, but glancing around again, he thought *Grim!*

Karl's queue edged towards the passport booth, and ten minutes later he found himself waiting by the red line on the floor. Now it was his turn, and he moved forward, stopped in front of the booth, handed over his passport and smiled at the uniformed woman in the booth. No response. Just a dour expression on her face. She seemed to take an eternity in examining his passport, glancing down at a machine, checking the passport again, looking at Karl, back to the machine, then finally she returned his passport. He smiled again and muttered "Thanks", but she simply waved him on. He headed for the baggage reclaim section, collected his case then joined another queue for the customs check. The passenger in front of him had to empty his case, and was then escorted to another control booth, but Karl was just waved through. *At last!* He was able finally to pass through into the arrivals hall, where he searched the crowd for Irina. He spotted a waving arm at the back of the crowd, pushed his way through the throng and reached her. They hugged, kissed each other on both cheeks, then Irina introduced Karl to her husband, Mikhail, a giant of a man.

"Welcome to Moscow!" he said heartily, shaking Karl's hand vigorously. "Come, let us get away from here. Be careful of pickpockets," he warned. "Follow me to my car". He grabbed Karl's case and forced a path through the crowd for Karl and Irina.

***

Karl enjoyed a leisurely shower and reflected on a busy few days since arriving in Moscow on Thursday evening. Irina and Mikhail had been perfect hosts, as well as guides, as they first settled him at the Ismailovo Hotel, then gave him a quick tour around the most popular city sights on Friday. Using the efficient Metro system, they accompanied Karl to Red Square, where he visited St Basil's Cathedral and the huge GUM department store, and then they passed the afternoon in the Kremlin. Saturday was taken up looking around the extensive Ismailovo market, just a short walk away from his hotel, where Karl was introduced to some of the artists and craft-sellers. By the end of the afternoon, he was exhausted after viewing stall after stall offering a wide range of nesting dolls, painted trays, wooden toys, lacquered boxes, Ghzel blue-and-white pottery, Christmas decorations, and so on. Several of the stallholders insisted on sharing a vodka toasting session, and when Karl was eventually allowed to walk back to his hotel, laden with samples and other purchases, he enjoyed a basic meal in the restaurant then fell into a deep sleep on returning to his room.

"We've been invited to a party at Grigori's dacha!" Irina had told him. "Sunday afternoon, Karl, and some of the other artists will be there. Mikhail and I will call for you around 2 o'clock, and we'll drive there. His dacha is just outside Moscow. I think you will enjoy it!" she said, grinning.

Now, as he dried himself after a late-Sunday-morning shower, Karl reflected on the party invitation. *This is going to be Russian-style.* Lots of food, lots of dancing and music, lots of vodka. *I hope I'm not going to be the cabaret!*

***

Mikhail slowed down and took the exit from the main road to Yaroslavl. They had only travelled a few miles beyond the Moscow boundary, and were now on a narrow country lane. It was an overcast, cloudy afternoon. Flecks of snow appeared on the windscreen, and patches of early snow lay by the roadside. Mikhail continued to drive cautiously along the twisty road, until there was a break in the trees and lights could be seen in a cluster of houses in the distance. Irina spoke quietly to Mikhail, and he slowed and stopped outside a green-painted wooden cottage set back on the right-hand side of the road.

"This is Grigori's *dacha,*" she said, turning towards Karl. "Mikhail has not been here before, so I had to tell him where to stop."

Karl smiled, and nodded. "It looks cosy," he remarked, as they got out of the car. He reached for a carrier-bag containing some presents, and followed Irina and Mikhail as they headed for the front door. Suddenly it was opened by Elena as her husband Grigori, singing at the top of his voice, held out a tray of small glasses filled with vodka. Karl glanced at Irina, who laughed at his puzzled expression.

"It's a traditional Russian greeting for you, Karl. Take

a glass, and let's go inside." He followed her instruction, and walked into the hallway, where half-a dozen other guests were standing, with glasses poised. Grigori gave a brief toast in Russian, they downed the vodka and then there were hugs and handshakes all round. Elena collected the coats and Karl handed out his presents – bottles of whisky and wine for the hosts, plus chocolates and small English cottage ornaments for the ladies and Yorkshire glass tankards for the men. Karl smiled at their delight in receiving the gifts, which were items he saw every day in the shops in Scarborough, then he followed the others into the main room. He glanced around, then gasped, staring at a long table laden with a wide range of food: various salads in bowls, dishes of gherkins, plates of various sliced meats, a selection of cheeses, bread, cakes, and a large tureen of steaming soup in the centre of the table.

"My God," he exclaimed, turning to Irina, "this can't be just for us? They must be expecting other guests, Irina?"

"I'm afraid not, Karl," she replied, laughing. "This is just the start. There will be more to eat … and drink." The others laughed when they realised what Irina had said, and Grigori slapped him on the back.

"Please, Karl, sit down," he said in Russian, and pointed to a seat at the head of the table. "You are our special guest," he continued, smiling, as bottles of vodka and Russian champagne began to appear as if by magic. Karl shook his head and laughed with the others.

"This is going to be a long evening," he whispered to Irina.

"Don't worry, Karl," she smiled. "You will be fine, but while you are still sober, I must remind you that you are going to stay with Dmitri tomorrow afternoon. He lives in a village not too far from Moscow, but you will travel there by train. Mikhail and I will call for you after lunch and take you to the station. You must make sure that you have a few things packed for your stay. Try to remember that when you wake up in the morning!" Karl looked blank. "Honestly, don't worry about today. Mikhail will return you safely to the hotel when we have finished here." Irina laughed again, as Grigori passed some shot glasses to the men around the table and opened a bottle of vodka. Elena handed a bottle of Russian champagne to Grigori and he made sure that the women each had a glass. Everyone cheered as Grigori popped the cork and filled the women's glasses with the foaming champagne. He then filled the shot glasses with vodka.

"*Stalichnaya!*" he roared, lifting his glass.

"It's a good brand of vodka," Mikhail whispered to Karl. "You'll have to drink it in one go, but make sure that you have something to eat afterwards." Karl looked puzzled. "It will help you to stay sober, or perhaps to avoid a hangover," Mikhail smiled. They both looked at Grigori as he completed a toast to Karl.

"*Nasdrovya!*" They all stood up and the vodka glasses were drained. Karl followed Mikhail's lead and ate a gherkin. They all sat down, there was a brief flurry of smiles and conversation, and the glasses were filled. Karl had a sudden rush of inspiration. He stood up, grinned and looked around the table.

"I just want to thank you all for making me so welcome in Moscow, and I would like to propose a toast to friendship." Mikhail whispered *Druzba* to the others, and they immediately stood up, smiled at Karl and drained their glasses again. Karl ate another gherkin, while Elena passed around some bowls and began ladling some soup into them.

"This is *borscht*," Irina explained to Karl, "beetroot soup. It's very popular in Russia. You might like to add some sour cream." She handed him a dish, and he swirled a small amount into his soup. Elena passed the bread to everyone, and the eating began. Karl smiled at her, then at Irina.

"Delicious!"

As the soup course finished, another guest, Sergei, filled the glasses and, glancing at the ladies around the table, proposed a toast to women. This was loudly supported, and the glasses were drained again. There was a buzz of conversation until Elena returned with a large, steaming pan. "What are those?" Karl asked Irina.

"They are called *palmeni*," she replied, "Siberian dumplings, filled with meat or vegetables." Elena ladled a couple of dumplings to every guest, and the room fell silent as they were devoured. The plates were cleared, and an inevitable toast followed. This time, one of the other female guests, Svetlana, proposed a lengthy tribute to the men in the room. Karl, warming to the atmosphere, joined in with gusto. More plates appeared, and everybody started filling them with meat and salad from the dishes on the table. Karl noticed another bottle of vodka being opened, and braced himself for the next toast.

And so it went on......

CHAPTER FOUR
SCARBOROUGH

Tim Sharpe glanced at his watch, yawned and looked across the CID incident room to DS Debbie Chapman, who was buried in her computer. Sharpe pushed aside his notebook and stood up, stretching. "Christ," he muttered to himself, "what a boring afternoon. Fancy a coffee, Debbie?" he quizzed loudly. She took a few seconds to answer.

"What? … oh yeah, Sharpie, please. Not too much sugar this time. Got any biscuits?" Sharpe shook his head, as she returned to the screen. He returned a few minutes later with two steaming plastic cups, and placed one of her desk.

"You're in luck," he grinned, "someone left these by the coffee machine." He dumped half a packet of Hobnobs on her desk, and glanced at her computer. "What's so interesting?"

"Well, it's hardly *interesting*, Sharpie," she muttered, dunking a Hobnob in her coffee and munching half of it. "It's that druggie, Jake Palmer, who was caught nicking last week. I'm just checking on his previous, and reading what the witnesses had to say. It's filling the time, I suppose. How about you?"

"Bugger all, Debbie, just typing up one or two reports. What a waste of a Saturday afternoon."

"Not really," she laughed, "if you were at home, you'd be lying on the sofa, watching *Grandstand* on the telly, or more likely snoring your head off!"

"Hmm, you're probably right. At least this is another shift down, and I'm due a few days off next week. I'm planning to take my girlfriend to Manchester for a few days."

"Ooh, last of the big spenders, eh? It's not like you …" The phone buzzed loudly, and Sharpe grabbed it quickly, while Chapman took a swig of her coffee.

"Hello … Scarborough CID, DC Sharpe speaking." He listened intently for half a minute. "Right, just hang on while I get my pad." He reached for a pen and notepad. "OK … Tony Johnson … you and your wife were out walking … found a body … on a pathway near the Saltergate Inn on the Whitby-Pickering road. The body's in a bad way?" he raised his eyebrows and glanced at Chapman. "Right, don't worry about that, Mr Johnson. Give me your address and phone details, please." He scribbled them down. "OK, Mr Johnson, thank you for letting us know so promptly. We'll get a squad out there straightaway, and someone will call at your house to take a statement." A pause. "Thanks again. 'Bye." He turned to Chapman.

"A body, sounds like he's been shot, on moorland near that old inn at Saltergate." Chapman looked puzzled. "You know, halfway along the main road from Pickering to Whitby." She nodded, pushed back her chair and moved to the large map of North Yorkshire on the wall. She traced her finger until she located Saltergate.

"Right, I'll give Bentley a ring. Can you contact someone from SOC, Sharpie? Who else? The local plods at Pickering, and perhaps George Ryan, the Wonder Kid. Bentley will want him involved too. Let's get cracking."

***

The skies had darkened and it was starting to rain as Detective Inspector Don Bentley pulled his Granada off the road and eased into the car park alongside the Saltergate Inn. The local police had cleared both customers and cars away from the inn to afford the convoy of police vehicles and ambulances somewhere to park. A yellow-clad constable came over to Bentley's car to check his credentials, then stepped back and pointed the pathway to the crime scene. Bentley fumbled in his pocket for a jelly baby before grabbing his coat and getting out of the car. He opened the boot and removed a pair of wellingtons before sitting on the back seat and changing his footwear. He reached for a large torch on the back seat, then, shivering, he glanced at the constable who pointed again at the pathway up the hill. Bentley slammed the car door and trudged up the muddy path.

As he reached the summit, Bentley could see that a group of the main players had already arrived at the crime scene. A large white tent flapped in the distance and, against the backdrop of the lights, Bentley could just make out one or two figures inside. He dug into his pocket for another jelly baby, a green one, grimaced and popped it into his mouth. "I wish they'd stop making bloody green ones," he muttered to himself, as he plodded along the muddy path. A tall, bulky man, overweight and in his early fifties, Bentley was breathing heavily by the time he neared the tent. He pulled his coat tightly around him as George Ryan, a young DC, spotted him in the growing darkness and moved out to meet him.

"Hello, Sir," he said, half-smiling, "foul afternoon, eh?" He glanced upwards. "Quite a mess in there, Sir. The pathologist is there," he pointed, "she's expecting you." Bentley just grunted as he brushed past Ryan and walked to the entrance of the tent, where Debbie Chapman was waiting.

"Thanks for getting everybody here, Debbie. Always seems to be shitty weather when something happens on the moors," he moaned, glancing up at the rain, which was coming down more steadily. "Where the hell are we anyway?"

"There is an area close to here called the Hole of Horcum, Sir. It's like a huge moorland amphitheatre, very popular with walkers, they say."

"Is that right?" Bentley replied matter-of-factly, grimacing at the thought of having to walk anywhere on the moors. "Have you had a look in there?" She nodded.

"Not very nice, Sir. Angela Dawson's in there. I'll wait outside for you." She opened the flap, and Bentley moved just inside the tent, where three figures in white overalls were taking photos and measurements. He stepped forward a couple of paces, leaned over and squinted beyond the kneeling pathologist. He could just make out a body lying on its side, surrounded by a large, dark stain.

"Hello, Angela," Bentley said softly, standing up straight as she looked up at him. "What have we got?"

"White male, around forty, shot in the back of the head. Face is a mess, unrecognisable. His hands have been tied behind his back," she said, pointing at them. "You've got another murder on your hands, Don."

"This mess was meant to be seen, Angela, meant to be public. That's no murder," Bentley snorted, glancing past her and pointing at the body, "that's a fucking execution."

CHAPTER FIVE
BYELAVAYA

Karl slowly opened his eyes and peered around the room. He blinked, closed his eyes and opened them again, slowly realising that he was in his hotel room. He was lying, fully-clothed, on top of the bed. He tried to swallow, coughed softly, then eased himself off the bed and tottered towards the bathroom. After urinating, he steadied himself against the door, then he reached for a glass and poured a little cold water into it. He drank, swirling the water around his mouth, then spat it into the sink. He returned to the bedroom and sat on a chair, head in hands, trying to recall the events of the day before, and thinking furiously about the day ahead. *Dmitri … I'm going to Dmitri's house today!* He glanced at his watch … 9.45 in the morning … time for a coffee. He had a quick swill, then exited his room and caught the lift down to the restaurant. A few glances in his direction made him run his fingers through his hair and straighten his clothes before looking for a table. A waitress walked across the room to his table.

"Tea or coffee, Sir?" she asked quietly, looking him up and down.

"Coffee, please," Karl croaked. She nodded and headed

for the kitchen. Karl looked around for the breakfast counter, walked slowly over to it and put some cheese, ham and bread onto a plate. *I don't feel ill,* he thought to himself, *just totally wrecked.* He picked at his food until the waitress returned with a jug of coffee. He quickly drank a cup, continued eating unenthusiastically and had another cup of coffee. After he had finished, he returned to his room, showered and changed, and packed a small bag ready for his journey to Dmitri's house. *Whatever next?*

***

Karl checked his watch, sat forward and peered out of the train window again. *More forests, mile after mile of birch trees, and more snow!* Earlier, Irina and Mikhail had collected Karl from his hotel, checked that he had not suffered any ill effects from the party, then they brought him via the Metro to the Yaroslavsky station. Within minutes he had a ticket and had boarded his train, which was already packed with passengers, most of them suitably attired for the wintry weather.

"Your journey will take about forty minutes, Karl," Irina had informed him, "so don't fall asleep! Look for the station sign – **БЕЛАВАЯ** – and also for Dmitri. He will be there to meet you. Have a good time!" She and Mikhail waved as the train moved slowly away from the platform. Karl waved back, and settled into his seat. The coach was comfortable, not as basic as he had expected, and he glanced around at his fellow passengers. A few smiled, but most ignored him as he stared out of the window as the train left the outskirts of Moscow and chugged into the wintry countryside.

***

True to Irina's advice, after about forty minutes the train slowed and halted at Byelavaya station and Karl grabbed his holdall and got off the train, the snow swirling around him as he glanced along the platform, looking for Dmitri. "Karl!" a shout to his right, and there was Dmitri, waving furiously, a woman standing alongside him. Karl moved briskly to join them, and suddenly it was all hugs.

"Dmitri," Karl gasped in the cold air, "it's great to see you again." The woman smiled at Karl.

"Welcome to my village, my friend," Dmitri continued, turning to his side. "This is my wife, Maria." Maria was a pretty, short dark-haired woman, about forty Karl guessed. He stepped forward and kissed her on both cheeks.

"Hi," Karl muttered, picking up his holdall and smiling at Maria. "I'm really pleased to meet you." She smiled and nodded.

"Let's go," Dmitri instructed, and they slowly padded their way through the slush on the platform to the road and headed into the village darkness. Dmitri led the way along the snowy lane, passing several *dachas,* the traditional Russian wooden cottages, as they made their way towards the centre of the village. Karl peered at the windows when they passed by a *dacha* which was brightly lit, and jumped as a large dog barked loudly in the darkness as they passed a wooden gateway. "Do not worry, Karl," Dmitri laughed, "lots of the villagers have a dog to protect them. Maria and I have an Alsatian who lives outside our house. You'll meet him soon, he's called Samson."

"Samson?" Karl quizzed. "He sounds big."

"Yes, he is," Dmitri laughed again. "I will try to stop him eating you."

Soon they turned a corner and Dmitri halted near a large, brick-built house with a sizeable garden. Maria touched Karl's arm. "This is our home." She smiled and moved towards a wooden gate. "Dmitri will go first," she cautioned. Karl could hear movement inside the garden, and Dmitri unlocked the gate. He shouted something in Russian, opened the gate and stepped inside.

"OK," he shouted, "I have Samson." Maria ushered Karl inside the doorway, and locked it behind them. Dmitri clung on to Samson's collar as Maria led Karl along the path to the front door. Karl glanced up at the house, then behind him at the darkened garden.

"This is amazing, Dmitri," he gasped, "what a fantastic house."

***

Maria headed for the kitchen and began preparing the evening meal, so Dmitri grabbed Karl by his arm and whispered: "Maria will not want you to watch her. Come with me, I will show you my house."

"Great," Karl nodded and smiled, "lead on, my friend." He followed Dmitri out of the spacious lounge, and they made their way upstairs.

"I have four bedrooms," Dmitri boasted, "so you can choose which one you would like, but not that one." He pointed. "That one is mine," he laughed, and opened the door. "It is the biggest in my house." Karl stepped just inside the door and looked impressed. "The bathroom is over here," Dmitri continued, "and there are many … towels, is that right?"

"Yes," Karl muttered, "thanks. I think I'll have the room next to the bathroom, just in case I am ill." Dmitri laughed.

"OK, OK, my friend, but you will not be ill. My wife is a good cook, and my vodka is good also, the best. I have a nice Georgian vodka, *Cha Cha,* 50% proof. You will like it! I also have some homemade vodka, if you wish to try?"

"I'll stick to the *Cha Cha,* thanks, Dmitri. Where to next?"

"Follow me." They headed downstairs. "You have seen these rooms. Now for my studios." He led Karl down some more steps into a large cellar. "This is where I prepare many of my sculptures," he said, sweeping his arm around the room.

"Wow," Karl gasped, caressing a small bronze nude and gazing around at other works in progress. "You're a bloody talented guy, Dmitri!"

"Yes, I agree!" Dmitri laughed loudly. "Now, come through here." He walked up a few steps into a lofty studio with large windows. "This is where I finish most of my work." A life-sized Crucifixion dominated one of the walls, and a variety of large and small sculptures were stacked on shelves along two of the walls. Karl examined a Nefertiti-style bust.

"She looks familiar," he pondered.

"Of course," laughed Dmitri, "it is Maria. She is my wife, and my model." He laughed again at Karl's astonished face. "Our meal will soon be ready, but we have time to look outside." He opened the door, paused to check that Samson was locked in his shed, then ushered Karl through the snow towards a group of small wooden buildings. "I grow vegetables in my garden, but I also have this, my *banya*."

"A *banya*," Karl asked, "is it a store for your tools?" Dmitri began laughing again.

"No, my tools are over there, near Samson's house." He pointed across the garden. "Come inside," he grinned, opening the door. "This is a room where we can relax - with vodka, of course - and this is my *banya*." He opened a second door, and Karl saw a large stove, surrounded by stones, with wooden seats in the background. Bundles of narrow branches hung from the walls.

"Wow!" enthused Karl. "Bloody Hell, it's like a massive sauna, right?"

"Perhaps," nodded Dmitri, "but you will find out tomorrow." He moved to the door, and listened. "Maria is calling for us. Dinner is ready, my friend." They moved outside onto the snowy path, and spotted Maria waving by the corner of the house. Karl walked gingerly along the path.

"Come on, Karl," Maria opened the door, grabbed his arm and pushed him inside. "My husband talks too much! It is warmer in here." Dmitri appeared behind them, grinned widely and slammed the door.

"Welcome to our home!" he beamed. "Now, where is the vodka?" Karl looked up to the heavens.

***

Karl sat back on his wooden kitchen chair, and rubbed his stomach. "That was a fantastic meal, Maria. Thank you very much, and thank you for inviting me to stay in your beautiful home!"

"You are welcome, Karl." He smiled and looked at Dmitri.

"Tell me, Dmitri, how did you buy this wonderful house? It's brick-built, and so much bigger that the wooden *dachas* I have seen in the rest of the village."

Dmitri poured two more glasses of vodka, and pushed one over to Karl. "What do you say in England ... Cheers?" They drained the glasses, and Dmitri leant forward on the table. "I did not buy this house, I built it!" Karl looked agog. "I was very lucky, Karl. I am a good sculptor, and I won many prizes in my country, when it was still the Soviet Union. I had some money, but I dreamed of building my own house," he paused, "a big house, where I had a lot of room to do my work. I bought this land, and asked the government if they would lend me some money to build a house." Karl listened intently. "This was about twelve years ago, you know. Well, the government agreed to lend me the money to build the house and continue my work, even though it would take me many years to repay the loan." He sat back. "I was very lucky. You know that about six years ago our government changed? The Soviet Union was gone, there were many changes, and our money - the rouble - lost a lot of value."

"Yes, I remember," Karl interrupted. "There was massive inflation here, yes?"

"Inflation, yes, that is right. Well, that was good for me," Dmitri spoke more quickly, eager to tell Karl about his good fortune, "because the thousands of roubles I owed quickly became a small amount of money, almost nothing." He laughed loudly. "I was able to pay the money back in two months!" At the sink, Maria turned and smiled. Dmitri looked at Karl. "I was not the only lucky man in Russia," he said, more seriously. "Many others became rich quickly. We call them the *New Russians*." He turned to Maria and spoke in Russian. She dried her hands and brought some large boots and heavy coats from a cupboard. "Let's go for a walk, Karl," Dmitri commanded. "The moon is bright, and it has stopped snowing. I want to show you something." They dressed for the cold weather outside, and Dmitri took a dog lead from a hook in the cupboard. "Samson can walk with us," he said, opening the door. Karl and Maria followed him into the garden.

***

It was very quiet in the village. A few lights glimmered from the *dachas*, but nobody was around. Snow lay undisturbed in the gardens and on the roofs, and occasionally dropped from the trees as they made their way along the village lanes. Soon they were passing fields, with heavy forest in the background. A full moon illuminated their path, and Dmitri pointed to an open area on their right.

"That is a lake, Karl. It is possible to walk across, because the ice is ... big." He raised his eyebrows.

"Thick, Dmitri, not big. You can walk across it if you like, but I'm staying on the road!" They all laughed. They continued along the lane as it slowly veered to the left between two clumps of trees, then they halted. Karl gasped, struggling to make sense of what he could see. Ahead of them was the beginning of a city street, with pavements and streetlights, and a few large modern brick-built houses on either side. "What the hell is this, Dmitri? It looks more like a London street than somewhere in Russia." They continued slowly towards the street and looking around, Karl could see security cameras and heavy gates attached to every house. He stepped onto the pavement, the snow crunching under his feet, and tried to peer through one of the gates. The others had moved slowly forward, and Karl joined them back on the street. About fifty metres ahead, in the centre of the street, stood a dimly-lit cabin, and as they moved a few paces further, a uniformed figure stepped out of the door. He was holding what appeared to be a rifle. Samson began to growl, and Dmitri passed the lead to Maria. The guard called out in Russian, and Dmitri answered him. They had a brief, one-sided conversation, then Dmitri turned to Karl.

"We need to leave," he said sternly and, glancing back at the sentry, he grabbed Samson's lead and ushered Karl and Maria back the way they came.

"This is weird," Karl remarked to Dmitri, glancing back towards the street. "What's going on there?"

"*New Russians*," Dmitri answered glumly. "The buildings are about three years old. They have their own private road. Nobody knows who lives there, they don't speak to anyone in the village. They are not part of Byelavaya." He looked very angry. "Someone told me that the man in charge of Sheremetyevo Airport lives there, but I do not know. Nobody knows, there are many secrets. We cannot find anything out. Everywhere is guarded." Maria smiled sympathetically at Dmitri, and they walked slowly back towards the village.

***

Karl drained his coffee and smiled at Maria. "Thanks, Maria. That was another lovely breakfast."

"You're welcome," she replied. "Would you like some more coffee?"

"No thanks, I'm fine," Karl muttered, standing up and crossing to the window. "It has snowed overnight and is still snowing lightly now. It looks like a *Winter Wonderland* outside, so I am going to take some photos of the village. May I have a coat and boots again, Dmitri?"

"Of course. Would you like me to come with you?"

"No, I'll be fine. I won't be long."

"OK, my friend, but do not walk on the lake." They laughed, then looking more serious, Dmitri added: "And do not go near those New Russian houses!" Karl nodded in agreement, and opened the cupboard door, looking for suitable clothes. "Oh, and don't get lost, Karl," Dmitri continued. "We are going to use my *banya* this afternoon. You are returning to Moscow tomorrow, so you must be clean before you go!" Karl grinned, popped his camera into a coat pocket and headed for the front door.

"See you later! Oh, what about Samson?"

"He is in his shed, so don't worry. Go!" Dmitri instructed. "Take some nice photos!" Karl opened the door and waved at Dmitri and Maria, before disappearing into the garden. He crunched his way along the path, exited via the gate and trudged along the lane. It was a wintry paradise, and Karl stood and gazed around at the snow-laden branches and pretty *dachas,* their roofs thick with snow, slowly dripping to the gardens. It was snowing lightly and Karl looked up at the grey clouds above, but noticed small patches of blue sky in the distance. *Just like Dr Zhivago,* he thought as he turned and began slowly making his way along the lane. He paused, taking a couple of snaps of Dmitri's house, then turned left at the end of the lane and continued taking shots of the trees, glistening in the snow. It was so quiet and peaceful, with most of the villagers out at work or tending to their stoves inside. Here and there a wisp of smoke twirled out of a chimney. Karl selected two or three of the prettier *dachas* and took some more photos before heading down the lane and turning left again. A small clump of trees caught his attention, then he spotted the onion-domed village church beyond. A narrow shaft of sunlight suddenly touched the golden dome, and he quickly took four more photos, twisting around for a better shot, then there she was ... a golden-haired young woman, tall and slim, clad in furs and brown boots. A few tiny snowflakes glistened on her face and on the long strands of her blonde hair cascading from under her fur hat, and she smiled at Karl. He gasped, muttering "Hello," and placed his hand on his chest. "You surprised me," he said, smiling widely.

"I'm sorry, please excuse me," she said, "I did not mean to shock you. I was just walking down this road when I saw you taking photographs. Would you like me to take one of you?"

"Please," Karl replied, handing over his camera. "Are you Russian? Your English is so good."

"Thank you," she said, a beautiful smile on her face. "I studied languages at Moscow University. Right now, I am staying with my grandparents in the village while I decide on a career. Move back a little," she instructed, and took a couple of photos of Karl. "What about you? What brings an Englishman to this small village?"

"Well, I have come to Russia to look for traditional crafts and artwork to sell in my parents' shops in England. I have a friend in Moscow who knows lots of artists, but I am staying for a couple of days with a sculptor who lives here in Byelavaya. He visited my hometown last summer. I am leaving for Moscow tomorrow." Karl paused and smiled at the girl. "I'm sorry, what is your name? I'm called Karl."

"Karl," she mused, smiling, "that's a nice name, I like it. My name is Natalia, but most of my friends call me Natasha." Karl nodded with approval.

"Natasha ... that's a nice name as well. I must admit that my favourite Russian name is Lara, probably because I enjoyed that old film *Dr Zhivago*".

"Lara, it is short for Larissa," she smiled. "True, it is another pretty name, quite popular in Russia." Karl grinned.

"I still need to take some more photos, Natasha. Would you like to come with me?"

"Of course, I can be your guide. I think I know most of the interesting parts of the village. Follow me, but walk carefully. There may be some ice on the road."

***

More than an hour had passed by the time Karl and Natasha neared Dmitri's house, having toured the village and the area near the lake. They had both taken many photos and had exhausted Karl's film, and had chatted comfortably all of the time. There was an obvious physical attraction between them, and the time passed quickly. Karl glanced at Dmitri's house, and pointed. "That's where I am staying." Natasha nodded. "My friend Dmitri is preparing his *banya* this afternoon. Would you like to join us? I am sure Dmitri won't mind."

"That would be lovely," Natasha answered, "but we

need to ask Dmitri first. It would be rude not to do so."

They made their way to the house, and Karl opened the front door, shouting: "Dmitri! Maria!" His friends appeared quickly from the kitchen.

"What's the matter, Karl?" Dmitri asked, a worried look on his face. "We thought you had got lost!"

"No, I'm fine," laughed Karl, "but I met someone when I was walking around the village." Natasha emerged from behind him. "This is Natasha."

"Come in," Maria ushered them inside. "It is too cold outside." They followed Maria into the hall and took off their coats and boots. Karl could not help admiring Natasha's figure when he saw her dressed in jeans and a jumper, and he smiled at her.

"OK?" he whispered, touching her arm. She smiled and nodded.

"I will prepare some tea." Maria walked into the kitchen, as Dmitri moved across and spoke quickly in Russian to Natasha. They exchanged a few sentences, and Natasha glanced anxiously at Karl before Dmitri reverted to English.

"I'm sorry about that, Karl. It was rude, but Natasha is a stranger to me and I had to ask her a few things." He grinned. "Everything is fine, don't worry. I have invited her to my *banya* later this afternoon."

***

Dmitri returned from the garden. "Everything is ready," he announced, "the *banya* is hot and waiting for us!" He put a couple of bottles of vodka and some towels into a bag as the others put on coats and boots for the short walk through the garden. Dmitri led the way along the snowy path to the *banya* and opened the door. It was warm in the outer room, and they removed coats and boots as Dmitri filled some glasses and placed them on the small table in the centre of the room. Maria added some small plates and jars of the predictable gherkins and cucumbers. Dmitri handed out the glasses and proposed a toast.

"Welcome to our *banya!*" he smiled widely and drained his glass. The others followed suit, and Karl took some cucumber and offered the plate to the others. The glasses were refilled and Karl stood up.

"To our hosts, Dmitri and Maria. Thank you for welcoming us to your home!" The glasses were drained again and refilled, and Natasha took the floor. She said something quickly in Russian and smiled at Dmitri and Maria before continuing in English.

"I cannot believe that I have only met you this morning! Let us drink to friendship!" The others chorused "*Druzhba!*" and the vodka disappeared again. There was a lull as they ate some of the salad that Maria had brought. Dmitri emptied the first bottle into the glasses, then moved to the inner door and opened it. The blast of hot air left them all breathless.

"Christ!" Karl exclaimed, grinning at Natasha. "It's red hot and I can't breathe. Surely you don't expect us to go in there, Dmitri?"

"Don't worry, my friend. You will feel better without your clothes." He moved into the *banya* and opened the outside door, pointing to the garden. "And if you still feel too hot, or need some cold air, then go into the garden. You can lie in the snow, or break the ice in that small pond!" He laughed loudly at Karl's blank face, then closed the door and re-joined the others. He drained his glass, then started to undress. "Come on," he said, glancing around at the rest, "let's enjoy ourselves." He continued undressing. "Come back in here if you want some more vodka or gherkins." Maria removed her clothes quickly and joined Dmitri, now naked, in the *banya*. "Hurry up, Karl and Natasha," he called from inside, "before you get cold!" Karl looked at Natasha, smiled and moved over to kiss her, then they began undressing. He dropped his pants on his heap of clothes, and turned to see that she was standing naked in front of him. He gasped at her beauty, admiring her full breasts and slim body, and felt himself getting aroused. Natasha glanced down and laughed.

"Come on, my big boy! The others are waiting." She turned quickly and Karl paused for a few seconds, blushing, before following her into the steaming room.

"At last!" Dmitri roared, flicking them lightly with some birch twigs as they entered the room, before pausing to admire Natasha's figure. "You can model for me," he grinned, and smacked them with the birch twigs again. Karl and Natasha joined Maria on the wooden seats, as Dmitri splashed some water onto the hot stones by the stove. Clouds of steam filled the room, and Karl began choking again.

41

"Have mercy, Dmitri," he shouted, "we can't breathe over here!" Dmitri sat down and punched Karl playfully.

"Wait for a minute or two, when the steam has died a little. Then you can breathe!" The others laughed as Karl tried to relax. As the steam clouds faded, they sat with eyes closed, taking in the heat, sweating slightly, their hair matted on their heads. Karl glanced at Natasha and saw that strands of her damp long blonde hair had moulded around her breasts. She smiled at him, then eased her head backwards, wallowing in the warmth in the room. It was very quiet, conversation was unnecessary, and Karl was feeling relaxed to the point of sleep when Dmitri reached for bowl of water and threw more of it on the hot stones. Clouds of steam and heat once again engulfed them, and this time Karl could stand it no longer. He lurched from the seat to the door, thrust it open and threw himself on the snow on the garden. He flipped over onto his back, then grasped handfuls of snow and moved them up and down his body, cooling himself down and creating rivulets on his body. Seconds later, he began shivering and headed quickly back into the steamy room. Natasha stood up and embraced him, and he caressed some of the colder water onto her body.

"My God, you are so cold, Karl!" she laughed, as Dmitri grabbed another bunch of birch and began smacking the others on their buttocks. Karl reached for another bunch and a play-fight ensued. Maria poured some more cold water on the stones, as Dmitri roared again.

"Be careful, Karl!" he warned as he thwacked Karl again.

"Do not stand on the hot stones!" Clouds of steam filled the room again, and Natasha headed for the door. Karl chased after her and, laughing, threw her onto the snow and they rolled around as one, massaging and melting handfuls on their bodies. They kissed passionately, hungrily until their shivers reminded them to return to the seat. They sat together, their thighs touching, their hands caressing softly. Karl peered through the steam and saw Dmitri and Maria both grinning and laughing, then Dmitri got up and went into the other room. He returned with more vodka and gherkins, passing the glasses around.

"*Snegurushka*", he shouted, raising and downing his drink in one. Karl looked puzzled. "Don't worry, Karl. This is a toast for your *Snow Maiden* ... Natasha!" He laughed again as the others downed their vodka, and then they were all laughing, standing and embracing each other. More cold water hit the stones, and as the choking clouds again filled the room, Dmitri ushered them all out of the room. "Quickly" he ordered, and hand-in-hand he guided them to the frozen pond and they jumped in as one, shattering the thin ice as they hit the freezing water. The pond was only a little over a metre deep, but within seconds they were scrambling out and dashing back into the steam room. Panting and gasping, they relaxed on the seat until their bodies were warm again. Dmitri broke the silence. "Maria and I will leave you soon and return to the house for a hot shower. After that we will prepare a meal. I will call you in some minutes when you can use the shower. Keep warm!" He and Maria headed into the other room, threw on a few clothes and dashed along the path to the house.

Karl looked at Natasha and they stood up and embraced each other, their hands exploring their bodies. Karl ran his fingers through Natasha's hair, then turned her round and found her breasts, fondling them gently, her nipples hardening. He eased his fingers downwards, finding her soft hair, as she reached behind for him and he responded quickly to her touch. As he turned her back towards him, she laughed and grabbed the bowl of water, tossing some onto him and the rest onto the hot stones. The steam engulfed them once again as Natasha took Karl's hand and they dashed out of the room and threw themselves on the snow.

In the house, Dmitri watched out of an upstairs window and smiled to himself as the naked couple writhed in the snow in the garden.

CHAPTER SIX
SCARBOROUGH

Seaside resorts always look tired and miserable out of season, and Scarborough was no exception. The cold, easterly wind discouraged all but the hardy shoppers, and they trudged around the main streets in the light drizzle, concentrating on the essentials then looking for the welcoming warmth of one of the town's cafes. Here and there a small group of pensioners, staying in the resort for a mid-week cheap break, huddled together, unsmiling, some thinking *Why didn't I stay at home?* As lunchtime approached, groups of schoolchildren appeared, lively despite the bitter weather as they looked for some hot fast food.

In the CID room at Scarborough Police HQ on Northway, Bentley's team shifted impatiently in their seats, waiting for him to finish his meeting with the stranger who had appeared at the station earlier that morning. Tim Sharpe stood up and started for the toilet, just as Bentley and the stranger appeared in the corridor.

"At last!" Debbie Chapman rasped, glancing around at the others. "About bloody time, eh, Ryan?" George Ryan watched as Sharpe sat down again, and nodded thoughtfully at the sergeant.

"Looks serious, Debbie," he muttered, and turned to face the table near the whiteboards, which were decorated with labels and photos of the recent murder at Saltergate. A projector had been set up, pointing towards one of the blank boards. Inspector Don Bentley ushered the stranger, a stocky man, towards a seat, then turned to face his team.

"Quiet, everyone," he instructed. "Sorry for the delay, but DCI Jefferson has been filling me in with some background details to our latest Moors murder. I'd like to welcome DCI Jefferson, from West Yorkshire Police, who is head of Leeds CID, and he'll now enlighten you." Bentley gestured to his guest, who stood up and placed a few sheets of paper on the table, then surveyed the faces in front of him. Bentley, meanwhile, sat down, pulled a jelly baby out of his pocket and popped it into his mouth. Jefferson glanced back at Bentley, then addressed the team.

"Thank you, Inspector, and *Good Morning* everybody. I've been asked to liaise with you today, to share some information and to see if I can help you identify and catch your killer. Before we think about him, however, I'd like to give you some background information about events that have been happening in Leeds. I'm sure that you're aware that the city has experienced problems with drug abuse and dealing over recent years ..." one or two nods in the room "... and we've had some gang warfare, but in the main it hasn't really affected the local population. The feuds have mainly eliminated a few nasty drug barons, so no loss there." One or two smiled

46

briefly, as the DCI opened a small bottle of water and took a swig. "Would someone dim the lights, please?" has asked as he moved to the projector stand.

"In the past three or four months, however," Jefferson continued, "things have got much worse, more sinister, and people are getting worried. The main gang operating out of Harehills, run by an evil Scouse bastard called Alan Murrell, have taken a number of hits." He switched on the projector and an image of Murrell appeared on the board. "Some of his key men have disappeared ... killed or moved away, we're not sure, but last month Tony Morran, one of his top men in the city, was found dead in Roundhay Park. Single shot to the back of his head, just like your man. Another big player, Jack Callaghan, was shot in his car at Birch Services, on the M62. He was on his way from Liverpool to Leeds, and the stash of drugs in the boot was stolen. And now we have your murder victim." He flicked another face on the board. "Gordon Ryan."

"George's brother!" quipped a voice at the back of the room, and one or two laughed softly.

"Quiet!" warned Bentley, who then glanced apologetically at Jefferson. The DCI had another sip of water, then continued.

"Gordon Ryan, a vicious thug, Murrell's right-hand-man. Now he's dead, and Murrell seems to have disappeared. We know that he's got a fancy yacht, the *Mersey Belle,* moored in Whitby harbour, but he's not there."

"Bispham and Williams from the Whitby station checked it out," Bentley added. "They got the keys from the harbour-master and searched the boat. It's massive, but there were no signs that anyone had been on board recently."

"It's quite likely that Murrell has fled to Liverpool," Jefferson continued, "and has gone underground. The manner of the killings would frighten anybody off."

"Who's taken over now, Sir?" Sharpe quizzed. "We know that supplies of drugs are still getting through to Scarborough."

"Nathaniel White, he's the main man now," replied Jefferson.

"White," muttered Debbie Chapman, "Nathaniel White … a black guy?" Jefferson nodded. "Wasn't he a big cheese years ago?"

"Yes, he was," Jefferson acknowledged, "but then he became involved in drug wars against other gangs, including the Scousers, was betrayed, then banged up for the past few years. Since his release from prison, he seems hell-bent on regaining the league title. Here he is." He flicked on the next slide, a handsome, well-built man in his late thirties.

"He's a looker," Debbie smiled, "should have been in the movies."

"Only the violent ones," Bentley added.

"I assume he's not operating on his own, Sir," George Ryan remarked, "so who's helping him? He must have some serious muscle behind him."

"You're right, of course, but at this stage we don't know who." Jefferson flicked onto another image, showing an older brute of a man. "James Masterman, or *Monsterman* as some prefer to call him. He's got form for all sorts of violent crime, and has served time, but he's getting on a bit now and just seems to be Nathaniel White's personal bodyguard. The recent murders are not his style."

"Any idea whose style are they, Sir?" Ryan pushed again.

"This is what we need to find out, and quickly, before more enemies are executed. This may help us." He moved on to the next image. "This is the type of gun that murdered Tony Morran and Gordon Ryan. It's a Makarov PMM pistol, a recently-updated version of the Makarov PM, a gun used extensively by Soviet police and military personnel … and the KGB." Gasps around the room.

"The KGB?" Sharpe asked, a worried look on his face. "Isn't this a bit out of our league, Sir? Shouldn't Special Branch or MI6 be involved here?"

"I can understand your concerns, of course, and we have been in touch with London to see if they can throw any light on the people involved. They are working on it, but in the meantime we still have a lot of work to do here, in Yorkshire."

"You mentioned that Morran and Ryan were killed by this gun, Sir," George Ryan spoke again, "but what about the other gun victim, the one of the M6?"

"Good question, young man," Jefferson smiled at Ryan. "Jack Callaghan was killed at Birch Services, and we think that he was shot by a similar gun, only a Polish version."

"So we've got a killer with two different guns, or two killers?" Bentley asked.

"I can't tell you, Inspector, but don't get too alarmed with the guns ... or the KGB. I'm told that these Makarov pistols, which were based on the German Walther PP, were used all over Eastern Europe and thousands became readily available after the collapse of the Soviet Union."

"What next, Sir?" Debbie asked. "It seems to me that the focus of these investigations is really in Leeds, not here."

"To some extent you are correct, but you still have a murder on your patch, and we need to know the new people involved in the drug supply chain to the coast. You have plenty of work to do in this operation." He smiled at Debbie, then continued. "There is something else. We have been told that Nathaniel White purchased a large house here, in Scarborough. As yet, we don't know the location. I hope you can find it for me." He turned to the projector, and flicked on to the last image. It showed a dark-haired shapely woman, with a floral tattoo near the top of her left arm. "Oh, I almost forgot," Jefferson turned apologetically to the others. "How could I forget her? This is Stephanie Garrett. Quite a stunner."

Sharpe grinned and leaned over to Slater. "What a pair of tits," he whispered, "she's got the sort of body that would make a bishop kick a hole in a stained-glass window!"

"Got something to say, Sharpe?" Bentley scowled at him.

"Er, I just said that she looks like a model, Sir," Sharpe replied meekly.

"She tried for a year or two," Jefferson continued, "but she was too short, so she turned to glamour modelling, then to porn. She was a prostitute in Leeds, but she's spent the past few years down in London, we think with her own set-up, very exclusive, high class, expensive. She was close to White years ago, and the word on the block is that she's back in the area."

"Drugs, killers, prostitution, big houses," mused Debbie Chapman. "It seems to me that this Nathaniel White bloke is empire-building, and that part of his empire is going to be here in Scarborough." Bentley and Jefferson just glanced at each other.

CHAPTER SEVEN
MOSCOW

Karl slipped out of bed and pushed the curtains apart in the hotel room. It was snowing outside and the parkland surrounding the hotel was white as far as the eye could see. Karl smiled to himself, *cold out there, warm in here,* then he glanced back at the double-bed where Natasha was sleeping peacefully. He went to the toilet, then moved quietly to the edge of the bed and sat down. The past few days had been idyllic. Natasha had accompanied Karl back to Moscow and to the Ismailovo Hotel, where she had efficiently arranged with Reception to have Karl's room converted to a double. They had spent the days touring around the areas of Moscow which were not familiar to Karl, had visited the Bolshoi Theatre on Friday evening, and had made passionate love in their room every night. Natasha had taken Karl around the area close to Moscow University, where she had lived and studied for three years, and they had spent some of the weekend with Irina meeting artists and making purchases in the souvenir market near the hotel. One of Karl's suitcases was now filled with samples to show his parents when he returned to Scarborough. *Scarborough* ... it seemed a million miles away, and Karl found it difficult to contemplate returning to his humdrum lifestyle there.

Natasha stirred, reached slowly across the bed and opened her eyes quickly. She smiled when she saw Karl sitting on the edge of the bed, and sat up, the duvet slipping down to reveal her breasts. "Come back to bed," she urged, and pulled back the covers as Karl moved towards her. He slipped in beside her, and they embraced each other, until Karl lay back on his side of the bed. "What's the matter?" Natasha whispered.

"You know that I am returning to England tomorrow?" he said, looking glum. Natasha smiled briefly and nodded. "We both know that, and yet we haven't spoken about the future. I've only known you for a few days, a few marvellous days, but it seems like years to me. We've got on so well, outside in the city, and here in this bed," he held her close, and released, "but we've not spoken about the future, our future. What are we going to do, Natasha?"

She looked thoughtful. "I haven't mentioned the future, because I think you may want to forget about me after you leave Russia."

"Forget about you! How can you say that when we've been so close since we met? In fact, we haven't been apart since that day in Byelavaya."

"Yes, I know that, Karl, my darling, but you haven't really spoken about your life in Scarborough. I don't know if you have a girlfriend, or even a wife." She laughed. "You may not have room in your life for a Snow Maiden like me."

"That's true, Natasha, I haven't talked about England

very much, and I haven't asked you if you have a boyfriend in Russia. You're so beautiful. I was frightened to ask in case you said that you have somebody special in your life." He paused, then held her shoulders. "I don't want this to end. I want you to be in my life, and if you feel the same, then what are we going to do about it? You told me that you haven't decided on a career, so why don't you come with me and we can live together in England? You speak English very well, and I'm sure that I could easily find work for you. What do you say? I can buy a flight ticket for you this morning!"

"Oh Karl, if only life was so simple! Yes, I would love to come to England and live with you, and it would be nice to return together, but to do that right now is impossible. I would need a visa from the British Embassy, and that could take a week or two to arrange. They will need a lot of information about me before they can issue a visa, and it could only be a student visa, perhaps for three or six months. They would not allow me to work in England."

"I'm sure that you will love living in Scarborough. It's only a small town in the north, but it's by the sea and very busy in the warmer months. Another thing: it's easy to drive or take a train to cities like York, Manchester or Leeds."

"I have two friends who are students in York, and another who lives in Liverpool. Is that in the north?" Karl nodded, then he thought for a minute or so.

"Right, so you do want us to stay together, and you do want to come to England and live with me?" Natasha laughed, mouthing *Yes!* "In that case, we have no time to lose. We must visit the British Embassy today and find out what information they need, and how long it will take to obtain a visa. Then we can book your flight, and you can start packing for your new life!" Natasha embraced Karl, then pushed him onto his back and started kissing him passionately. He responded briefly, then pushed her off him, looking serious. "Come on, woman. Get up and get dressed. We have a lot to do today!"

CHAPTER EIGHT

WHITBY

Following the meeting with DCI Jefferson, Bentley had assigned his team to various tasks - updating the drug scene in the Scarborough area, searching for witnesses or any new evidence relating to the murder on the moor near Saltergate, and checking recent purchases via the local estate agents to identify the location of Nathaniel White's house in Scarborough. He had just finished a phone call to Jefferson in Leeds when George Ryan knocked on his door.

"May I have a word, Sir?" Ryan asked meekly.

"Come in, Ryan, and take a seat. Drink?" Ryan shook his head. "Now, lad, tell me what's on your mind."

"It's about our murder on the moor, Sir? It's been bugging me. When DCI Jefferson told us that other members of the drugs gang had been shot in Leeds and on the M6, I couldn't understand why another gang member had been killed here on the moors. OK, so the Hole of Horcum is a beauty spot and a murder there would attract lots of publicity, but why would the killer drive all the way here instead of simply murdering his victim somewhere closer in the Leeds area? After all, there are many locations there which would grab the headlines. To my way of thinking, it has to link with Alan Murrell's yacht at Whitby."

"I understand what you are saying, George, but the yacht was thoroughly searched and no trace of Murrell was found there."

"Agreed, Sir, but he's still missing, isn't he? He may be in hiding in the Liverpool area, but I think he's around here. That makes sense, doesn't it? Killing the two main men at the same time would send a powerful message to other enemies or potential rivals. They must have missed something at Whitby, Sir."

"You're not going to drop this until you've had a look yourself, are you?" Ryan grinned and nodded slowly. "OK, go to Whitby and have a look around. Have a word with the harbour-master, then let me know. And another thing, George. Call in at that little sweet shop on the East Cliff and buy me a pound of jelly babies. I like them from there." He looked in his wallet for a £5 note and passed it over.

***

It had started to rain by the time Ryan was leaving the building, so he returned to the store for some wet-weather gear before driving to Whitby. Tim Sharpe noticed Ryan loading the boot of his car, and trotted over.

"Where are you off to, George?" he enquired.

"Whitby. I'm going to check around the harbour again."

"Lucky bugger. You get all of the interesting jobs. I'm back off to the moors in this pissing rain." He looked upwards and shrugged.

"It might brighten up later, Sharpie," Ryan grinned.

"There's more chance of you seeing a mermaid at Whitby, pal," Sharpe called back as he headed for his car.

***

Ryan parked on the harbour car park and looked around for the harbour-master's office. He spotted a sign on a low building further along the harbour side, and made his way to it. One or two fishermen were busy on their boats, but the rain had intensified and not many people were around. Whitby, like Scarborough, was quiet at this time of the year. Ryan knocked on the door, opened it and smiled at the harbour-master, who was busy at his desk.

'Morning," Ryan muttered, searching for his warrant card. "I'm DC Ryan from Scarborough police, and I would like to have a look around one of the boats here."

"I guess that would be the *Mersey Belle*?" the harbour-master replied, glancing at Ryan's warrant card. "The local police have already had good look around it, you know?" Ryan nodded. "I'm Jim Caine, by the way," he said, shaking Ryan's hand.

"George Ryan. I know that, Jim, and I don't expect to find anything they've missed, but I just wanted to have a nosey myself. Have you got the keys?"

Caine unlocked a cabinet and brought out a bunch of keys. "This one," he pointed, "unlocks the security gate on the pontoon, and the rest are for the boat. Do you want me to come with you? I'm rather busy at the moment." He gestured towards the paperwork on his desk.

"Oh no, I'm fine, Jim, but can you just point me in the right direction, give me a clue?"

"I don't need to, George. It's that big one on the far pontoon, where the water is deeper," he stood in the doorway and pointed across the harbour. "She's a Sunseeker Apache, just in case you're interested ... worth maybe a hundred grand and we don't see many of them around here. Give me a shout if you're struggling."

"Thanks," smiled Ryan. "I'll see you a little later." He exited the building, and glanced across the harbour where a variety of small and larger boats were moored. The largest boats were on the far side, but one stood out from the rest, and Ryan guessed that was the *Mersey Belle*. He made his way across the pontoons, nodding a *Hello* to a boatman as he passed by. Arriving at the last pontoon, Ryan pulled the keys out of his pocket and unlocked the security gate. He fastened it behind him and walked slowly down the pontoon, studying the other boats moored there. Gasping at the size of the yacht, he boarded the *Mersey Belle*, walked around the deck, then unlocked the cabin door and moved down inside the boat. It was spotless inside. The beds had not been slept in and the sink was clean, with no pots. There didn't seem to be anything out of place. Ryan checked around again, before climbing back up on deck. It certainly looked as though the boat hadn't been used for weeks. He glanced across the water to the East Cliff harbour side, and decided to have a look from there. As he walked back along the pontoon, Ryan studied the other boats and their moorings. All were tethered to the pontoon. Ryan locked the security gate, returned to the harbour side and walked out of the harbour towards the swing-bridge. It was lunchtime, and a few visitors were heading for one the town's cafes, probably to enjoy a portion of fish and chips, for which Whitby was renowned. The delicious odour almost tempted Ryan as he crossed the bridge to the east side, but then he noticed the row of little shops and remembered – *jelly babies*. Bentley would not be pleased if the young DC returned without a result for his examination of Murrell's boat and having forgotten to buy a bag of jelly babies. Ryan made the purchase and popped a green one into his mouth (*the DI doesn't like those!* he thought, justifying his theft). He left the cluster of shops and headed along the east harbour side, halting by the rails and studying the boats moored opposite. He was about to return when he thought – *there's something odd!* He looked again. The *Mersey Belle* was the only boat with a mooring rope on the side away from the pontoon. Ryan scratched his chin, then retraced his steps back across the bridge and to the harbour-master's office.

"Hello, Jim. It's me again." Caine looked up from his desk. "There's something I want to show you. Sorry to be a pain, but it should only take a few minutes." Caine stood up, and they both walked across the pontoons to the *Mersey Belle*.

"Right, George, what's bothering you?"

"Well, it's the moorings. I went to the other side of the harbour and noticed that this boat has an extra mooring rope, but not on the pontoon side. Is that normal?"

"No, that's not really necessary, George. Let's take a look." They climbed onto the boat's deck and Ryan pointed out the mooring rope. Caine knelt down and examined it. "This rope's different to the rest. Give me a hand, George." They both gripped the rope and heaved. It hardly budged. Caine looked over the side, then back at Ryan. "I don't like the look of this. You'd better give your boss a ring."

***

Just over an hour later, Bentley and Chapman arrived at the harbour from Scarborough. Two police divers were already waiting, and once their superiors were on board the *Mersey Belle* they slipped into the chilly water. A couple of minutes passed before one of them surfaced. He pushed his goggles onto his head and shouted: "A body, Sir. There's a body, and there's some chain wrapped around it."

"Can you undo it?" Bentley called down to him.

"We'll have a go, Sir". The diver pushed his goggles over his eyes and slipped beneath the water again. The minutes passed, then both divers reappeared. They climbed on board. Debbie Chapman moved away as water splashed around her ankles.

"We've managed to loosen the chain, Sir," the other diver spoke. "It looks like a man, and he's been gagged, with his feet and hands tied together. He's in a mess, Sir

… the crabs have been busy." He glanced over to the harbour side, where a few people were gathering.

"Thanks," muttered Bentley. "Debbie, nip over to the harbour office and call the cavalry. I want Angela to have a look before we start moving the body. Be quick, lass." Chapman went with Jim Caine to make the calls, and Bentley turned to Ryan. "Well done, George. It looks as if your hunch was correct, and that what's left of Murrell is down there." He pointed at the water alongside the boat. "It may take Angela a few days to prove who he is, as his fingers may have disappeared."

"Dental records should do it, Sir."

"Hmm, of course." He thought for a moment. "Oh, I almost forgot, young Ryan. My jelly babies and my change, please." He held out his hand.

CHAPTER NINE
MOSCOW

Mikhail manoeuvred his car through the sludge and found a tiny parking space outside the departure building at Sheremetyevo Airport. "Quickly!" he called to the others, "they will try to move me on soon. Please make sure that you have all of your luggage, Karl."

Karl, Natasha and Irina, swaddled in thick winter coats, tumbled out of the car and went around to the boot. Karl hauled his two heavy cases out onto the snow, and stretched to grab his flight bag. He moved his luggage off the road, then walked back to the driver's door. Mikhail opened the window. "Hey, Mikhail, you've been a great host and a great help! Thank you very much!" They hugged through the window as an official strode along, waving his arms to get Mikhail moving. "Don't forget … come to England soon, and we'll drink some more!" Mikhail grinned and lurched the car forward into the chaos. Karl slung his flight bag around his shoulder, then picked up his two suitcases and followed Natasha and Irina into the building.

"Be careful in here, Karl," warned Irina. "There are so many people, and somebody may try to steal your wallet or your passport. Go over to the right. There is more room there and we can say our goodbyes." Karl found a space and dumped his suitcases on the floor. "Well, Karl," Irina continued, "I hope you have enjoyed your visit to Russia."

"Of course, yes," beamed Karl, glancing at Natasha, "it's been fantastic, and it's all down to you. You and Mikhail have been marvellous, and have made everything possible. I am sure that we will do a lot of business in the future, and I look forward to the next time that you visit England. It will be my turn to be the host!" He kissed Irina on both cheeks and hugged her. She wiped a tear from her eye, then turned and said a few words to Natasha in Russian.

"Goodbye, Karl. Have a safe voyage, and we hope to see you again soon." She turned and pushed through the crowds, stopping near the entrance. Karl watched her go, then turned to face Natasha.

"Well, my love, I don't want to go but I must. Remember everything that we have discussed, and soon you will be in England. Make sure that you complete all of the forms correctly for the British Embassy, and we will be together in a week or two, just in time for Christmas!" Natasha looked really glum. "You are going to come to England, aren't you?"

"Of course, Karl, of course. I'm just so sad that you have to go without me. We have been together ever since we met, and I'm worried that you might change your mind when you get home."

"No way, I'm not letting you go. We're going to be

great together, and everyone will love you over there. Don't forget to call or fax me when you have all of your documents, and I'll book your flight and don't worry, I'll be there to meet you in London when you land. Everything will be fine, my Snow Maiden, just you see!" They kissed and hugged each other, then Karl broke away. "I hate long goodbyes, so please go now, pet. Irina is waiting for you by the entrance." He kissed the tears from Natasha's eyes, then she turned and walked quickly to join Irina. Karl waited until they waved, then he picked up his suitcases and headed for the Customs desk.

***

In the centre of Moscow, the traffic moved relentlessly through the broad streets, the snow heaped by the pavements. The early morning rush hour was easing, but many workers were still pouring out of the underground stations, like a human zoo, with fur hats, coats and boots to protect themselves against the bitter cold. It was a bright, sunny day but the temperature was still well below freezing.

In the *Lubyanka,* Sergei Rudnev had been summoned. He made his way to an office on one of the lower levels, and knocked on the door. He heard a grunt, and opened the door. The thick-set man who had chaired the September meeting glanced at him and gestured for him to sit down. "This Orlov," he spoke slowly, "has been like an eel, a slippery bastard. You must have trained him well, Rudnev," a brief smile, "but now we have an idea of what he is doing. This is what we know. When he was in London he met a prostitute called," he glanced at his notes, "Stephanie Garrett. He became obsessed with her and was persuaded to move to the north of England. He took with him a Pole called Jan Tobolski, who, I think, has worked for Orlov before?" Rudnev nodded.

"Muscle, not too bright, but reliable."

"Hmm, yes, well it seems that this trio moved to a city called Leeds, where the woman had links with the drugs underworld there. They have been working for a drug baron called … Nathaniel White, a black man." He laughed, saying: "He is black, but his name is white," then frowned again. "Orlov and Tobolski have been doing White's dirty work for him. They have eliminated many of White's rivals, and he seems to be the top man now. Some of the killings have been like public executions, and the police know that Makarov pistols have been used. It won't be long before they link these killings to the Mafia, or to us. It is imperative that Orlov and his friend are dealt with quickly."

"Some of this information I knew from my sources," Rudnev replied slowly, "but nobody seems to know where Orlov and his friends are living. Perhaps they are laying low, as they have finished their work for this man White, but I think it won't be too long before they are called to deal with some other rival. When we find out where they are living, we will be able to deal with him."

"You cannot just sit and wait, Rudnev. You must be ready to act as soon as the information is available."

"Of course, I realise that, Sir, and we have already set

the wheels in motion. We will be ready to take action as soon as we receive the necessary information."

"I hope you are right, Rudnev. Your head is on the block." He glared at him, nodded slowly then gestured for him to leave the office.

CHAPTER TEN
SCARBOROUGH

Karl was watching TV when someone knocked loudly on his door. He stood up as the hammering intensified. "Just a minute, hold your horses!" he shouted, as he stretched to open the door and Maggie Buxton almost fell into the flat. "Maggie ... what are you doing here?"

"Charming! What happened to *lovely to see you again,* or *I've missed you, Darling!* You must have been back for three or four days, so is your phone not working, or something? Why haven't you been in touch?"

"Sorry, Maggie, but it's been manic since I returned. I've had to catch up with shopwork and the accounts, sort out all of the new stuff, see my parents and ..."

"And what ... *forget about seeing my girlfriend.* What about me, you pig? You couldn't get enough of me before you went to Russia, and now I'm the Invisible Woman. When did you intend giving me a call? Are you seeing someone else, because God help her?"

"Calm down, pet ..."

"Don't call me *pet.* I'm not a bloody dog."

"It's like I said, I've been busy, and tired after my trip. I was planning to get in touch tonight, or tomorrow."

"Don't put yourself out," she said, turning for the door. "You're not the only fish in the sea. There's plenty out there who fancy me. Call round and see me if you're still interested, and I might think about it."

The door almost left its hinges as Maggie left the flat.

CHAPTER ELEVEN
HEATHROW

Karl glanced for the umpteenth time at the Arrivals board to check that the Aeroflot flight from Moscow had landed. It seemed hours ago as he waited impatiently for the passengers to clear Customs and collect their luggage. He was about to look again when the doors opened and a few more passengers filtered through, some to be greeted warmly by waiting relatives and friends. A larger group of new arrivals pushed their trolleys through the doors, and Karl studied them intently, searching for a slim young blonde. He pulled Natasha's fax from his pocket and double-checked the arrival time again, and was just replacing it when the door opened again and *there she was!* Karl waved wildly and pushed his way through the crowd to greet her. She let go of her trolley and they embraced each other.

"Wow!" he said, beaming, "you're really here, Natasha. I can't believe it! Here, let me take your luggage." He lifted the two cases off the trolley, bumping into other passengers and muttering brief apologies. "How are you? Are you hungry, or thirsty? Do you need the toilet? Would you …?"

"Please," she laughed, "slow down." Karl relaxed and

laughed as well. "I'm fine, Karl, and very happy and excited to be here. I would like a coffee, please, before we leave. The drinks on the plane were awful."

"Of course," Karl looked around and spotted a café, "over there." He pointed, then he placed Natasha's cases back on the trolley and found an empty table. He turned and embraced her again. "It's great to see you again, my Snow Maiden. I've really missed you!"

"Me too. I can't believe that it has only been ten days since we last saw each other in Moscow. I'm so excited to be here with you again!" Karl leant over and kissed her.

"Let me get some coffee, then I can tell you about our journey. Stay right there, Natasha!"

***

"We haven't far to go now, Natasha," Karl checked the motorway ahead then glanced briefly and smiled at her as she awoke from a quick nap. She rubbed her eyes and apologised.

"I'm so sorry for falling asleep. I wanted to see everything on our journey."

"Don't worry about it. There's not much to see on the motorways and main roads, and anyway it will be getting dark soon. We should be at Scarborough in about forty minutes."

"Everywhere is so green," she enthused, "and I love the houses in England. There are so many different designs. In Russia I only know horrible apartments or village *dachas*."

"Well I hope you won't be too disappointed with my flat," Karl replied, looking worried. "It's not very big, but it does have a good view of the sea and the harbour."

"The sea! I can't wait to see it. This is like an exciting adventure for me!"

***

"We're almost there now, Natasha. It's dark now, but I'll take you on a short drive around the town, then we'll go to my flat. We can go out for a meal when your luggage is inside."

"Just a meal? Is that all you want tonight?" They both laughed.

"I'm being polite, pet! You must be hungry after your long journey, but you will only see our bedroom after we have eaten. You can unpack tomorrow!" Natasha, smiling, placed her hand on his leg then glanced out of the window, as they entered the outskirts of Scarborough.

"Are we here?" she asked excitedly.

"Yes, we are. Welcome to Scarborough! I'll tell you a little about my town, Natasha. It is built around two bays on the coast." She looked puzzled. "Do you understand the word "bay"? It's like a big curve on the coast. Well, Scarborough has two of these, called North Bay and South Bay. We are going to start at the South Bay," he muttered, making his way through denser traffic, "and I'm heading for a high point where you will have a good view. The bays are divided by a headland, and there is a ruined castle."

"It sounds just like a fairy-tale," Natasha grinned.

"Look, we are almost there," Karl said, as he drove through a narrow street onto the lofty Esplanade. "There's the North Sea!" he pointed forward, then turned the car and looked for a space, parking outside a hotel. "Let's go," he said, opening the door. They got out and crossed the road to the railings, the strong wind catching her hair. "There you are," Karl whispered, putting his arm around Natasha. "This is the South Bay," he swung his other arm around, "and you can see the harbour below us and over there, the castle on the hill." Far below them, a myriad of colourful lights twinkled on many of the boats bobbing in the water within the harbour walls, and the powerful beam of the lighthouse flashed in regular intervals across the bay. Bright lights illuminated the promenade, and in the background the menacing outline of Scarborough Castle was just visible in the darkness.

"It's absolutely wonderful, Karl, a real fairy-tale. I love all of those pretty lights in the houses – is that a local tradition?" Natasha grinned.

"No, silly," Karl laughed, "it's Christmas soon. Most of those houses have Christmas lights and trees in the windows."

"What's that down there, another castle?" she asked excitedly.

"No," Karl laughed again, amused by the Russian's innocence, "that's the Grand Hotel, one of the oldest in Scarborough."

"It's very hilly here, Karl. It will be excellent for keeping fit. I'm looking forward to running up and down these hills."

"Good Luck to you," he muttered, guiding her back to the car. "Now for the North Bay." He set off, heading for the valley road and the harbour. Natasha was like a small, excited child as she gazed at all of the shops and cafes along the way, then the harbour and fairground appeared.

"I can't believe I'm here. It's like a dream, a fairy-tale, Karl."

"Well you are a Snow Maiden, after all," he laughed. "There's a lot more to see. I'm driving around the headland now, and soon we'll be at the North Bay. There's a big park, Peasholm Park, on this side and more cafes and amusements, but you need to see this side during the daytime." Karl continued driving along the North Bay, then turned and headed back towards the town centre, skirting around Westborough and the main shopping streets. "There are lots of shops around here, of course, but you'll have plenty of time to see them in the future." Natasha couldn't stop beaming, as Karl headed back towards the harbour and parked his car. "Now for our home, my love. Let's grab your luggage and take it to our flat. Put your coat on, Natasha … it's a few minutes' walk to the flat." He lifted out the two larger cases, while Natasha gathered together the rest of her belongings. She followed Karl through the narrow streets of the old town. "Here we are," he announced, sweeping his arm upwards. "Home!"

The lower flats were empty, and Karl ushered Natasha ahead of him on the stairs, finally placing the cases by the side of the door while he unlocked it. He caught his breath, pushed the door open, then bowed gracefully while grinning and pointing inside. "Madam … your room awaits."

"Thank you," she replied royally, and held her head high as she strutted into the room, then they both burst out laughing and embraced and hugged each other. Natasha walked to the window, opened the curtains and looked across at the sea and the twinkling lights in the harbour. "I love it, Karl!" she exclaimed, bending slightly to look around a corner. "It's great view, isn't it?

Karl studied her backside and, grinning, said: "It certainly is!" She turned and followed his eyes.

"Men!" she laughed. Karl moved to the window and put his arm around her.

"Come on, Natasha. Let's have a look at the rest of the flat." He took her hand and led her to another door. "This is the kitchen" … she took a quick peek, and he moved her to another door … "and the bathroom."

"Very nice," she said, smiling coyly. "Is there anywhere else?" He took her hand again.

"Just here," he muttered softly, as he guided her into the room and switched on a bedside light. "What do you think?"

"Very nice," she repeated, "is the bed comfortable?"

"Let's find out," he said, pushed her gently onto it, and kissing her softly. "Everything OK?" he whispered, and she nodded as they began slowly undressing each other. Their clothes tumbled to the carpet as they kissed and caressed each other's bodies, then Karl eased back as Natasha finally lay naked before him. "My God," he gasped, "I'd forgotten how beautiful you are!" He ran his hands gently onto her breasts, feeling her nipples hardening, then moved down her body as he felt himself becoming aroused, then he pushed her fully onto the bed.

"Did you say something about a meal?" Natasha asked, a cheeky smile on her face.

"Later, my Snow Maiden, later."

***

Karl's head was drumming as their movements gradually slowed down, and he eased himself off Natasha and lay on his back. Both of their bodies were glistening with perspiration, and he looked at her and kissed her on the lips. She put her arm around his shoulders, and they lay in an intimate embrace for a few minutes. Natasha moved her head to one side.

"That was a nice welcome," she smiled, and Karl grinned.

"Fantastic!" he whispered, gently massaging the sweat into her body. "You must call here again!" They both laughed heartily, and she punched him playfully on his arm.

***

Later, having showered, Natasha opened one of her cases and looked for something casual to wear. Karl had promised her a traditional Scarborough meal, but had told her that it wasn't necessary to get too dressed up. They both decided to wear jeans and t-shirts. "Make sure that you have a warm coat or jacket, Natasha," Karl advised.

"I come from Russia," she laughed. "I don't have anything else!"

They walked hand-in-hand through the narrow streets of the old town, Natasha pausing frequently to admire the houses, shops and alleys that they passed. "I am going to take lots of photos," she told Karl, "to show my family and friends what my new home is like."

"There'll be plenty of time for that," he replied, "especially in the warmer months, and there are lots of other interesting places nearby. You'll need a lot of films!" They were now nearing the town centre, and Karl guided Natasha into a side street, pointing to an illuminated sign on the other side. "That's where we're heading," he informed her, "fish and chips. This coast is famous for them."

"Chips?" she looked puzzled.

"You'll see," he said, smiling as he opened the door and they moved in, looking for an empty table. Karl called the waitress over, and ordered two haddock specials. "Tea or coffee?" he asked Natasha.

"You choose," she replied.

"A pot of tea for two, please, and may we have some bread and butter?" The waitress nodded, and Karl turned to Natasha. "You've had a lot of travelling today," he said, "so it is best that you have a good meal before we return to the flat. I think it would be best if you don't have any alcohol tonight … we can find a nice pub tomorrow and I'll introduce you to British beer."

"And after our meal, what next?" asked Natasha, feigning innocence.

"I'm going to finish welcoming you to England!" he grinned.

CHAPTER TWELVE
SCARBOROUGH

Narrow shafts of sunshine dappled the bedclothes as Natasha stirred from her deep sleep. It was already mid-morning and Karl was up and about, having showered, and was busy in the kitchen. He heard movement in the bedroom, and poked his head around the door. "Good morning, sleepy head!" he greeted her. She eased herself up and half-smiling, rubbed her eyes.

"What time is it?" she asked, yawning.

"Almost half-past ten."

"No!" she exclaimed, pushing back the bedclothes. "I never sleep for so long. I'm going to have a shower. I'm sorry, Karl. I can't believe that I have been asleep until now."

"Don't worry, Natasha," he said, laughing. "You had a busy day yesterday ... and last night! I'll make you some breakfast."

"Just some juice and some coffee, please, Karl" she called from the bathroom. "That will be fine. We can eat later."

"OK, but there's some toast and yoghurts here. You can decide when you've showered. It's a nice, sunny morning. When you are ready we can go into town, and I'll show you our shops. You might even meet my parents!"

"So soon? I will need some more time to get ready."

"Don't worry, pet. You'll be fine."

***

They wandered hand-in-hand along the harbour side. It was, as Karl had said, a sunny morning, but it was breezy and both were wearing winter coats. A few people were wandering around, and some fishermen were busy working on their boats. Karl led Natasha to a low wall, and they sat down. He pointed to one of the souvenir shops on the other side of the street.

"That's one of our shops, Natasha. We mainly sell cheap rubbish, souvenirs, you know" … she laughed … "but it's really busy in the summer time, especially when the children are on holiday. I'm not sure if our shop is open today. Most of the shops and cafes near the harbour are closed in the winter, but they will all be open in the town centre. After all, it is Christmas next week!"

"Christmas, oh yes, of course, I had forgotten. In Russia we celebrate Christmas *after* New Year, on the sixth of January. How exciting! It will be interesting for me to see how Christmas is celebrated in England."

"OK, well let's go to the town centre. All of the shops will be open there, including our other shop on Westborough. One or both of my parents might be there today. Are you ready to meet them?"

"Well, yes, I suppose. What do they know about me, Karl?"

"Oh, nothing yet," he smiled. "I wanted it to be a secret." Natasha looked thoughtful.

"You haven't told them because you weren't sure that I would come to England. Isn't that the real reason?"

"Partly, I suppose," Karl conceded. "I thought you may have had problems obtaining a visa, and maybe, after I left Moscow, you might have thought it crazy travelling to a foreign country to live with someone you hardly know." She still looked thoughtful. "I'm sorry, Natasha. I should have had more faith in you," then, grinning, added "but I'm so glad that you are here. This is just the beginning."

"I hope so, Karl," she smiled briefly. "This was a big decision for me, you know." He put his arms around her.

"You've been really brave, Natasha. Don't worry, I won't let you down. Now, let's go to town."

"OK, but not to your shop. I'm not ready to meet you parents, Karl. You must tell them about me before I do." He nodded, and they crossed the road, heading for the old town and the shopping centre.

***

"Anyone fancy a coffee?" Debbie Chapman broke the silence in the incident room, as the team waited around for DI Bentley to arrive and start the morning briefing. Dennis Slater gave a thumbs-up signal, but the others just ignored her. Bentley had travelled to Leeds the day before, and there was an expectant atmosphere in the room. A few minutes passed before Chapman returned with the drinks and passed one to Slater. He was poised to take a drink as Bentley entered the room.

"'Morning, everyone," he began, "sorry for the late start. We need to see where we are with this lot before Christmas and New Year messes us up. I saw DCI Jefferson in Leeds yesterday, so I have some new developments from his end. It's taken a little while longer to formally identify the body at Whitby because of its state of ..." he paused, apparently stuck for words.

"Preservation, Sir?" volunteered Sharpe.

"Yeah, that's it. God, I'm cracking up. Anyway, the dental records have secured it, and as we already knew, it was Alan Murrell."

"Were Gordon Ryan and Alan Murrell killed around the same time?" a voice asked from the back of the room.

"Looks that way. We think that both men were taken at the same time in Leeds, then bound and gagged and driven to North Yorkshire late at night. The killers stopped at Saltergate to shoot Ryan, then continued to Whitby where they dealt with Murrell. They must have timed their trip to avoid the late drinkers in Whitby, and the returning fishing boats in the morning. There weren't any reports of unusual activity in the harbour area around the time Murrell was killed." He paused ruefully. "Anyway, the double killing certainly sent out a powerful message to all of White's rivals. He seems to have total control of the drugs scene in Leeds now. What's the state of play here in Scarborough, Sharpe?"

"We've had words with Jake Palmer and some of the other key suppliers, Boss, and it looks like business as usual, except that new people are involved from Leeds."

"Any names?"

"No. It's all very hush-hush."

"I got the same picture from Jefferson. We know who are the top dogs, but very little about those in the middle of the operation. You need to keep digging … we need some bloody names." Bentley paused to look at his notes. "Next, Dennis, did you find anything else at Saltergate?"

"Not really, Sir. I checked with the landlord of the pub, and it seems that he has occasional bother with lovers in their cars – you know, in the car parks or on the rough moorland nearby – but beyond that, nothing. As you said before, it looks as if Ryan was killed well after midnight and the murderer probably had a silencer on his gun. Hardly anybody lives around there, Sir." Bentley listened quietly, then flicked through his notes.

"You're right about the gun. I've been informed there is a version of the Makarov pistol called PB, which has a silencer." Back to his notes. "OK, what about Nathaniel White's house here in Scarborough? Jefferson had whispers about that in Leeds. Any luck, Ryan, Debbie?"

"Nothing so far," Debbie Chapman grimaced. "We've checked all of the records for the past year, and there's nothing in White's name."

"We expected that, Sir," Ryan continued, "so now we're checking all of the purchasers from the past year to see if any of them has a link with Nathaniel White. It's likely that the purchase was made using a friend's or a relative's name, but there are a lot of properties to investigate."

"I realise that, Ryan, but concentrate on the larger houses, especially those with some privacy. White's made a lot of money out of drugs, hasn't he? He's not going to buy just a two-up, two-down terraced house, for Christ's sake. He'll want somewhere flash and private, somewhere to impress his guests. Concentrate on Scarborough to begin with, then slowly widen the net. You can give them a hand, Slater. I'll get DCI Jefferson to send a list of all of White's known relatives." He smiled briefly. "I know this search could take some time, but it's vital that we find out. White keeps a very low profile in Leeds. He may be more relaxed, more careless over here." Bentley crossed the room and poured himself a glass of water from the drinks dispenser. He took a couple of sips, then continued. "The big bit of news that I have concerns our possible killer. This has come from London, and it's something the Russians have been trying to keep quiet. One of their agents," he glanced down at his notes, "a Boris Orlov, has gone AWOL. We've found out that he's been seeing that Leeds prostitute, Stephanie Garrett, and has fallen for her big-time. Put two and two together, and it seems likely that he's done a flit with her, back to Yorkshire. We think that some kind of deal has been struck with White, to provide the muscle to clear away his drug rivals and then to expand into prostitution in the Leeds area."

"Wow! If that's true, he's taking a massive risk, isn't he?" Sharpe asked. "A Russian agent. I can't see the KGB, or whoever it is these days, just allowing him to go solo in Yorkshire. He'd be a good catch, wouldn't he, for our boys? Surely the Russians will get rid of him for us?"

"That's right," Ryan chipped in, "but they've got to find him first, haven't they? If we can't find him, it's going to be more difficult for the Russians. Do we know what he looks like, Sir?"

"They've promised to send us some photos," Bentley took another sip of his water, "but it's vital that we keep the lid on this information. Jefferson agrees. If the press gets hold of this, I'll have the culprit hung, drawn and quartered, mark my words!"

"Do we know if it's just one killer, Sir?" Ryan again. "Two guns have been used so far, haven't they?"

"True," admitted Bentley, "and one was Polish. We might get some more help from London on that one. Right, any more questions?" He looked around the room. "OK, there's lots to do. Let's get on with it."

***

Karl passed the rice bowl to Natasha, but she declined politely. "No thanks," she said, rubbing her tummy, "I'm absolutely full. That meal was delicious, Karl. I haven't eaten much Chinese food in Russia."

"Well, this is the best Chinese restaurant in the area. It's famous for its Cantonese style of cooking." Natasha looked puzzled. "Canton is just one region of China. There are lots of different variations, as well as Malayan, Vietnamese, and Indian, of course." He laughed. "Don't worry, pet. We've got plenty of time to sample some of the others." She nodded, and smiled.

"I'll have to cook you a Russian meal soon."

"Of course, I'll look forward to it. I bet you're a great cook!" He glanced around the room, where several couples were still eating their meals. "Now then, first impressions, Natasha. It's nearly the end of your first full day in Scarborough, your new home. What do you think?"

"It's been so exciting, I don't know what to say." She grinned. "I feel like a small girl on her birthday, or at Christmas time. The town is so beautiful, with lots of lights in the streets and the harbour is wonderful. There are so many new things, Karl, it's like a big adventure for me."

"And this is only the beginning. There will be lots of see, and people to meet, in the coming days, weeks, months … and years!" He smiled, then added more seriously. "This is not important now, but soon we must talk about our future. You are not allowed to have a job, but I will have to go out to work soon, so what are you going to do? You can't just sit in the flat all day."

"Of course not! Do you think I am a lazy pig? I think you need someone to keep your flat tidy," she said, pulling a face at him, "but I also want to be active, and to keep fit. I will enjoy running around this town, and I want to keep studying to improve my English. I would also like to travel, and to visit my friends who are living in England."

"Oh yes, you said. York and Liverpool, wasn't it?"

"Yes, that's right. I have some money, but I may need some help from you. Perhaps you could drive me to places?"

"That's true, but don't worry about money. As far as I am concerned, we are going to live like a married couple, and I can give you money each week … you know, for food, clothes, travelling, and so on. As for running up and down Scarborough's hills, yes, a little, but I want us to spend time together during some of the days. I will check with the authorities, but I'm sure that you can do some unpaid work in the shops. It will help you with your English too. Anyway, we can discuss these things again in the holidays. We will have lots of time together at Christmas and New Year." He looked at the dishes of food on the table. "Have you finished?"

"Yes, thank you. The meal was delicious."

"Good! I'll just go and settle the bill, then we can call in one of the pubs and have a drink … unless you are too tired?"

"Oh no, I'm fine. I don't feel tired at all."

"Great! When we've been to my local pub and had a beer or two we'll return to the flat, then I'll show you another way to keep fit." Natasha pretended to be bashful and she slapped his arm. "That's right, my dear. You won't be running up and down hills all of the time!"

CHAPTER THIRTEEN
SCARBOROUGH

"Oh, Mrs Griffin. I feel ill. I haven't eaten so much food in my life!" Natasha sat back on the sofa and held her stomach. She looked across the room at the dining table, still laden with the remains of the Christmas dinner. "What a feast!" she exclaimed, "and for only four people. I can't believe it!"

"It's a tradition in this country," Mrs Griffin explained, "that we always have too much to eat and drink at Christmas. We haven't had the pudding yet!" She laughed as Natasha placed her hand over her eyes. "We can save that for later."

"I'm confused," Natasha confessed. "Is Christmas pudding something sweet, or more like a pastry such as Yorkshire pudding?"

"It's definitely sweet," Karl's father continued, "with lots of fruit and a tasty sauce. I really like it!" he smiled. "And don't worry about the amount of food on the table, Natasha. We never eat it all on Christmas Day. We'll still be eating turkey by New Year!" Everyone laughed, as Mr Griffin went to the drinks cabinet. "Would you like some more wine, Natasha, or something stronger? Karl told us that you drink a lot of vodka in Russia."

"Oh, that's for the men, Mr Griffin. Wine will be fine, thank you."

"I'll refill your glass, and by the way, I'm called Ted and Karl's mother is Betty. Forget the Mr and Mrs!"

"OK, Ted. I'll try to remember. Things are more formal in Russia, you know." Karl joined her on the sofa and put his arm around her shoulder, as Ted passed the drinks around. He sat down on an armchair, as Betty left the room, returning a few minutes later with a carrier bag.

"Now that we're full and relaxed, we can open our presents." She smiled widely at Natasha. "After that we can have the Christmas pudding."

"I'll just go and fetch ours," Karl eased himself up from the sofa and brought another carrier bag from the hall. He passed it to Natasha, and she rummaged around for the gifts she had brought from Russia.

"This is for you, Ted," Natasha passed a bottle-shaped present to Karl's father, and watched him unwrap it. "It's *Stalichnaya,* one of the finest vodkas from my country. You should place it in the freezer before you open it, and drink it neat, down in one!"

"Thank you very much," Ted smiled, admiring the bottle and trying to read its label.

"Oh, and this is for you as well," Natasha handed over another package, and watched Karl's father unwrap a furry-looking Russian Army hat. "I hope it fits. Karl told me that you enjoy playing golf, so it should keep you warm!" Ted placed the hat on his head.

"It's great, thanks!" He stood up and admired himself in the mirror, as Natasha passed a parcel over to Betty. She revealed a small box, which contained an oil-painted portrait brooch.

"How beautiful!" she exclaimed, and hastened to fasten it onto her dark-blue top. "How lovely! Who is the lady in the portrait, Natasha?"

"She was Natalia Goncharova, the wife of the poet Alexander Pushkin. They said she was the most beautiful woman in Russia!"

"Oh, really? I'll have to remember that when I show it to my friends." She too posed by the mirror. "It's really beautiful, thank you." She turned and smiled at Natasha. "Karl told us that your name is really Natalia."

"Yes, my formal name is Natalia, but I prefer Natasha – most people call me that." She handed another small parcel to Betty. "This present is not so special, but it should be useful." Betty unwrapped a hand-painted round papier-mache box. "You can keep small pieces of jewellery in it."

"Very nice, thank you very much, Natasha." She crossed over and kissed Natasha on her cheek, and watched as she handed Karl a bulky parcel.

"I hope you like them, Karl. It's a hat and scarf from my favourite football team ... Dynamo Moscow." Mrs Griffin took over again.

"Now we have something for both of you." She dug into the carrier bag and passed a square package to Natasha and a larger, bulky package to Karl. Natasha carefully unwrapped the parcel and took out a large box of chocolates with an envelope taped to the top. She smiled at Betty, then opened the envelope, reading the card inside. "It's a voucher, a gift token, so that you may choose a nice perfume in one of the big shops. We didn't know which brand you use, so we thought a voucher would be better. Karl can take you to choose." Karl, holding up a purple woollen jumper and matching shirt, nodded to his mother.

"Thanks for these," he grinned, "I thought you would buy me some clothes."

"We never know what to buy," Betty explained to Natasha, "so clothes are always useful. You like the colour, don't you, Karl?"

"Yes, good choice," he said, reaching for two packages and passing them over to his parents. Ted unwrapped a pair of golfing gloves and watched his wife open a box containing some chocolate Brazil nuts, two cookery books and an envelope. "The envelope is for both of you," Karl explained. "There are two tickets for the Stephen Joseph Theatre. You can choose which show you want to see."

"Thanks, love, very nice. Now then, who's ready for some Christmas pudding?"

"Just before we do, Mam, I have a little something for Natasha. This is something special for you," he smiled as he passed over a small, wrapped box and watched as she carefully eased off the gift-wrapping. Natasha's eyes opened widely as she looked at the piece of jewellery inside.

"Oh Karl, it's beautiful, really unusual, but you must tell me more about it," she gasped as she lifted a silver and black pendant out of the box.

"That's Whitby jet, isn't it, love?" his mother asked, having a closer look.

"That's right, Mam," Karl said, turning to Natasha. "Jet is a black mineral found in this area, and it is often used for jewellery, but I think this pendant is delightful, very unusual. I think it is like a sunburst."

"Or a star," Natasha muttered, handing the pendant to Karl. "It's so delicate, Karl. Please put it on for me." She leant forward, and he fastened the pendant around her neck.

"It looks lovely on you, Natasha," Ted said, "a nice contrast between the black and silver pendant and your beautiful blonde hair."

"Hmm," muttered Betty, giving her husband a filthy look. "Now, can we have some Christmas pudding?"

***

It was a polite, almost formal evening as later on, Ted nodded off in his armchair and Natasha fended off a barrage of questions from Karl's mother. Just before nine o'clock, Karl and Natasha stood up and looked for their coats.

"Thank you for a lovely meal and some wonderful presents, Betty," Natasha smiled as she gave her a hug. "You too, Ted," she said, repeating the process after he had fully woken up. Karl kissed his mother and shook hands with his father.

"We'll see you soon," he announced as he opened the front door and led Natasha to the gate. They turned and waved to Betty and Ted, then walked to their car. Karl hugged Natasha before opening the car door for her. "Thank God that's over," he laughed.

"I really enjoyed it, Karl. My first English Christmas. I won't forget it, and thank you again for your wonderful gift … this beautiful pendant." She lifted it from her neck and studied it again. "I will treasure it for the rest of my life." She leant over and kissed Karl as he started the car and slowly drove off.

Across the street, in the darkened car, Maggie Buxton raised her head and watched the rear lights of Karl's car brighten as he reached the junction of the road, then she started her car and followed, keeping a good distance between them.

***

In Roundhay Park in Leeds, a young couple looking for some privacy headed into some bushes and stumbled over a body. The man shone the light on his key-ring and baulked as it revealed the body of a woman, hands tied behind her back, a pool of blood around her head. His girlfriend screamed loudly.

A few miles away, in Harehills, one of the area's notorious brothels went up in flames. Christmas revellers were evacuated from the neighbouring houses and watched in silence as the firefighters tackled the blaze.

Later that evening, a body of a man was found in the garden of a house close to Headingley Rugby ground. He too had been shot in the back of his head.

CHAPTER FOURTEEN
SCARBOROUGH

Don Bentley surveyed his team, glanced at the whiteboards on the wall, then rummaged for a jelly baby in his pocket. He popped it into his mouth and chewed it thoughtfully.

"I hope you all had an enjoyable Christmas." Nods and mutters around the room. "Make the most of it then, because it looks as if we're going to be busy for the foreseeable future. I expect you heard about the latest killings in Leeds?" More nods. "Helen Steel, one of the top toms in the city. She was shot, or rather executed, on Christmas night. Bradley Hogan, a well-known pimp, was killed around the same time. Both killed in the same way as Gordon Ryan at Saltergate … hands tied, shot in the back of the head. We're waiting for the test results, but I expect it to be the same killer." He paused briefly. "What you may not have heard is that Steel's brothel was torched on the same evening. No fatalities, but the building was gutted. The message is pretty clear, I think."

"Nathaniel White's moved on to the next phase?" suggested Sharpe.

"Looks like it, Sharpie," Bentley continued. "He obviously feels that he's dealt with his drug rivals, and now he's moving into prostitution. We desperately need a break here, some information to help us catch up with him."

"We may have something connected with his house in this area, Sir." Bentley glanced over to George Ryan's desk.

"Really? … go on, Ryan."

"Yes, Debbie and I think so, Sir."

"Where the hell is DS Chapman?" Bentley barked.

"She felt ill this morning, Chief," Slater explained. "She's gone to her doctor's, but hopes to be in later on."

"OK, thanks. Now then, young Ryan, spill the beans."

"Well, Sir, we've been concentrating on larger, more private properties in the Scarborough area, and we looked at a large detached house near Peasholm Park. It's situated right at the end of a secluded road, has an electric gateway and is surrounded by high walls. It's really private, and you can see some security cameras from the road."

"Have you already had a look?"

"Yes, just from the road. We haven't tried to have a look inside yet."

"What makes you think this has a link with White, George?" Sharpe asked. Ryan glanced at his notes.

"The house was purchased last August by someone called Richard Marshall, and White has a younger sister, Rebecca, who is married to a Richard Marshall." Smiles around the room. "We haven't completed the legal checks yet, Sir, but I think this looks promising."

"Too bloody right, it does," spluttered Bentley. "As soon as we have some confirmation, we can begin sniffing around, eh?"

"Yes, Sir," Ryan continued. "I thought we might be able to do some house calls about home security … that sort of thing, Sir. Deliver some leaflets and interview all of the nearby households. It's a big house. Someone must be looking after it for White, after all. What do you reckon, Sir?"

"I reckon you're right, Ryan. Keep pursuing the legal ownership, and let me know as soon as you get a definite link with Nathaniel White." He looked around the room. "Anything else to report?"

"We're still waiting for photos or any other information from London on that Orlov character, Sir," Sharpe looked up. "Have there been any sightings of his partner … Stephanie Garrett?"

"Nothing from DCI Jefferson in Leeds, as yet. It looks as if they're living out of the area, maybe out of Yorkshire. We could do with a lead on that one," Bentley confessed, as Debbie Chapman entered the room. "Ah, DS Chapman, feeling better?"

"A little, Sir. I wanted to get in today to see if we had any new leads before New Year."

"Not much. Young Ryan will update you." He glanced at Ryan, who nodded. "OK, that's all for now. Don't get too cabbaged at New Year, you lot. I want to see some real developments next year, and by that I mean starting on the second of January!"

CHAPTER FIFTEEN
SCARBOROUGH

"I've got a table-tennis match tonight, Natasha. Do you want to come along and watch?"

"Yes, please." She smiled widely. "I used to play a little when I was at university. It will be interesting to see how good you are."

"Well, I'm the weakest player in my team, but we're doing quite well this season. We're top of the second division, hoping to be promoted next year." He grinned at her. "Anyway, that's tonight. I have some work to do at the shops today, mostly pretty boring stuff, so what are you going to do, Natasha?"

"I want to phone my friends in York and Liverpool, if that's OK with you. I would like to see them soon, or perhaps stay for a weekend with one of them."

"Of course, pet, no problem."

"The weather's nice today, dry and not too cold, so after I make the phone calls, I think I'll go for a good run. I want to get to know this lovely town, and find all of the best places where I can keep fit."

"A good place to start might be the Esplanade, high up on the cliffs. You'll get a great view of the town from there, and you can run down to the harbour and along the promenade to the North Bay." He pointed cautiously. "Don't go too far and get lost!"

"Don't worry, Karl. I'll just look for the castle. Our flat is not too far from there. I'll be back here long before you finish work!"

***

"I'll just check my bag, then we'll be on our way. I can't play without a bat!"

"Where is your match tonight, Karl?"

"Oh, it's just in one of the local schools … not too far. We'll take the car, however, and perhaps have a drink afterwards. Mick might bring his girlfriend with him, so you may have some female company. I hope you can make friends with some of the girls here. I don't want you to spend hours on your own, Natasha."

"Don't worry about me, Karl. I haven't been in Scarborough very long. I have lots of time to make new friends!"

"I know that, of course you have. I've forgotten that you've only been here for a month or so, it just seems much longer. Now, wear a warm coat. It can get quite cold in these halls when you're just sitting around."

***

Karl and Natasha arrived as his team-mates, Mick and Jonny, were practising. Mick's girlfriend Jill was there, so Karl introduced Natasha and the two women were soon lost in conversation. Karl was getting changed as Mick and Jonny strolled over.

"Hurry up, Karl," Jonny barked. "We haven't much time before the other team arrives." He paused and glanced at Natasha. "Who's this then? She looks fit." He grinned at Karl.

"I'm Natasha," she replied, smiling and glancing up at Jonny. "How can you tell that I keep fit?" she asked innocently.

"I think he means something different!" laughed Karl. "I'll explain later," he added, when he saw Natasha's puzzled expression, then he turned to Jonny. "She does like to keep fit, as it happens. Natasha told me that she played a bit of ping-pong at university."

"Did she? In that case, Natasha, while we are waiting for that slowcoach over there, let's see what you can do. We've got a few spare bats here, so please take your pick." He passed over a sports bag and watched as Natasha looked through, before selecting a bat with reverse rubber on both sides.

"I think this one will be OK for me," she said, examining both sides of the bat, then standing up and removing her coat.

"Wow, you are fit!" Jonny gasped, ogling Natasha's curvy figure. "You're a lucky bastard," he smirked at Karl, then turned back to Natasha. "Now then, lass, let's see what you've got." He grabbed a ball from the bag and walked to the table. Natasha followed him and they began to knock up slowly. Jonny patted a couple of easy balls over the table, but it immediately became obvious that Natasha was no novice, as she firmly smashed a couple of balls past her opponent. Jonny's face looked more determined as he played some more attacking shots, but Natasha was equal to them, blocking some and smashing others past her astonished opponent on the other side of the table. As she warmed up, the Russian added more spin and power to her game, and was soon making Jonny work hard just to keep the ball on the table. He was quickly working up a sweat, whereas Natasha was coolly controlling the exchanges. Within minutes, Jonny realised the hopelessness of the situation and called a halt to the practice session. He grabbed the ball as it was passing by him once more. "OK, point made, Natasha. Not bad, not bad at all. I don't want to try too hard, of course, as I have a match to play, but if you keep practising, you might make a decent player." He stretched for his towel and began mopping his brow, as the others roared with laughter. Natasha returned the bat to the bag, and sat down next to Karl.

"Christ, you are a dark horse!" he exclaimed. "I didn't expect that, Natasha. You didn't just "play a bit" at university, did you?"

"Well, I did play against other university teams in Russia, and one or two abroad," she confessed. "I really enjoyed that," she added, as she watched Jonny continue to wipe the sweat off his head.

***

After the match finished, Jonny made his excuses and the other four went for a drink in a nearby pub. "That was fantastic … you were fantastic," enthused Jill, as Karl and Mick went to the bar for drinks. "I couldn't believe how good you were," she laughed as the men returned. "That Jonny," she turned to Mick, "has always been a big-headed bugger, but Natasha really put him in his place."

"Too true," Mick replied, "that was the best laugh I've had for ages."

"I was really proud of you," Karl added, kissing Natasha. "I wonder what else you have up your sleeve?"

CHAPTER SIXTEEN

YORK

Bishopthorpe Road was busy with early evening shoppers, and couples perusing the menus outside the area's varied restaurants, before deciding where to eat. There were few tourists at this time of the year, but the city's large student population always added a vibrancy to the nightlife in York. The traffic was busy with many vehicles passing through the area on their way to the outskirts of the city and beyond, others finding a parking space locally to return home or to enjoy an evening in the area.

Away from the main thoroughfare, streets of terraced housing afforded cheaper accommodation for lower-paid workers in the city or for students. Around 7.30 in the evening, a couple exited the back door of an end house of a large Victorian terrace, and made their way slowly towards Bishopthorpe Road, before crossing the river via Skeldergate Bridge and heading towards the city centre. They turned right near the ruins of Cliffords Tower and walked along the ring-road, until they reached a popular pub on the bank of the River Foss.

Stephanie Garrett and Boris Orlov shared the large apartment on the first floor of the house with their friend Jan Tobolski, but they rarely went out as a trio. They took their privacy, and security, very seriously, and tried to avoid drawing attention to themselves in the city. They rented the other flats to students, who had busy social lives or conscientious studying to worry about, and so largely ignored their landlords. Stephanie was the main contact with the tenants, and most of the repairs were sorted out by Orlov and Tobolski. They communicated with Nathaniel White via mobile phone, and despite several attempts to trail his three partners, he still had no idea where they lived. Orlov was determined to keep it like that.

Today was Boris' birthday, so he and Stephanie decided to relax and enjoy a pub meal, where they could discuss their next moves regarding Nathaniel White. Orlov chose a corner table, where he could speak privately to Stephanie, as well as keeping an eye on the doorways for any potential threat. Old habits died hard with Orlov. Though he was disguised, wearing false glasses, he had his gun discreetly concealed … just in case. They looked through the menu, and Stephanie ordered and paid for their meals and drinks at the bar. Wearing a figure-hugging dress, with her long brown hair cascading over her bust and her shoulders, Stephanie, as usual, caught the attention of some of the male customers, but they soon lost interest when she returned to the bulky Orlov at their table.

"Everything's gone well so far, don't you think, Boris?" she asked quietly, taking a sip of her drink.

"Too well, in my opinion. We have removed most of White's drug rivals, and made a start with taking over prostitution in Leeds, but it's been too easy for my liking. I'm surprised that both the police and my Russian friends have not found us."

"That's because we've been very careful to keep a distance from Nathaniel White, and to live well away from Leeds. The police haven't really bothered our operation in Leeds, let alone look for us."

"The police are obviously stupid. In Russia they would not have been so polite. They would have made some arrests by now and would perhaps have been on our tail, but here … well. The security services cannot be so stupid. They must know that we are involved, yet they still have to make a move. We must look for another place to live - somewhere away from this city, perhaps a remote farm on the moors."

"I don't think we need to panic just yet. It's safe in the city because we are surrounded by students who have no interest in us. We have melted into the background, and as long as we remain careful we should be safe here until our operation has finished. When we have control of the prostitution scene in Leeds, we can break away from Nathaniel White. He needs us, well you mostly, at the moment, but when we have eliminated the opposition we can do a deal with him." She paused as a waitress placed their meals on the table. "Thanks," she smiled, as Boris began tucking in to his mixed grill. "Don't wait for me, dear," she added sourly, "Happy Birthday!" Boris, his mouth full, just nodded *thanks.*

***

Boris sat back in his seat, as Stephanie finished her trifle. "Very nice," she smiled across the table. "You know, I've been thinking. Once we get established and get rid of White and the drug scene, we might be able to expand into porno films, and perhaps open a club or two. I think there's a lot of potential there."

"Maybe," mused Boris, "and I think Jan would be happy to help out there." They both laughed, drawing some attention from the other diners.

"Jan, in porno films!" Stephanie snorted. "He'd have to wear a bag over his head, or a mask ... the ugly bugger!"

"True, but he has got a big cock. He might be a porno star in the future!" They laughed heartily again, then Stephanie returned to the bar for some more drinks.

CHAPTER SEVENTEEN
SCARBOROUGH

George Ryan pulled up his scarf and collar around his neck to ward off the bitter cold, as he waited for Debbie Chapman to finish saying goodbye to the lady owner of a large detached house near Peasholm Park. He shivered as she approached the gate.

"About time, Debbie. I'm bloody freezing here. What were you doing … swapping life stories?"

"Shut up, you wimp. Mrs Ashton knows my mother, so she was asking how she is. I was only being polite."

"And the rest." He glanced along the road. "Just two more to go, and this next one overlooks Nathaniel White's house. Let's hope that the owners can give us more information than the ones we've seen. They all seem to keep themselves to themselves around here. Are you ready?" She nodded and they walked to the next gateway, crunching along a pebbled drive to an imposing wooden front door. "Got a leaflet?"

"Of course," she replied stonily, as she rang the bell, then smiled as she heard footsteps in the hallway. A petite lady in her fifties opened the door slightly and peered around the safety chain.

"Yes, can I help you?" she asked timidly.

"Good afternoon, Madam," Debbie continued to smile widely. "I'm DS Chapman and this is DC Ryan from Scarborough police." They held up their warrant cards so that she could see them. "There have been a few burglaries in the area recently, so my colleague and I are interviewing local homeowners to check their security arrangements and to give them some advice. Can you spare us a few minutes to check your house?"

"Yes, that should be fine. My husband isn't in at the moment, but he ought to be back soon." She unhooked the safety chain. "Please come in," she said, ushering them into the hall. "Would you like a hot drink? It's very cold today."

"Lovely," Debbie rubbed her hands. "Tea would be nice, thank you, Mrs … ?"

"Mills, Joyce Mills. Go through to the lounge and find a seat, while I make a pot of tea." She opened a door, and Chapman and Ryan walked past her and sat down on a leather settee.

"Nice room," Debbie called to her disappearing hostess. George stood up and walked to a large window, surveying the well-planted back garden.

"Nice garden too," he muttered. Debbie joined him at the window. "I wouldn't fancy all of the work though," he added, as Mrs Mills returned to the room, carrying a large tray.

"Please, sit down and make yourself at home. Help yourself to milk and sugar, and there's some biscuits if you want one." They all sat down and busied themselves with the tea.

107

"You're very kind," Debbie said, sipping her tea. "Lovely … it is really cold today, Mrs Mills. This is just what we needed, eh George?" Ryan nodded enthusiastically. "Now this is why we're here." She passed a leaflet to Mrs Mills. "I'll leave this with you, and you can discuss things with your husband later. The leaflet gives you up-to-date details about the latest security devices for your home – door and window locks, alarms, the whole works. I see that you have a safety chain on your front door, but you need to make sure that other doors are equally secured, and that your upstairs windows have modern locks. We often find that the upstairs is forgotten in these large, older houses." Mrs Mills flicked through the leaflet.

"Do you have any alarms, Mrs Mills?" Ryan asked.

"No, but we have been thinking about getting some installed. My husband has made some enquiries. One of his friends on the other side of town was burgled recently, so it made us think."

"That's good," Ryan continued. "Do you think you could show us around the upstairs rooms? I'll soon be able to tell if you need any extras there."

***

"That's a big house next door," Ryan looked at Mrs Mills, as they all looked out of one of bedroom windows.

"Yes, it's probably the biggest house in the road. It changed hands last year, but we don't know who lives there. It's somebody from away, we think, though I have seen a woman once or twice. She looks like some kind of housekeeper. I think that's her car parked over there."

She pointed to an area behind the house. "There have been two or three weekend parties, with lots of visitors, but they've kept themselves well-hidden. Some of the guests arrive by taxi. Those high walls and the trees make that house really private."

"You're right there, Mrs Mills," Debbie looked thoughtful. "It looks a bit grim, doesn't it?" They laughed briefly. "Well, I think we're about done, Mrs Mills. Thank you for your time and oh nearly forgot, here are our cards. Please call us if you have any questions, and one of us will call round and see you."

"Thanks again for the tea," Ryan smiled as they walked downstairs.

"You're welcome," Mrs Mills patted him on his arm. "The police seem so young these days," she remarked to Debbie Chapman.

"True, but he's a clever lad, is our George," she smiled at Mrs Mills. "Goodbye." Chapman and Ryan walked slowly along the driveway, and they turned and waved at Mrs Mills as they moved into the road. "Now for the big one, George."

"Hmm, well at least, there should be somebody at home. The housekeeper's car is there, so hopefully we'll be able to have a good look round and find out some information about the mysterious owner." They walked along to the large gateway. The gate itself was solid, and there was an intercom on the wall. Ryan peered through the crack near the hinges as Chapman pressed the intercom button. A minute or two passed before a voice answered.

"Hello. Can I help you?"

"Hello, yes," replied Chapman. "We're from Scarborough police, and we're advising local residents about house security. Can you spare a few minutes to talk to us?"

"Oh, I'm not sure. How do I know that you are the police?"

"We have some ID cards here. If you come to the gate I can pass them through, and you can phone headquarters if you want. We've interviewed most of your neighbours today."

"Give me a minute or two. I'll come down to the gate." Ryan watched through the crack as a young woman came out of the house and approached the gate. "Put your ID cards in the letterbox, please." Chapman dropped them in, and within a few seconds the door began to open. "Can't be too careful," a dark-haired young woman smiled at them both. "Please come in." She pushed her glasses onto the knot of hair piled on her head and led the way. Ryan glanced at Chapman, raising his eyebrows, as they followed her to the front door. He was studying her casual dress from the back – trainers, jeans and a loose jumper – as she suddenly turned and welcomed them inside. Ryan looked embarrassed, but she just smiled briefly. They followed her to a huge lounge, where she pointed to a range of armchairs and settees. "Please, sit anywhere," she muttered, as she watched them find separate seats. "I'm sorry about before, but I've been told to be wary of strangers."

"Very sensible," Ryan remarked, "told by whom?"

"The owner of the house ... he lives away from Scarborough most of the time."

"And the owner, Miss...? Sorry, we haven't introduced ourselves. I am DS Chapman, and this is DC Ryan." They held up their warrant cards again.

"Oh right, I'm Elizabeth Coward," she muttered, glancing at the cards, "but most of my friends call me Liz."

"OK, Liz," Chapman flashed a formal smile, "and the house is owned by...?"

"I'll need to find the paperwork, as I don't really know him, but didn't you say you are here to check security? This seems more like an investigation." She laughed shyly.

"Sorry about that, Liz. Yes, we are here to check your house security and to advise about improvements, but as you are not the owner, we may need to contact him to confirm changes, that sort of thing. Don't worry, you are not under suspicion!" They all laughed. "You can find the details later. George?"

"Right, well as DS Chapman was saying, we've been interviewing local residents because there have been a few burglaries around here recently. We've been checking people's doors, windows, alarm systems and so on, and giving them advice when we feel improvements are needed. Here's a leaflet for you." He passed it over, and the young woman glanced through it. "Burglars are becoming more sophisticated, you know. It's wise to have your security checked regularly, especially if you live on your own in a big house like this. Are you the housekeeper, or do other people work here?"

"No, it's mainly just me. I do most of the cleaning, but from time to time a man comes to do the gardening and I arrange for any repairs that need doing. As I said before, the owner doesn't stay very often, but when he does it's usually at the weekend and he often invites lots of guests to stay as well. He phones me to tell me how many people are going to be here, and I have to make arrangements for the food and drink when we have a guest weekend. There's always a lot of cleaning and tidying up after they've gone." She smiled at Ryan, who made no reply but just waited until she continued. It seemed to him that she was glad of the company. "I'm a sort of secretary as well, you know, dealing with the post, that kind of thing."

"It must be a bit lonely, Liz?" Chapman asked.

"I suppose so, but I don't mind. I quite like my own company, and I have plenty to do most days. I try to keep a regular routine, and I also do some studying. I had a bad time at university last year, but I hope to go back and continue with my course." She glanced at the two police officers. "I'm sorry, I'm going on too much. Where else would you like to see?"

"Everywhere really," said Chapman. "You lead the way, Liz." They all stood up, and made their way to the kitchen. Ryan examined the door lock, then looked at the windows.

"These look old, Liz. A burglar would get in here easily. Let's look at the other downstairs rooms." They moved into another lounge, which had been converted into a games room, with a snooker table in the middle. "Very nice," Ryan muttered, looking around the room. "This looks like a recent conversion to me, as the locks are more modern."

"I don't know," said Liz, "it was like that when I started here." She led the way into the hall. Ryan pointed to a door.

"Where does that lead?"

"To the basement I think, or a cellar. I'm not allowed to go down there."

"That's bad, Liz," Chapman studied the padlocked door, "because if there was a fire down there, the whole house could go up before you or the Fire Brigade could get it open. You need to get that changed. You must have a word with the owner." Liz nodded. "Let's go upstairs." The young woman led the way, taking Chapman and Ryan into a labyrinth of bedrooms and bathrooms on the next two floors.

"Everything's old-fashioned up here, Liz," Ryan explained. "No modern window locks, one or two damaged fittings. It's not good." He pointed to a smaller door. "More rooms?"

"Yes, this is where I sleep." She ushered them into a comfortable attic room, with a medium-sized bed and a small wardrobe.

"This isn't much," Chapman looked around, then

smiled at Liz, "when you compare it to the rooms downstairs."

"Oh, I don't mind," Liz replied, "in fact I like it up here. It's much cosier that those big downstairs bedrooms, and in any case, I don't have much."

"Typical student!" Chapman retorted, and they laughed.

"What about friends, boyfriends, Liz?" Ryan asked, as they reached the hall. "It must be lonely living here on your own, a young woman like you." They looked at each other for a few seconds, then she smiled and replied.

"Like I said before, I don't really mind. I've got lots of studying to do, and I've not been encouraged to have company." Ryan smiled sheepishly, then glanced away.

"By the owner?" Chapman enquired. Liz nodded. "Can you find his details for us, Liz? If he refuses to do any improvements, we may need to get in touch with him." Liz went into a small office at the back of the games room, and returned with a piece of paper.

"This is the contact number I have," she pointed to a phone number on the sheet, "and his name is Richard Marshall. I don't have any address information."

"What's he like, Mr Marshall?" Ryan asked. "Do you get on well with him?"

"Well, as I've already told you, I haven't had a lot to do with him. He made it clear that if I do my work properly, he won't interfere much. I've spoken to him when he's been here for the weekend, but he spends most of his time with his guests. I try to keep in the background."

She smiled.

"Finally, Liz," Ryan continued, "is Mr Marshall young, middle-aged or old?"

"I'm not very good at guessing ages," Liz confessed, smiling, "I would say late thirties, early forties, I think. He always dresses smartly, and he's good-looking. Yes, a good-looking black man." Ryan glanced at Chapman.

"Well, thank you very much for your time, Liz, but don't forget … you need to contact Mr Marshall and get him to improve security here. A lot of work needs to be done, some of it for your personal safety. If you need any more advice, or want us to speak to Mr Marshall, please get in touch." Chapman handed Liz a card, and turned to leave, but Ryan paused, smiling at Liz.

"Thanks again for your help, Liz. Can I just take your number for our records?" She wrote it on a piece of paper, smiled at him, then he followed Chapman out of the gate. She walked a few metres along the road, then waited for him to catch up. "What do you reckon, Debbie?"

"I reckon that you fancy her, you sly little toad!" Ryan blushed and turned away. "I can read you like a book, George Ryan."

"I feel a bit sorry for her, Debbie, you know, stuck on her own in a huge house like that. I wonder why a good-looking young woman agreed to take a job like that?"

"I don't know, or why she dropped out of university. Perhaps you can find out, my son?" She pinched him on his cheek. "Let's see what Bentley makes of all this."

***

"Hello ... Liz?"

"Oh hi, Mr Marshall. How are you?".

"I'm good, thanks. Now listen, I'm bringing some friends to Scarborough this weekend, so you'll need to make up a few rooms and get some food in."

"How many guests will there be, Mr Marshall?"

"Not too many. Let's see ... me, Masterman, a couple of partners, and three others. We'll need four rooms, I think. If it's any different, I'll let you know."

"OK, I'll have everything ready for you."

"Good, that's my girl. Anything to report?"

"Not really, except that two police officers called today. They..."

"POLICE! Fucking Hell, what did they want? You didn't let them into the house, did you?"

"Well, yes, I had no choice. They told me that there had been some burglaries in the area, and they were checking everyone's security."

"Jesus Christ! And you just let them into my house?"

"They both showed me their warrant-cards, Mr Marshall, then said that they needed to check all of the doors and windows, and to see if we had any alarms. The woman gave me a leaflet, and told me that the locks and everything are old-fashioned, out-of-date."

"Did she? Well listen, don't let them in again. I don't want any police snooping around my house. If they call again, tell them that I'll sort out the security I need.

Tell them to piss off, you understand?" He paused for a minute. "Listen, Liz, try to have a word with that old woman who lives next door, or any other neighbour you see. Find out if the police visited them as well, then let me know."

"Yes, I will," Liz sounded worried.

"I've been pleased with your work so far," he spoke in a softer tone, "but we both know what might happen if you mess things up, don't we, Liz?" Silence. "OK, don't worry, I'm sure they were just doing their job, but be careful and double-check. You can tell me what you found out at the weekend. Understand?"

"Yes, Mr Marshall." She sounded more assured.

"Good girl, then I'll see you on Friday evening. Four rooms, don't forget." The line went dead.

CHAPTER EIGHTEEN
MOSCOW

Sergei Rudnev shuffled along the darkened corridor, took a deep breath and tapped the door. He heard a grunt, and opened the door, glancing at the occupant sitting at a desk. "Ah, Rudnev," he muttered, placing a drained vodka shot glass on the desk. "Sit down!" he instructed, waving a chair. "What news do you have?"

Rudnev cleared his throat, and tried to appear relaxed. "Our searchers still have to locate Orlov and the others. We know that they are not living in Leeds, where the gang wars have been taking place, but at the moment we do not have an exact location for them. They must be living in the area, however, not too far away. At the end of last month, Orlov and Tobolski murdered a pimp and a prostitute in Leeds, and probably burnt down her brothel."

"Hmm, so they have moved on from just a drugs war, Rudnev? I expected a result by now, not a new development." He looked very angry.

"Of course, but as we have said before, agent Orlov is very clever. We know that the police and the British Secret service do not have his address, so he has covered his tracks very well."

"Do not call him *agent!*" the bulky man said furiously, adjusting his collar. "Orlov has betrayed us, remember? This could still be a huge embarrassment for our country if he is captured by the British." He paused to light a cigarette. "How quickly can we act when we do have a location for Orlov?"

"Everything is ready, I can assure you. It is frustrating, but I am confident that we can deal with this problem successfully."

"That *you* can deal with the problem, Rudnev. Remember, Orlov is *your* responsibility. If you fail, we will have somebody ready to eliminate you. Watch your back, my friend," he added sarcastically.

"That won't be necessary. Orlov will cease to be a problem soon. I plan to travel to England next week to be there when he is removed."

"I don't want any bad publicity from this, Rudnev. We need to have Orlov dealt with discreetly. I don't want a cowboy-style shoot-out when he is found. I hope you understand this, and are not using any agents who are known to Orlov. It *must* be hush-hush. The British Secret Service will not want the public to know that there has been a Russian agent on the loose, so they will keep things quiet, but the police ... and the newspapers, well, they will love it. Everything has to be done so carefully, Rudnev. This is a mess, an embarrassment, but we can still have a good conclusion. I am relying on you to achieve it."

"Of course, I understand everything. There will be a

successful outcome to this problem, but I must confess that I did not expect Orlov and his friends to give us so many problems." He sat back, flustered. The other man stared at him sternly, then laughed.

"Do not worry, Rudnev. I know you will not let me down. Here," he said, finding another glass and pouring two shots of vodka, "let us drink to a successful conclusion!"

CHAPTER NINETEEN
SCARBOROUGH

Natasha wiped the sweat from her brow as she paused from her run on the Esplanade. It was early evening, with a bitter easterly breeze, a darkened sky and the threat of rain. She had now developed a running circuit around the town which was demanding, but still enjoyable, and Natasha smiled to herself as she looked at the harbour lights and the darkness around Castle Hill, where she would soon find warmth in the flat. She generally timed her runs to coincide with Karl's return from the day's business, and today she was looking forward to a drink and a meal in one of the local pubs. She wiped her brow once more, then set off jogging along the road, ignoring the flight of steps which led to the footbridge over the valley. She preferred instead to take the winding footpath which also led to the footbridge. As she descended towards a bend on the steep path, she collided with a woman who had moved slightly to block her way, and knocked her over. "Oh, I'm sorry," the Russian said, stooping to help the woman back onto her feet, "are you alright?"

"No, I'm bloody not," said Maggie Buxton, brushing her coat and holding her arm. "Christ, that hurts … you did that deliberately."

"Honestly, I'm sorry," Natasha replied, "but you moved in front of me. It was impossible for me to stop." As she spoke, two men moved forward from the bushes by the side of the path.

"No, it wasn't, you bitch! You knocked me over on purpose, and you've injured me. Now we'll see how you like it." She moved forward and aimed a swipe at Natasha. She swayed slightly and the blow missed. Maggie rushed forward, but Natasha sidestepped her deftly and pushed her to the ground. The two men moved quickly, and one tried to grab Natasha, but she kicked him in the balls and moved to face the other man. He aimed a vicious punch at Natasha's face, but she swerved quickly enough to parry the blow and hit him in the stomach. He staggered backwards, and she moved forward to punch him again, making him tumble into the bushes. As she turned, Maggie and the other assailant dived towards her, but she caught the man with a smart chop to his face, then she kicked Maggie karate-style into her chest. The other man roared out of the bushes, but Natasha tripped him neatly and he thundered onto the path, knocking out a tooth and grazing his face. He lay groaning on the ground, as the other man made a last attempt to punch Natasha. She grabbed his arm and somersaulted him onto his back, knocking him out on the concrete. Maggie moved away up the path as Natasha turned towards her. "You'll bloody pay for this, you mad bitch!" Maggie gasped, holding her chest. "You haven't heard the last of this." She staggered into the bushes as Natasha straightened her grazed knuckles, then, glancing at the two men on the ground, she began jogging down the path towards the footbridge. Tears of anger were in her eyes, and the wind jostled her bunched hair as she quickened her steps towards the town centre. One or two passers-by looked at her quizzingly as she hurried past them, then she paused for breath at the Grand Hotel, looking around to make sure that there was no pursuit.

*****

"Hi, Natasha," Karl shouted from the bedroom as he heard the door close. "Had a good run?" He walked into the lounge and gasped when he saw Natasha's tears and her bloody hand. He rushed over and held her carefully. "Christ, pet," he kissed her forehead, "what's happened? Have you tripped over? Let me find the first-aid box."

"It's alright, Karl. I'm not really hurt, I'm just angry." She sat down on the settee, and looked up at him. "I was running down the path from the Esplanade when I was attacked by a woman and two men."

"Attacked! Bloody Hell! I can't believe it … attacked." He stretched for the phone. "I'm going to call the police."

"No, Karl, no police! Please, it is not necessary. I'm not really hurt," she managed a brief laugh, "but they are." Karl sat down next to her.

"Would you like a drink?" She shook her head. "Right, Tash, tell me what happened. Take your time." He put his arm around her.

"Well, it was quite strange. I was just jogging down

the pathway when this woman stepped in front of me, and pretended that I had knocked her over. I tried to help her up, but she just pushed me away, then tried to punch me. I knocked her away, then two men appeared and attacked me." She paused and looked at Karl.

"So, have you been hurt … injured?"

"Oh no, they weren't very good. I left them all lying on the pathway." Karl laughed, and held her tightly.

"What are you, some kind of Ninja warrior? Bloody Hell, you're full of surprises, Natasha. First you hammer my friend at table-tennis, now you're beating up the locals!"

"Honestly, Karl, I was not looking for trouble. I tried to avoid a fight, but I had to defend myself when they wouldn't stop."

"Don't worry, pet, I'm proud of you." He kissed her again. "But are you sure about the police? This should be reported. They were probably after money, trying to rob you."

"No, Karl, we do not need the police. I am not hurt, only them. Now, I'm going for a shower, then you can take me for a nice meal."

CHAPTER TWENTY

SCARBOROUGH

Dennis Slater looked along the incident boards as he and the team waited for Debbie Chapman and George Ryan to report back on their recent visit to Nathaniel White's house. Inspector Don Bentley popped a jelly baby into his mouth as Chapman began the report.

"On Tuesday, George and I visited several houses near Peasholm Park to check their security arrangements. As you know, this was just a cover to check out what we believe to be Nathaniel White's house in Scarborough. We gave out a few leaflets, and tried to get a bit of information out of his neighbours. Most of them knew very little, though the lady at the house next door…" she paused.

"Joyce Mills," Ryan offered.

"Yes, Joyce Mills, well she was more helpful. She told us that the house changed hands last year, and that there have been some weekend parties with lots of guests, some of whom arrive by taxi. Mrs Mills also mentioned a housekeeper who lived there. OK so far, George?"

"Yes, Debbie. The useful thing about Mrs Mills' house is that she has a bedroom which overlooks White's house. You can't see much from the outside because there is a secure gateway and it's surrounded by high walls and large trees."

"Yeah, that's right. Anyway, we then called at White's house and managed to speak to the young woman who looks after it …" she glanced at her notes …"Elizabeth Coward. She let us in and allowed us to have a look round."

"Did she seem worried about a police visit?" Bentley asked. "I can't imagine that White would want her to give the police a guided tour." A few titters.

"She seemed OK, Sir, a bit naive to be honest. She certainly swallowed our story about checking security arrangements, and told us that she would pass on our recommendations to Mr Marshall."

"Marshall?" puzzled Sharpe.

"Come on, Sharpe," Bentley glared at him. "Were you asleep at our last briefing? We think that White used his brother-in-law to purchase the house." The penny dropped, and Sharpe smiled sheepishly. "OK, it would be interesting to know White's reaction when she told him about your visit."

"We might be able to find out, Sir. I think that Liz Coward took a fancy to our young George … and I think it was mutual." A chorus of "ooohs" and wolf-whistles, followed by laughter. Ryan blushed deeply.

"Hmm, I suppose we could try a follow-up visit, Ryan, but we'll have to tread carefully. I don't want White getting suspicious. Let's have a think about that one." He glanced down at his notes. "In the meantime, we have a visitor … Tom Maynard-Smith, from MI6, the British Secret service. He's going to speak to us tomorrow morning. DCI Jefferson from Leeds will be here as well. I'll make a decision about future visits to White's house and young Ryan's love life after we've heard what London has to say." He grinned at Ryan. "Is anyone making coffee?"

***

Bentley's phone rang. He listened for a few minutes, nodding and saying "hmm" a couple of times. "Thanks." He put the phone down and turned to Debbie Chapman. "Debbie, there's a woman downstairs, wants to make a complaint about an assault. Can you and Slater go and sort it? Cheers." Chapman and Slater got to their feet and headed out of the room.

"I wonder what this is about?" mused Slater, as he descended the stairs. "Violent boyfriend or husband, no doubt?"

"We'll soon find out," Chapman replied, as she made for reception. Maggie Buxton was sitting there, her arm in a sling. "Hello, Miss…?"

"Buxton … Maggie Buxton."

"OK, Maggie, we believe you've been a victim of an assault. Would you like to tell us about it?" She ushered her into an interview room. "Please, sit down, Maggie. Would you like a drink, tea or coffee?"

"No, thanks, I'm fine."

"Well, if you change your mind, just shout out. Now," she said, pointing at Maggie's arm, "would you like to tell us what happened to you?"

"It was last night, just after tea-time. I was on the pathway down from the Esplanade with my brother and my boyfriend."

"Names, please."

"Michael Buxton and Scott Warriner." Slater noted then down, as Chapman nodded and smiled. "We'd had a meal at my parents' house, and were slowly making our way towards town when this woman came running down the path and crashed into me. She knocked me over, then started cursing at me as I tried to get up. My brother and my boyfriend quickly came over to protect me, but she began lashing out at them with hands and feet. She was like some kind of beserk kung-fu fighter, and she's injured all three of us. Michael's in hospital after she knocked him out." Maggie looked angry and agitated.

"OK, Maggie, slow down. Take your time. Now, have I got this right, this one woman kicked off just because you were in her way, and she managed to beat up all three of you … two blokes included? She must have been one hell of a fighter. Was she a big woman?"

"She was tall, and fast, not bulky. She must have had a lot of training. She sounded a bit foreign." Maggie held her arm, as if in pain.

"Tall and thin, can you remember anything else about her appearance?" asked Slater.

"She had blonde hair, tied back, and was wearing a track suit. I'd guess that she was in her twenties, she was quite young."

"After she assaulted you, what then?" Chapman continued. "Where did she go?"

"She carried on running down the path towards the footbridge. My boyfriend managed to get up and stagger down the path a little way. He watched her stop near the Grand Hotel, then she carried on towards the old town, and disappeared."

"Have you seen her before?"

"I'm not sure … not in a tracksuit, but I think I may have seen her in the town centre. Her hair was loose. I think it was her."

"Ok, Maggie, can you think of anything else? Was there anybody else on the path when she assaulted you?"

"I didn't see anyone."

"Right, Maggie, I think that's all for now. Please give your contact details to DC Slater, and we'll let you know if we get any leads. Let us have some photos of your injuries, please. We'll certainly have someone patrol that area for the next few nights, and see if the woman returns. In the meantime, please get in touch if you think of anything else, OK?"

"Of course, thanks." Chapman left the room, and returned upstairs.

"Anything interesting?" Bentley asked her.

"A bit odd, Sir. This woman reckons that she and two blokes were taken out by a female jogger near the Esplanade. She beat them up, and put one of the men in hospital."

"Hmm, sounds like we've got Wonder Woman on the loose." Bentley grinned and massaged his right earlobe. "Take Slater with you and interview the two men, Debbie. It sounds far-fetched, doesn't it? Interview them this afternoon, and check if they're singing from the same hymn sheet."

"Shall I have a word with Bill Tomkinson from the local rag? He'll like the story, and it might unearth one or two witnesses."

"Do the interviews first, then if they all check out, have a word with Tomkinson. Tell him not to make it too sensational, mind."

***

"'Morning, everybody. I'd like you to welcome Tom Maynard-Smith from MI6, who will update us on the search for Boris Orlov and Co, and I am pleased to welcome again DCI Jefferson from Leeds, who will also bring us up to speed on events there. First of all, Tom." He gestured towards his guest. "Many thanks for taking the time to travel from London to darkest Yorkshire," some polite titters for Bentley's joke, "to widen our knowledge about Orlov. The floor's all yours." He smiled at the smartly-dressed Maynard-Smith, who stepped forward and sat on the edge of the desk.

"Good Morning," he smiled at the team, then glancing behind him, he added: "and thanks for your introduction, Don. By the way, I was born and brought up in Yorkshire – near Harrogate – so I'm glad to be back home." Bentley nodded, and smiled thinly. "We have known Boris Orlov for over ten years. He's lived in London for some of that time, but has also operated in other areas of Europe. For all of that time he seems to have been a model agent, and a loyal servant of Russia, so recent events have really taken us by surprise." He handed around A4 sheets of paper with composite photos of Orlov. "These are the best shots we have of him, I'm afraid. He's not caused us any real bother, until now, that is. We think that he used London as a base, and to have carried out most of his tasks elsewhere in Europe, working discreetly ... well at least until he met Stephanie Garrett about two years ago, and then he seems to have lost his head. She had long-standing links with the Leeds underworld," he said, turning this time to DCI Jefferson. "I am sure that you have been given the background details. We are quite puzzled, it has to be said, for an agent who has been loyal to Russia for so long to flip his lid. It's a crazy situation, we feel. However successful he has been in dealing with rival gangs in Leeds, he must surely know that either MI6 or his Russian masters will track him down eventually. In normal circumstances, we would be very interested in turning an agent who has gone AWOL, but this man is obviously too unpredictable, too violent. The Russians would love to get him back to Lubyanka, but I can't see that happening. Anyone in his right mind would prefer to die." He paused to take a sip of water.

"Have you any idea where he and the others are based?" asked Slater.

"We know as much as you do, that they are living

in a very secure location, probably in Yorkshire, not in Leeds but not too far away. They have been very clever to jettison all of their previous phone records and identities, and have not contacted any of their known associates. My guess is that they are not holed out in some remote farmhouse, but are living in a close, busy community where nobody pays them any attention."

"But that Garrett woman is such a good-looker," Sharpe chipped in. "It's hard to believe that no-one has spotted her."

"Well, yes, not so far, but as I said before, they have been very clever, probably used a lot of disguises. If Nathaniel White does not know where they are … that is still the case, DCI Jefferson?"

"As far as we know, but there have been some developments here in Scarborough, which may lead to a sighting." He nodded to Bentley.

"Ryan, your turn." George Ryan sat up alertly.

"We think we have found Nathaniel White's house in Scarborough. It looks as though he only uses it occasionally at weekends. DS Chapman and I interviewed a housekeeper when we were pretending to do a security survey, and she gave us some useful information. We think he may be entertaining some guests this weekend, so we are hoping that Orlov and the others may be among them."

"What are you planning to do?" asked Maynard-Smith.

"We'll have some discreet surveillance," Bentley

continued, "and may be able to have some access to the house next door. White's house is very secure, with high walls, but we'll try to identify anyone who enters."

"This may help you," the MI6 man passed around some more photos. "This is Jan Tobolski, a Pole, and another dangerous character. He and Orlov make a lethal team. I'll have a word with my superiors, and see if I can join your watchers."

"We may be able to contact the housekeeper again, Sir, and see if she has any information about this weekend's guests … you know, numbers and suchlike."

"If I may say so," Maynard-Smith interrupted, "I have a feeling that this operation could get out of hand. I've already stressed just how dangerous these men are. They are *professionals,* and I am worried that some kind of Indiana Jones response could lead to a lot of bloodshed, especially in a residential area. I would advise the utmost discretion at this stage, with any kind of sighting being invaluable. What do you think?" he glanced at both Bentley and Jefferson.

"Definitely," Bentley agreed. "We need to plan this operation carefully. I don't think we should have any armed police officers at this stage, but if any of our trio visit this weekend, we should try to follow and find out where they are living. That's the most important thing at this stage."

"Yes, I agree," Jefferson continued, "after all, we don't have a really clear idea of what the two men look like. They will probably be disguised, and we can't be accused of shooting at innocent people." He too reached for a glass, and took a drink. The others took the opportunity to stretch their legs, and to mutter to each other.

"Have things quietened down in Leeds, Sir?" Ryan asked Jefferson.

"To some extent, yes, they have," he replied. "Those murders on Christmas Day and the fire that followed have sent shock waves through the criminal community. Most of the regular prostitutes are wary, keeping off the streets. I think they're waiting until they see if new people are taking over. What do they say – the lull before the storm? As far as the drug scene is concerned, White's definitely got a stranglehold there." He glanced at Bentley.

"OK, let's take a break … fifteen minutes, then back here everyone." The room began to clear. "Oh, Debbie," he beckoned, "just before you go. How did you get on with those two men who claimed to have been assaulted yesterday?"

"Well, I interviewed one of them – Michael Buxton, the woman's brother – in hospital. He's badly bruised, lost a couple of teeth and has a couple of cracked ribs. Dennis Slater saw the other guy, her boyfriend, at home. He's just bruised, but lucky that he's still got a pair of bollocks! Anyway, Dennis and I compared notes, then checked with Maggie Buxton's original statement, and they all tally."

"Is that right? That does surprise me. OK, have a word with Bill Tomkinson, but tell him to keep it brief, and not sensational. We don't want a load of vigilantes battering an old granny on the prom just because she gave them a dirty look or waved her stick at them." Debbie laughed. "Oh, and while you're at it, check out the three who've made this complaint. See if they've got any form."

***

Later in the afternoon, when a second briefing had broken up, Bentley ushered George Ryan into his office. "Sit down, George. We need to decide on how to proceed with this housekeeper … what's her name?"

"Liz Coward, Sir."

"Yes, well she could be very useful for us, but I'm worried that she might alarm White and stop him using the house for a while."

"I see what you mean, Sir, but I think Debbie Chapman and I were quite convincing. After all, we did interview other neighbours. I don't think a follow-up phone call to Liz Coward could do much harm. If White has flipped over this, at least we'll know." Bentley thought for a minute or two.

"Give her a ring, then we'll decide on the next move. If you get a positive response, then I think you and I can pop round and see if her next-door neighbour will allow us to do some surveillance." He sat back, happy with his decision. "Jump to it then, lad."

CHAPTER TWENTY-ONE
WHITBY

Karl steadied himself as he balanced on two rocks whilst attempting to take an unusual angled shot of Natasha among the ruins of Whitby Abbey. The camera clicked.

"Is that OK?" she asked.

"Just a couple more," he said, adjusting his position, "then we're done. It's such a beautiful winter's day, so clear. Blue sky, hardly a cloud to be seen, and a blue sea!" He pointed to the horizon. "The photos should be great, Natasha." He clicked a couple of times more, then jumped off the rocks. "All done." He walked over to Natasha and hugged her. "Have you enjoyed today?"

"It's been so lovely, Karl," she beamed. "The scenery in this part of Yorkshire is fantastic. I'm so happy." She kissed him passionately, then broke off as a couple of visitors passed close by. "So just remind me where we have been today."

"We haven't been far from Scarborough. First to Pickering, where we had a look around the shops and a coffee. Then I drove you through the moors to Goathland, that little village where they used to film a popular TV series called "Heartbeat".

"Is it still on TV?" He nodded. "Well, we should try to

watch an episode."

"If we must," he conceded. "Then we drove along the River Esk to here … Whitby."

"I love it here," she enthused. "There's so much to see. We must come here again."

"Of course," Karl agreed, "but it's always best to visit when the weather is good. Whitby is so busy during the warmer months, just like Scarborough, as you will see. We have been lucky with the weather today. Anyway, we're not finished yet, Natasha. Many people say that the best fish and chips are served here, in Whitby, so let's find out! Head over that way, towards the steps, then we can look for a good restaurant."

***

They returned to Scarborough as the light was fading, and Karl drew up alongside a corner shop. "Won't be a minute," he muttered to Natasha, "we need some milk." He left the radio playing and headed inside the shop. He grabbed some milk from the fridge, plus a small loaf and a packet of biscuits, then waited at the counter as another customer was being served. His eyes drifted to the *Scarborough Evening News*, and to a story covering part of the front page:

TRIO ASSAULTED BY FEMALE JOGGER

He skimmed the first few lines, then added the paper to his other purchases. Muttering *thanks,* he hurried back to the car and thrust the paper into Natasha's lap. "Have a look at this."

On Tuesday evening, a woman and her two male friends were assaulted by a female jogger on the pathway leading down from the Esplanade. Following an accidental collision with the woman, the jogger became violent and threw the woman to the ground, injuring her arm. The men came to her rescue, but were set upon by the jogger, who then ran away after the incident. One of the men was left hospitalised.

Police are appealing for anyone who may have witnessed the attack, or for any information about the jogger, who is tall, with blonde hair, and is thought to be in her twenties and possibly a foreigner.

"Oh, my God," Natasha gasped. "How awful! This is not the truth about what happened, Karl. What shall I do?" She was near to tears.

"We'll do what I advised on Tuesday – go the police and tell them what really happened. We've got to clear your name, Natasha. There's no way you can go running in this town again until we do." She looked frightened. "Don't worry, pet. The police aren't animals … they won't lock you away. We'll go first thing in the morning and get this sorted out. The woman who reported this is the criminal, not you."

CHAPTER TWENTY-TWO
SCARBOROUGH

George Ryan was just settling to his desk when Bentley opened his office door and beckoned him. "Ryan," he called, "a word, please." He collected his notebook, and glancing through it, walked slowly across the room and sat down near Bentley's desk. Bentley waved at him to close the door, then muttered: "Any luck, lad?"

"I think so, Sir. I rang Liz Coward last night and pretended to be following up the security survey. I'd only managed a sentence or two when she burst into tears. Apparently, White had phoned her the same day to tell her to prepare for some guests this weekend, then she told him about our visit, and he went ape-shit."

"Ape-shit? What the hell is that?"

"Sorry, Sir, I meant that he went mad with her, but when he calmed down he seemed to believe her that it was only a routine visit. Mind you, he told her to check with the neighbours to see if they had been surveyed as well."

"Good job we covered our backs, eh?"

"Yes, but she seemed pretty frightened and she asked if she could see me tonight. What do you think, Sir?"

"I'm not sure about that, Ryan. We all know that we've got to tread carefully on this one."

"She's got to go shopping for this weekend's party, so she has a valid excuse for leaving the house. I might be able to find out why she's so frightened, and what sort of hold White has over her. It might be a good …" The phone rang, and Bentley grabbed it.

"Bentley," he snapped. "The assault … downstairs … just a minute." He put the phone down. "Sit tight, Ryan." He opened his door and called Debbie Chapman over. "Debbie, there's a couple downstairs, come about that jogger assault. Take Slater down with you and find out what they have to say. I'll catch up with you later. Alright?" Chapman crossed to Slater's desk, and they both left for the stairs. Bentley returned to his office, sat down and thought for a minute or two. "Listen, George, you might be able to find out some crucial information about this weekend's party if you see this Liz woman, but you must be really careful, otherwise we could frighten all of the bad guys away. Tell her that on no account must she tell White that she's seen you outside hours, otherwise it might be curtains for both of you. Take a back seat and listen to what she has to say. She sounds lonely to me, as well as frightened. Does she know anything about the expected visitors? In the meantime, I think I'll go and see Mrs Mills. It's too risky having people sat in cars outside White's house, but if we can set up some surveillance in that bedroom … well, photos, car registrations, possible gold dust for us. I'll have a word with that MI6 bloke and Jefferson in Leeds, then decide what to do. I won't tell them about your date, however, so keep everything under your hat. It's our secret, George. You're a clever lad, and I think it's worth taking a risk. Don't let me down, young Ryan! Now run along, and make your phone call away from the incident room, OK?" Ryan nodded, picked up his notebook and left the office.

***

Debbie Chapman approached the nervy-looking couple sat in reception. "Good morning," she smiled reassuringly, "I believe you have some information about the assault on Tuesday night?" Karl nodded, and Natasha looked down. "I'm DS Chapman, and this is DC Slater. Would you like to follow me?" She pointed towards an interview room down the corridor, and ushered them inside. "Would you like a tea or coffee?"

"No, thank you, we're fine," Karl said quietly, pulling out a chair for Natasha. He waited until everyone had sat down, then continued. "I'm Karl Griffin, and this is my girlfriend Natasha Petrova."

"Petrova - that's an unusual name, Natasha?" Chapman looked at her full in the face.

"Well," Natasha replied shyly, "I am Russian."

"Really, and how long have you lived in Scarborough?"

"Just for a few weeks. Karl and I met in Russia in November and he invited me to stay with him here in Scarborough, to see if I like living in England." She cast a desperate look at Karl. He took up the story.

"I'll start at the beginning, DS Chapman. My parents

have two giftware businesses in Scarborough, and I've been helping them for the past couple of years. Last year, I met some Russian artists in Oxford and they invited me over to Russia to see if we could sell their crafts in our shops. When I was there, I met Natasha and we clicked." He smiled at her, then continued. "Before I returned to England, we went to the British Embassy in Moscow to see how we could obtain a visa for Natasha. A couple of weeks later, I collected her at Heathrow."

"Have you brought your passport, and visa?" Chapman asked. Natasha rummaged in her bag, and handed the document to DS Chapman. She studied the visa, then handed it to Slater. "OK, so you're here for six months, Natasha?"

"Yes, initially, but if things go well, I hope to extend my visa."

"Alright, so now that we know a little bit about you both, perhaps you can tell us what you know about this assault?" She stared again at Natasha. "Take your time, please." Natasha took a deep breath.

"Since I have been living in Scarborough, I am not allowed to work, so I have tried to keep fit by running around the town. There are many hills, so it is a good place for running!" Chapman and Slater smiled, then waited for her to continue. "On Tuesday evening, I was running down from the top of the cliff ..." she paused, and looked at Karl.

"She means the Esplanade, you know, where there are steps and a footpath leading down to the footbridge over the valley."

"OK, we know where you mean. Natasha?"

"I was running down the footpath, around a bend and I saw a young woman just standing on the path, but I when I ran near her she moved suddenly in front of me. I almost fell over, and she fell onto her back. I tried to help her to stand up, but she kept shouting at me, then two men came out of the trees and tried to grab and hit me. I was frightened, but when they attacked me I defended myself. I did not know what else I could do. I stopped them from attacking me, then I continued my run down to the bridge."

"You certainly stopped them, Natasha," Chapman said seriously. "One of the men is in hospital, and the other two have injuries."

"I'm sorry about that," tears appeared in her eyes, "but I did not want to fight. I think the woman planned to get in my way, and I tried to help her, but they were very aggressive. I do not know your laws, but I had to defend myself." She wiped her eyes, then glanced again at Karl. He put his arm around her shoulder.

"You can see why she's upset, officers," Karl added sternly. "These people have deliberately attacked Natasha, and she had every right to protect herself."

"I am not so sure about that, Mr Griffin. Why didn't Natasha just run away? She's obviously a lot fitter than the people she attacked, so was there any need to set about them and put them in hospital?"

"I would have reacted just the same if I had been attacked," Karl responded angrily. "If one of the men had managed to hold onto her, the others could have beaten her up really badly."

"The problem we have, Mr Griffin, is that the victims all claim that Natasha started the trouble by deliberately colliding with the woman, then dealt with the men, even though they hadn't provoked her."

"Then they are lying, DS Chapman. Who are they? They must have had some reason for doing this?"

"I'm afraid that we cannot divulge the names of the victims. At this stage we are only interested in finding out exactly what happened on the pathway."

"What about eye-witnesses? Did anyone else see the assault?"

"We don't know, Mr Griffin. We have asked for witnesses, and have left a notice-board on the footpath, but so far nobody has come forward."

"So it's just Natasha's word against these others?"

"It's a little bit more than that, Mr Griffin. We have three people who have been injured in an assault." She looked again at Natasha. "I am sure that even in Russia you are not allowed just to go around attacking people?"

"Of course not," a tearful Natasha replied, "but *I was attacked.* I had no choice but to protect myself."

"I think that's all for now," Chapman sighed. "DC Slater will take a written statement, and you will have to leave your passport with us, Miss Petrova. I will consult with my boss and the CPS, and will let you know what will happen next. At this stage, you will not be charged, but that may change if we receive fresh information from an eye-witness. Do you understand, Miss Petrova?" Natasha nodded slowly, glancing at Karl and looking like a frightened rabbit. "In the meantime, Miss Petrova, I must ask you not to leave the house where you are staying."

"What kind of justice is this?" Karl shouted angrily. "Natasha came here freely to tell you what really happened, and now you're treating her like a bloody criminal. I'll get in touch with my lawyer and see what he has to say."

"You've every right to do so, Mr Griffin." Chapman held out her hand. "Your passport, please, Miss Petrova."

***

Debbie Chapman tapped on Bentley's door, opened it slightly and poked her head inside. "Have you a minute, Sir?"

"Yes, Debbie, come in. How did you get on downstairs?"

"I'm not sure, Sir. It was the woman who carried out the assault, and her boyfriend, and she's admitted attacking the three of them, but claims that they provoked her."

"Provoked her? That sounds a bit far-fetched ... explain, please."

"She told us that as she was running down the hill, the woman, Maggie Buxton, deliberately stepped into her path, and as she was trying to help Buxton back onto her feet, the two men appeared out of the bushes and tried to grab her and attack her. We know what happened next, don't we?"

"She gave them a good beating."

"That's right," Chapman paused. "Oh, by the way, she's Russian, Sir."

"Another bloody Russian! What's wrong with these people? Can't they stay at home and cause trouble? After all, the bloody country's big enough." Bentley sat back in his seat. "What action did you take?"

"I've confiscated her passport and visa, and told her to stay at home until we've reviewed the evidence and decided what to do with her. I didn't charge her, but told her that she might be charged later. I thought she was telling the truth, Guv, but when all is said and done, she did assault the others. She could have just run away."

"Not if they did grab her, I suppose. If she's telling the truth, she must have been frightened, but she can certainly handle herself." He paused in thought. "Did you check Buxton and the men?"

"Maggie Buxton is clean, but both men have been involved in some petty crime, theft *et cetera*, years ago."

"We'll give it a day or two, and see if anyone else comes forward, eh? It's a pity she's Russian, Debbie. We could use a few women on the force who can handle themselves like her!"

"Trust you to think that way!"

***

George Ryan placed two mugs of coffee on a tray and walked over to the table in a café near Safeway where Liz Coward was waiting. He put the tray down on the table and smiled at her. "Help yourself to sugar or a biscuit."

"Thanks, George." She glanced around the room, where a few other tables were occupied by early evening shoppers. "This is romantic, isn't it?" Ryan laughed.

"Hardly, but it's safe, Liz. We're anonymous in here." He opened a sachet of sugar and poured it into his coffee. "Thanks for agreeing to see me here, Liz. It sounds like things got nasty with Mr Marshall?"

"Yes, he wasn't too pleased when I told him that you had looked around the house. He went ballistic, in fact, but calmed down a bit later."

"We surveyed other houses in the street, Liz. It was all quite innocent, after all we were only trying to help people to be more secure in their homes."

"I think he accepted that, but he did tell me to ask some neighbours if they had been surveyed as well."

"Why is he so concerned, I wonder?" Ryan looked thoughtful, dangling the bait.

"I don't know him that well, George, but he likes his privacy. He doesn't seem to like the police very much."

"Perhaps he has something to hide?" Ryan paused for a response which never came. "Does he use the house much?"

"Not really. He lives somewhere else, and just use the house occasionally at weekends, when he invites his friends to stay."

"Like this weekend? I watched you loading bags of shopping into your car."

"Yes, he's told me to prepare four rooms, so not too many guests this time."

"I'm worried about you, Liz. You lead a pretty lonely life, and that's not good for an attractive young woman like you." She smiled widely, as Ryan handed her a piece of paper. "How did you get involved with a job like yours?"

"Another time perhaps," she muttered, looking at the note.

"That's my phone number, not a works number, just in case you need any help, or someone to talk to." They smiled at each other. "In fact, I'd like to see you again. Would you like to go out for a drink, or a meal?"

"That would be lovely, George. Perhaps sometime next week? Let me get this weekend out of the way, then I'll give you a ring."

"I'll look forward to that, Liz."

***

Don Bentley sat on the edge of the settee and took a sip of his cup of tea. "Lovely," he smiled at Mr and Mrs Mills, "perfect."

"Please help yourself to a biscuit, or a piece of cake."

"Thank you. I've not long had my tea, but that gingerbread looks too good to miss." He smiled again at the smartly-dressed lady sitting opposite, and devoured a piece of cake. "Delicious!" he exclaimed, and took another sip of tea. He relaxed back on the settee, and continued. "I expect you're wondering why I'm here?"

he asked. "It isn't about window locks and such, but something far more important, and something which must remain a secret." The couple looked at each other like a pair of excited schoolchildren. "I need some help, a favour from you. It concerns next door."

"That's not a surprise, Inspector," Mr Mills said, looking for support from his wife. "There have been a few mysterious goings-on since the house changed hands. The new owner's so secretive."

"True," continued his wife. "The young woman who looks after the place seems pleasant enough, but I don't like the look of some of the people who stay there at weekends."

"How do you know," asked Bentley, knowing the answer, "as the walls are so high and there is a secure gate?"

"Well, Inspector," she said furtively, "we can see a bit from one of our bedroom windows."

"Ah, I thought so," Bentley waggled his finger at her, "you wicked lady." They all laughed. "On a more serious note, you might be able to help us here. We need to find out a little more about these weekend parties, and in particular, who attends them. Would you be willing for a surveillance team to use your room with a view? We think there will be some guests this weekend." He held up his hand. "Before you answer, however, I must stress the need for secrecy, and tell you that some of these guests may be very dangerous people."

"Of course, Inspector, we'd be happy to help," Mr

Mills opened his arms in welcome. "What do you want us to do?"

"Very little, Mr Mills, apart from showing us the room layout and somewhere we can make coffee. We will try to disturb you as little as possible."

"How exciting!" enthused Mrs Mills, prodding her husband in his ribs. "My friends will be ever so jealous!"

"OK, Mrs Mills, please don't get carried away. I can see that this can look like an exciting adventure," warned Bentley, "but as I said before, we need absolute secrecy on this matter – both during the operation and afterwards. You must never mention it to your friends and family, unless we give you permission to do so. The people we are dealing with here may be extremely dangerous, possibly even to you. Do you understand?" Mrs Mills looked very serious, briefly smiled then nodded.

"May I ask, Inspector," Mr Mills asked calmly, "does your operation have anything to do with those terrible murders on the moor and at Whitby?"

"I'm sorry, Mr Mills, I can't tell you anything about the operation, only that it is very important and that in allowing us to set up watch here, you may be helping us get rid of some evil and dangerous criminals." He paused for some brief reflection, then stood up to leave. "Right, we'll contact you later today with the arrangements … and thank you again."

***

Karl and Natasha lay in bed in the flat. They had tried to keep busy after visiting the police station but now, with

150

time for reflection, Natasha had become weepy again. Karl did his best to comfort her, but with little success.

"Oh, Karl, I'm so sorry. I wish I had continued running, just as that policewoman said. I could have easily run away from them, then there would not be any problems. I was so happy here with you, and beginning to feel that I belong in this town, and now I might end up in prison or be deported back to Russia."

"Come on, Natasha, try not to be so worried. After all, the police did not arrest you. It's your word against hers, and anyone can see that you're telling the truth. I have an idea, and there's somewhere I must go tomorrow. I am sure that this matter will be finished soon, then we can get on with our lives. You will be happy here, don't you worry, love." He comforted her again, and she tried to lose herself inside him as they slowly began to make love.

CHAPTER TWENTY-THREE
MOSCOW

The controller closed his office door and lit another cigarette, glancing through a file as he exhaled clouds of smoke. He looked for a phone number, then lifted the phone and dialled, puffing away as he waited for a reply. Finally, a voice answered softly: "*Da?*"

"Rudnev ... you took your time. Was there a problem?"

"No, no, I was on the toilet, actually. Have you some news?"

"Yes, finally we have a sighting of the pig Orlov ... or rather his woman and the Pole."

"Good! Where were they seen?"

"In a town called, hmm, York." He had difficulty in pronouncing the name. "York, yes, there is a university there. One of our students saw them at a local shop and followed them to this address." He spelled it out slowly. "He told me that many students live in that area."

"Any sign of Orlov?"

"Not yet, but this student is continuing to watch the house. He is quite clever, I think, and is being patient. He has not asked students in the house for information, but he will find out exactly where they are living soon. Is your man ready?"

"Of course!" Rudnev replied confidently. "We just need confirmation of the exact location, then we can take action. Everything is ready. Have you decided on the preferred method of disposal?"

"Naturally we would like Orlov to be returned to Russia, but I can't see that he would allow himself to be kidnapped, or that he could be persuaded to return. He would rather die. I would if I were in his shoes." He shuddered at the thought of some of the inquisitors he used in *Lubyanka*. "It will be easier to take him out in England, but remember ... no shoot-out, no fuss, no big publicity. Try to make it look like an accident, or suicide. You may need to eliminate the others as well. We want a conclusion to this matter as quickly as possible, but it must be achieved in the correct manner. Understood, Rudnev?"

"Yes, fully."

"Good. You say that you are ready to make a move, so I look forward to receiving some good news soon." He put the receiver down.

In Manchester, Rudnev glanced around his room and wrung his hands together until they hurt. He sat looking worried for a few minutes, thought about making a call himself, then went to the kitchen for a cold drink. *Orlov, the bastard,* he thought to himself, *how has he managed to get his brains into his dick after all of these years?*

CHAPTER TWENTY-FOUR
SCARBOROUGH

Karl Griffin drove slowly into the car park at Scarborough Hospital and looked around for a space. He spotted a gap between two cars on the far side and parked his car.

The car park was filling up with other afternoon visitors as Karl made his way to Reception. He checked the various wards on the information board, then headed for the medical wards. A nurse was busy at the entrance desk to Ward 6 as he waited for her to look up.

"Excuse me," he smiled, "but I wondered if you can help me? A friend has asked me to visit a patient who was admitted here after being attacked by a jogger. Am I at the right ward?"

"Oh," she replied, "I read about that. How awful! He's not on this ward, so perhaps you could try the other medical ward, Number 5? It's on this level."

"Great. Thanks for your help." Karl walked across the building and scanned the lists of patients on Ward 5. He checked them a second time, nodded slowly to himself, then looked for bed 15. Most of the patients were talking quietly to their visitors as Karl approached the bed. "Well, well, if it isn't Michael Buxton. What a surprise!" The two visitors turned around on hearing Karl's words, and he put on a wry smile when he saw Michael's mother and Maggie. "I *knew* that this would have something to do with you," he spoke angrily, glaring at Maggie.

"You want to keep that bitch of yours under control," Maggie screetched, getting to her feet. "She needs to be locked up somewhere." She pushed Karl on his chest, as heads swivelled towards them, and a nurse ran in from the corridor. "Look what she's done to my brother," she pointed at the bed, "vicious bitch."

"It's pretty obvious what happened on the promenade," Karl spoke calmly, as Maggie's mother was about to join the argument. "You've waited for Natasha and tried to assault her. They're the vicious ones, Mrs Buxton," he pointed at Michael and Maggie, "but luckily my girlfriend can handle herself. You deserved everything you got." As he turned to leave, Maggie tried to grab him and other nurses arrived to intervene. "We'll see what the police have to say about this, Maggie. I wouldn't like to be in your shoes," he grimaced as he left the ward.

***

Karl drove to the police station at Northway, then paused to consider his options before switching the engine off. It was late on Friday afternoon, and he wasn't sure if there would be any CID staff available to arrange an interview. Natasha would have to be there, in any case, and she didn't know about Maggie. The police, he thought, would only have viewed the assault as low priority, so would probably delay sorting things out until after the weekend. He decided to leave everything until Monday

155

morning, and to spend the weekend making a fuss of Natasha.

When he arrived at the flat Natasha had just showered and was sitting on the edge of the bed, about to dry her hair. She had a dressing-gown fastened loosely around her. She looked anxious as Karl entered the room. "I've been worried. Where have you been, Karl?" He smiled, sat on the bed next to her and took hold of her hands.

"Relax, Darling. I think I have found a solution to our little problem."

"A solution … what do you mean?"

"I've just been to the local hospital, and I know who assaulted you."

"You do? Have you told the police?"

"Not yet. I thought I'd better explain everything to you first." He glanced out of the window, then continued. "Before I visited Russia, I had been seeing a girl called Maggie. She lives here in Scarborough, and I guess I must have taken her out for about six months."

"Did she live here with you?"

"God, no, it wasn't that serious, at least on my part. I think she wanted to get engaged or for us to live together, but I wasn't ready. She was quite annoyed that I didn't take her to Russia."

"You were still seeing her when you left for Russia?"

"Yes, I was, but when I returned I didn't contact her, and we finished badly."

"Why didn't you want to see her again?"

"The answer to that is quite simple, silly. Because I met you ... and even though I wasn't sure that you would come to England, I didn't want to see her again. Meeting you spoilt everything for me, Natasha." He leaned over and kissed her. "When I met you it was like eating fillet steak, and I didn't want to go back to burgers again." He laughed at her puzzled face.

"Fillet steak, I don't understand."

"Maggie's a pretty girl, but the feelings I have for you are way above anything I felt for her. I love you, pet."

"Did you tell her anything about me?"

"No. She must have found out from someone, or spied on us."

"Spied on us! Well, she must be a very jealous person."

"That's certainly true. I hadn't seen it before, but all of this is down to her jealousy. She must have found out that you went jogging in the evenings, and set a trap to beat you up. The man you put in hospital is her brother, and the other is an ex-boyfriend of hers. Actually, she may have been seeing him again. Anyway, when I went to the hospital, I saw her brother's name on the list of patients and then I knew what must have happened. Maggie was there when I went to confront him, and there was a bit of a scene." Natasha loosened his hands, stood up and went to the window. She looked across at the harbour, then turned to face Karl.

"I wish you had told me about Maggie."

"I'm sorry, Natasha, but I didn't consider it to be

important. Maggie was history, we were finished. That happened before you flew over to England. If you had decided not to come to England, I wouldn't have started seeing her again." Natasha moved back to the bed, sat down and hugged Karl. He turned her head and kissed her passionately.

"What happens next, Karl?"

"We're going to enjoy ourselves this weekend, then on Monday morning we'll go to the police and tell them about Maggie. After that, we can get on with our lives."

"Oh, Karl, I'm so relieved. Now I can start running again, and I can phone my friends and make some plans to visit them." She smiled widely, then lay back on the bed, her dressing-gown gaping open to reveal her breasts and thighs.

"No problem, my Snow Maiden, but before you do any of that, there's something else that we need to do first." He untied her dressing-gown, eased it off her shoulders and began kissing her breasts and running his fingers up and down her body. Natasha held Karl close to her, running her hands tenderly up his back, then unfastened his shirt and eased it off his shoulders. He caressed her more eagerly as she reached forward and felt the hardness in his jeans, then she began unfastening his belt.

***

Tim Sharpe eased himself off the bed in the darkened room, quietly made his way onto the landing, and yawned and stretched. He glanced back at the three

158

officers from West Yorkshire CID, who were silently watching the house next door, their cameras ready to record any activity. They had arrived at different times during the afternoon, so as not to arouse suspicion. As he walked to the bathroom, he longed for a cigarette. *Why was I chosen for this job?* he mused. *What a waste of a Friday evening, possibly night.* Sharpe knew that the surveillance would probably last all night, so plenty of coffee would be needed. He flushed the toilet, then headed back into the bedroom.

"Coffee, anyone?" he whispered.

"No need to whisper, son," one of the officers laughed, "they're not going to hear us over there. I'll have a coffee, thanks." The other two nodded, then one muttered: "Hang on a minute, Tim. The gateway's opening." A taxi could be seen in the road, and a bulky figure hurried along the drive to the main door and entered the house. The cameras clicked. "It's difficult to see who that was," someone remarked, "with no lights on the driveway and the main door in darkness." They sat back and relaxed as Tim went downstairs to make some coffee. He returned ten minutes later carrying a tray full of coffee, cakes and biscuits.

"God, it stinks in here," he gasped.

"Sorry lads," the older of the Leeds men confessed, "it's me. I had a great curry in town last night, but I'm suffering today. I could shit through the eye of a needle." He looked in pain.

"So, we've got to put up with that all night, have we?"

Sharpe asked. "Your arse will be like a blood orange in the morning!" The others sniggered. "In the meantime, that woman downstairs is determined to put weight on us," he joked. He placed the tray on a low table.

"At least we won't starve," one of the others muttered, and they began helping themselves, as another taxi drew up, followed by a car which drove into the drive and quickly parked around the back. Peering into the darkness the watchers could just make out three women and a man who had arrived in the taxi, and another man who had driven the car.

"How many are we expecting?" asked Joe, one of the men from West Yorkshire CID.

"We only know that the woman who looks after the house has been told to prepare four rooms, so that could be it," Sharpe informed the others. "She wasn't told us how many people would be here."

"Right, so we've got three couples so far, plus the housekeeper. What's she like, Sharpie?"

"I haven't seen her, but Ryan said that she's in her early twenties. She doesn't seem to be part of the top table. My guess is that she's there to prepare the refreshments for everyone, and to make up numbers if they're short."

"Very cosy," Joe sniggered, and sat back in his chair. "If no-one else appears in the next hour or so, we'll need to pair up and work in shifts, and try to get some shut-eye. Let's say two hours a shift? I'll take the first spell with Sharpe, OK?"

"Yeah, whatever," one of the others muttered. "That

gingerbread's lovely," he reached for another piece.

"Don't forget, everybody," Joe continued, "no lights. If you wake up suddenly needing a piss, don't switch the bathroom light on!"

"Here we go again," Sharpe whispered, as the gateway opened and a man and woman made their way across the drive and into the house. A taxi completed a three-point-turn in the road and drove off at speed. "That's four couples now, plus an emergency spare woman."

***

Nathaniel White ushered his guests into the dining room, where Liz Coward had prepared a cold buffet and plates of kebabs, sausage rolls and chicken legs. "Help yourself, everyone," White swept his arm across the table. "We've opened a bottle of champagne, and we've plenty of red and white wine, but shout out if you'd like something different. Liz will sort you out, won't you dear?" He smiled at Liz as she moved around the table, filling up the champagne glasses. "Well done, Liz, by the way ... that's a nice spread and you're looking very smart tonight." One or two of the guests half-smiled or nodded, and Jan Tobolski grinned leeringly at her. Liz turned away, blushing, and smoothed down her dark blue dress. She glanced at the other women, who were all wearing short dresses, with a lot of cleavage on display.

"Thanks, Mr Marshall," she said quietly, and continued filling the glasses, before walking to the kitchen for the bottle of wine.

"Mr Marshall, who the fuck's that?" asked Stephanie Garrett.

"Me, it's me, Steph," White laughed. "Remember that name while you're here. The least Liz Coward knows about us, the better. Try not to use any of our real names, or make one up, Betty!" He laughed again, as Liz returned to the room with the wine. "Tuck in, everyone. When we've finished eating I need to have a word with you two," he pointed at Boris and Stephanie. "After that, we can all relax and enjoy ourselves. There's enough booze here to float a battleship, right, Liz?" She smiled briefly, then continued filling up the glasses.

***

Nathaniel White ushered Boris and Stephanie into a small lounge, leaving the others to continue drinking. James Masterman was in his element, cracking jokes and touching the women intimately, while Tobolski kept quiet, sipping his drink and staring at Liz Coward every time she came into the room to clear up. White closed the door and sat down.

"This shouldn't take too long," he smiled at the others. "Things are going great in Leeds, don't you agree, Steph?" She smoothed down her tight skirt, crossed her legs and was about to speak, but White beat her to it and continued speaking. "Really great, better than I could have hoped for. We've got the drugs scene pretty well tied up, but I think we need another push at the pros. Steph?"

"Yes, things are going well, but we haven't made as much progress in Chapeltown as I had hoped." Boris Orlov remained quiet, as White picked up the thread.

"Are my people proving a difficult nut to crack?" he said, pointing at his black face, and smiling. "Perhaps they need a reality check, or a bomb underneath them. What do you say, Boris?"

"Well, violence has worked for us in the past. They are not frightened enough yet. Perhaps they need a reminder of who is now in charge." He glanced at Stephanie. "I think Jan and I can arrange something. Stephanie and I need to discuss possible targets."

"We agreed that prostitution will be your pigeon when we've eliminated all of the opposition," White looked more serious, "so do what you have to do. Just be careful, be discreet. I don't want you to rock the boat in Leeds now that we're doing so well. Agreed?" He studied both of their faces. "OK, then let me know when you have an action plan. In the meantime, let's enjoy the rest of the evening." He turned to Orlov. "Is Jan alright, Boris? He seems a bit quiet, sulky even. The women we've brought are all fit. He should be happy once The Monster and I have taken our pick."

"He's not that bothered, Nathaniel, though he does seem to like your housekeeper."

"Liz, really? I can easily have a word with her, if that's what he wants. She'll do as she's told, but the women have been paid for tonight. It would be a pity to waste the money." Orlov got to his feet.

"I'll just go and have a word with him, and make sure that he is alright. I won't be long, Stephanie." He left the room.

"You're looking great tonight, Steph," White crossed over to her seat, and touched her shoulder, letting his hand slip down to the swell of her breast. "Mind you, you've always been a stunner. We had some good times before I got banged up, yeah?"

"I guess we did, Nathaniel."

"We could do again, you know, pick up where we left off." She stood up and moved away.

"That ship sailed years ago," she snapped. "I moved on, did well in London, and now I'm happy with Boris. I like the arrangement we all have just now. We understand each other, yes?" White nodded, and grinned. "Then let's keep it that way." She scowled at White. "Enjoy the girl out there, Nathaniel." The door opened and Boris came back in the room.

"Jan's OK, I think. He gets depressed at times, misses Poland, you know. He likes Liz, but he'll be happy with one of the other girls. You alright?" he smiled at Stephanie.

"I'm fine, Boris, and thirsty."

"Me too," White muttered, "and the women will be fed up of Jim Masterman by now. Let's join them." He ushered Stephanie forward, and they moved for the door.

***

Later in the evening, Liz drew a breath as Jan Tobolski and one of the blondes staggered their way upstairs. He glanced back at her, but she turned away and made for the lounge, where she continued clearing away bottles and glasses into the kitchen. *I'll have time to wash everything*

164

in the morning before they all get up, she thought, before returning to the lounge and making sure that it looked tidy. After that, she hastened upstairs, glancing at some of the bedroom doors and then across at the darkened house next door, before reaching her room at the top of the house and bolting the door. She collapsed on the bed, exhausted and relieved, before burrowing under the covers, fully-dressed.

CHAPTER TWENTY-FIVE
SCARBOROUGH

"Morning, everybody, let's get started," Bentley barked as he breezed into the incident room and sat down behind the main desk. "We seem to have got this case moving a bit faster now, so let's keep up the momentum. I want to show Leeds CID and those lads at MI6 that we're perfectly capable of dealing with things here at Scarborough. How did you get on with the surveillance, Sharpie?"

"There was a lot of activity on Friday evening, Sir," Sharpe scratched his neck, "one car and some taxis. It was difficult to get any clear photographs because they kept the house in darkness, but in total there were four male and four female visitors."

"Did they all arrive together?" Bentley continued.

"No, at intervals, only one person driving the car. We're assuming that most or all of the women were prostitutes, but it was difficult to tell who was who." He glanced around the room. "They all stayed until Saturday evening, then left in dribs and drabs after it became dark. I was knackered ... so were the other lads from Leeds." He looked around for sympathy, but in vain. "We got the car's reg, but it was a false plate."

"No surprise there," Debbie Chapman muttered. "Waste of time and money, if you ask me," she added cynically.

"Not at all," Bentley scowled at her, "as we can guess who was probably at the house. I don't think they were there for a billiards session, more likely planning their next move in Leeds. Now that we know how they all get there, we can be better organised the next time there's a meeting and have some surveillance cars away from the road." He paused for a few seconds. "Then there's Elizabeth Coward. Ryan, what's next as far as she's concerned?"

"She agreed to meet me sometime this week," Ryan announced, glancing at Sharpe, who pursed his lips and grinned. "If she doesn't phone soon, I'll contact her, Sir, and arrange a meeting."

"Or a date," Sharpe whispered.

"Will you grow up, Sharpe, for Christ's sake?" Bentley bellowed. "Go on, Ryan."

"I hope that she can give me descriptions of the people who were there at the weekend ... perhaps some names. She was a bit frightened, Sir, after White had told her off for showing us around the house, but I think she'll be OK. She's our best hope for making some progress on this case."

"Very true, Ryan, so tread lightly, lad." He glanced down at the desk. "Any more developments, other news over the weekend?" He looked around the room.

"There's one thing, Sir," Debbie Chapman spoke up.

"Yesterday a young woman called in to Reception, and told the duty officer that she has some information about that assault near the Grand."

"Oh, that Russian jogger?" Bentley asked.

"Yes, she's left a number, so I'll contact her this morning and hear what she has to say." A phone rang, and Slater answered it quietly, as Debbie continued. "She might be able to help us decide what to do with the Russian woman."

"Keep me informed, Debbie, and you, young Ryan, let me know when you have some news."

"Sir?" Bentley looked across at Slater. "It's that Russian girl and her boyfriend. They're downstairs, reckon they have some important information about the assault."

"Get downstairs and find out what they have to say, you and Debbie, then afterwards you can contact that witness. I want this matter tied up quickly. Right, everybody, get to it. Sharpe, go and get a coffee and liven yourself up. You look like a zombie." He glared at him as Chapman and Slater left the office. Sharpe waited until he and Ryan were alone, then he cornered the young DC.

"Listen, George, a quiet word of advice from someone who's experienced a bit more life than you. Be careful with that Coward woman. If she's been working for White for some time, she must be involved in his drugs scene. If I were you, I'd assume that she's not all that innocent, and treat her like a 4F girl."

"A 4F girl, what the hell's that?"

"Find 'em, feel 'em, fuck 'em and forget 'em," Sharpe muttered, grinning widely. "Remember that when she's doe-eyed, smiling at you like an English rose!"

***

"Please," Debbie Chapman ushered Karl and Natasha into an interview room, "take a seat. Would you like a drink?"

"No, thank you, we're fine," Karl replied.

"OK," Chapman continued, "I'm told that you have some new information, yes?" She switched on the recording machine, and dictated the standard introductions.

"That's right," Karl smiled at Natasha. "I visited the hospital on Friday and saw the man who claimed to have been assaulted by Natasha. His mother was at his bedside, and his sister ... Maggie Buxton."

"I take it that you know her?" Chapman asked.

"Yes, she is an ex-girlfriend of mine."

"When did you stop seeing her, Karl?"

"In December, just after I returned from Russia." He paused, then carried on with his story. "Let me explain. We had been seeing each other for about six months before I travelled to Russia. She was more serious about our relationship, but when I was in Russia I met Natasha, fell in love," he smiled again, "and asked her to come to England and live with me. I finished with Maggie as soon as I got back, but she didn't take it very well. At that point I did not know if Natasha would come to England, but I did know that I didn't want to see Maggie any more. In the light of what has happened, I think that she must have found out about Natasha, and her jealousy has led her to plan the assault on the prom with her brother and an old boyfriend. What she didn't know was that Natasha can handle herself, resulting in the injuries that all three suffered." He sat back in his chair. Debbie Chapman glanced at Slater, then looked across the table.

"I have to admit, Karl, that this new information *may* put a different light on what actually happened." Natasha looked shocked and was about to speak as Chapman continued. "Yesterday a new witness, a woman who was walking on the promenade that evening, has come forward, claiming to have witnessed the assault. DC Slater and I plan to visit her today and to take a statement from her. If she backs up Natasha's version of what happened, then we will interview Maggie Buxton and the others again and make a final decision on what action to take."

"Natasha and I have discussed this, DS Chapman, and we don't want to press charges. Natasha just wants to put this behind her and to have her passport and visa returned."

"I can understand that, Karl, but you are jumping the gun. We need to interview this new witness first, then I have to discuss the matter with DI Bentley. After that we'll ask you to call in the station again and tell you how we may proceed. Don't forget that at this stage

Natasha is facing a possible assault charge." Karl turned to Natasha, who looked frightened and close to tears. Chapman switched off the machine. "Don't look so worried," she smiled. "It looks a lot better for you than it did last week!"

***

After returning home from work, George Ryan phoned Liz Coward.

"Hello", she said softly.

"Hi Liz, it's me, George Ryan. How did your weekend go?"

"Oh George, thank God it's you. I'm so pleased to hear a friendly voice again."

"Are you alright, Liz? Did something terrible happen at the weekend?"

"No … not really, but well, let's say that I'm glad it's over. I'm sorry, George, but I can't say too much on the phone." She sounded frightened.

"That's OK, Liz. Don't worry. Look, let me take you out for a meal, and we can relax and talk more easily then. How about tomorrow evening?"

"I think that should be alright, but where will I meet you?"

"Drive your car and park at Safeway. I'll meet you there around seven." A pause. "OK, Liz?"

"Yes, sorry, that will be fine. I'll look forward to it, George, but if there's a problem, I'll ring you."

"Good. I'll look forward to it as well. See you tomorrow then."

"Bye, George." The phone went dead, and Ryan sat back on his sofa, and smiled to himself.

***

The following morning, DS Chapman and DC Slater called in one of the larger stores in the town centre. Chapman spotted a supervisor and headed in her direction.

"Excuse me," she said, "I'm looking for Molly Sanders. I think she works here."

"Oh yes," the woman replied, "you'll probably find her on Women's Fashion." She pointed towards the rear of the store. "Would you …?"

"I am sure that we'll easily find her, thanks," Debbie called back, as she and Slater walked away. They made their way through the racks of clothing and saw a young woman working on the right of the store. Chapman approached her, peering at her "Molly" name badge. "Molly Sanders?" she enquired.

"Yes, that's me." she turned, smiling.

"Hello Molly. We're from Scarborough Police. I'm DS Chapman and this is DC Slater. I believe you called in the station yesterday with some information about the recent assault on the promenade?" Molly nodded. "Can you spare a few minutes to tell us what you saw?"

"Sure, just give me a minute." She dashed over to another supervisor at the tills, had a quick word, then returned. "Follow me, please. There's a staffroom over there where we can talk in private." She led them across the store, checked that no other staff were using the room, then pulled out some chairs for them.

"Thanks, Molly," Chapman smiled, sitting down. "What do you have to tell us?"

"You're not recording this, are you?" Molly asked, a concerned look on her face. Chapman shook her head. "I was with a friend, you know, just out for a walk."

"Boyfriend?" Chapman raised her eyebrows.

"No!" she said, looking down. "That's why I don't want this recording. My boyfriend knows him." She smiled briefly. "Anyway, we'd been walking along the prom, along that path up to the Esplanade, joking, larking around a bit, when Will dragged me off the path into the bushes. We hid behind a tree, and ..." She looked down again.

"It's OK, Molly, you don't need to go into details. Tell us what you heard, or saw, on the path."

"I saw this girl, well young woman, further up the path, talking to two men, then they moved away just off the path, into the bushes. Seconds later, another young woman wearing a track-suit came running down and the other woman stepped right into her path and they collided."

"Are you sure that she deliberately moved into the jogger's way?"

"Oh yeah, definitely, then she played fuck ... sorry, hell with the jogger and hit her. The jogger was trying to help her up but she kept hitting her. That's when the jogger pushed her over, and the two men rushed out to try to hit her." She laughed. "Bloody Hell! The girl in the track-suit gave them all a right pasting, then she ran past us and down the path towards the Grand. Will and I thought it was brilliant, and we kept hidden until they limped off down the path. One of the men was holding his arm … it looked broken. I didn't think any more about it until my Mum read out something from the paper. Will didn't want me to come in, but I had to because the newspaper story was wrong." She stopped talking suddenly, and looked at the two police officers. Slater closed his notebook.

"Thanks for contacting us, Molly. Your information will be valuable in sorting out this matter."

"You're welcome, but I don't want to give a written statement or evidence in court … you understand, don't you?"

"We can't guarantee that, Molly. I understand that you don't want your boyfriend to find out, but there may be charges involved here. We'll have to see what the jogger wishes to do. We'll let you know, and thanks again for your help." She and Slater got up and left the room.

"What now, Sarge," Slater muttered, "who do we see next – the Buxton woman or the Russian?" Chapman thought for a minute or two.

"I'll run it past Bentley, but the Russian girl, I think. She must be worried about all of this, so deserves to know quickly that she is innocent of the initial assault. We also need to know if she wants to press charges. Let's get back to the station, then we can wrap this one up."

**

"As you can see, Natasha, the witness who has come forward has backed up everything you told us. I don't think we need these now," she smiled, handing over Natasha's passport and visa. Chapman looked at Karl and Natasha, who had been sitting anxiously on the settee in their flat as she summarised Molly Sanders' statement. When Chapman's words had sunk in, they embraced each other and Natasha began crying.

"Oh, Karl, I was so worried. I'm sorry," she sobbed, wiping away her tears.

"Don't be sorry, Natasha," Karl said sternly. "You did nothing wrong. Now, DS Chapman, what happens next?"

"DC Slater and I will interview Maggie Buxton, her brother and her ex-boyfriend and charge them with assault, attempting to pervert the course of justice, and with wasting police time. You may be required to attend court to act as a witness, Natasha." She looked frightened.

"Oh no, I don't want that. I just want this thing to be over and to get back to enjoying life with Karl in Scarborough. I don't want any fuss." She glanced at Karl for support.

"Natasha and I need to talk this over, DS Chapman, but if she does not want to press charges, will that be the end of the matter?"

"Possibly, but what if Maggie Buxton tries something else in the future? She seems to be a jealous, malicious bitch, if you ask me."

"Can you just caution them … a bit like a suspended sentence?"

"If you want my advice, Karl, I think that's the least we ought to do," Chapman replied.

"OK, can we just have a few minutes to discuss things?"

"Of course, go ahead."

"OK, enjoy your drinks. We won't be long." He helped Natasha off the settee, and they went through to the kitchen, returning a few minutes later. "Natasha wants to draw a line," Karl explained, "so we don't want to press charges, but we would like you to caution Maggie and the two men."

"Are you sure? We now have enough evidence for a conviction."

"No, we've decided, DS Chapman. We want to get on with our lives without worrying about the fuss and publicity a trial might bring. One thing, though. Would you let us know when you've seen Maggie and the others, and how they've reacted to the action you've taken?"

"Of course, not a problem."

"Thanks very much for all of your help. We're really relieved that it's all over." He led Chapman and Slater to the front door. "Thanks again," he smiled as they left the flat.

"Oh Karl, I've got my passport back," she shrieked, clutching the precious document. "I am so glad that this is over. Now we can get on with our lives." She thought for a few seconds. "Karl, would you mind if I visit some of my friends this week?"

"Not at all. Where are you thinking of going?"

"York, I think. I've looked on the map and I can take a train there. Oh, I'm so pleased that I can travel again!" She brandished her passport again.

"York isn't too far away. I can drive you there if you like."

"Thanks for your offer, but I'd rather travel on my own. I need to be more independent, and in any case, you have work this week!"

"Yes, I suppose you're right. A change will do you good, I think."

"Right, no time to lose. I'm going to pack a small case, then I'll phone Ella in York. If things are OK there, I'll travel in the morning."

"York's a beautiful city, there's so much to see. You'll love it, Natasha. Away you go," he laughed, patting her bottom, "go and get sorted, then we can go out to eat. If I'm not going to see you for a few days, we'll need to say *Goodbye* properly when we return."

"I think I know exactly what you mean, Karl," she waved her finger at him, "but it's only *au revoir.*"

"*Goodbye, au revoir,* whatever, but it's straight to bed when we get back!" They both laughed.

***

Debbie Chapman glared at Maggie Buxton in the interview room at the station. "As you can see, Maggie, we now know everything about this assault - your former relationship with Karl Griffin, your jealousy over his new girlfriend, how you planned it with the others, and exactly what happened on the promenade. We even have a reliable eye-witness to testify against you if need be. I could throw the book at you now, and charge you with common assault, perverting the course of justice, wasting police time, and the rest. You and the others would go down for this," she barked, staring at the tearful woman across the table. "Crocodile tears don't fool me, lady." She paused while the waterworks continued. "In fact, you're a very lucky woman, Maggie. The jogger you tried to assault does not want to press charges," Maggie sat up and breathed a sigh of relief, "but don't think that this is the end of it. When we leave this room, you will be formally cautioned as to your future conduct, and if you or any of the others have any contact with the victims, the charges I mentioned before will be activated, believe me. Treat this as a suspended sentence, Maggie. As I said before, you're very lucky. You don't deserve it."

***

George Ryan leaned over the table and poured more wine into Liz Coward's glass. She smiled at him. "Thanks, George. Wow, that was a lovely meal! I'm stuffed. I'm not used to eating that amount of food."

"Yes, it was good. One of the lads at work recommended this place to me, you know, if I wanted somewhere for a special occasion." Liz blushed, and glanced around at the other diners.

"It is nice here, and I'm glad we're out of Scarborough. It's more relaxing for me." She took a sip of her wine, and sat back.

"Let's take our drinks into the lounge. It will be more comfortable there, and we can have some coffee later." He picked up the bottle of *Pinot Grigio* and their glasses and they made their way through to the lounge, where they found a quiet corner. Liz eased herself into a soft seat, pulling down her red dress as it rode up. She blushed again, and crossed her legs. "You look lovely tonight, Liz," George said nervously. "That dress really suits you."

"Thanks," she said bashfully, "I don't get many opportunities to dress up these days, except when Mr Marshall has guests." George felt it was the right time to begin some discreet probing.

"It's odd, you know, someone as young and as pretty as you, looking after a big, old house ... spending so much time on your own ... why on earth did you take this job in Scarborough? You're not from here, are you?"

"It's a long story, George, and I don't want to bore you with the details tonight. You're right about Scarborough, though. I was brought up in Bradford."

"I can understand a move to Scarborough, as it's such a nice place to live, but you don't enjoy the work that you're doing, do you?" Liz looked away. "Each time I've spoken to you you've seemed frightened by this Mr Marshall." Liz remained silent, so George probed deeper. "You're an intelligent, attractive young woman, Liz. Why aren't you at university or doing, I'm sorry, a better job?" Liz sat up.

"As I said before, it's a long story and I don't want to spoil this evening. I'm having such a lovely time, please, George."

"Don't worry, Liz," he laughed, trying to lighten the atmosphere, "I'm not the Spanish Inquisition." She smiled, and relaxed again. "It's just that I'm worried about you. I like you a lot, and want to know more about you. I can't help being nosey, it goes along with my job." They both laughed, and Liz took another drink.

"But what about you, George? I don't know much about you either."

"How about this. I'll tell you something about my background, if you tell me more about yours. Do we have a deal?" She nodded. "Are you alright for drink?"

"I think I'd like a coffee now, please. I can't be out too late, just in case Mr Marshall calls again."

"Has he phoned today?"

"Yes, but forget about that. You were going to tell me more about yourself, remember?" she smiled cutely.

"OK, but there's not really a lot to tell. Let's see. I was born in Cumbria, but when I was about eight we moved to Darlington. When I say "we", I mean just me and my parents. I don't have any brothers or sisters. My Dad's had a variety of jobs, but right now he's a postman. My Mam works in a solicitor's. We're just an ordinary family, you see." He smiled, and paused, waiting for her to reveal her story.

"Go on, please."

"Oh, well after leaving school I went to Sheffield University. I studied History, but hadn't really thought about a career until my last year. That's when someone suggested a career in the police. I've got an inquisitive mind, you see. They thought I would make a good detective." He laughed, then sat back as the coffees arrived. "Thanks," he smiled at the waitress, then poured some coffee into each cup. "Please help yourself, Liz. I don't know how you like yours."

"Just milk, thanks. And are there any girlfriends, or wives even?" She grinned, as George looked shocked.

"Wives, God no! I've had one or two girlfriends, but no-one serious. I did quite like a girl back home in Darlington, but we finished after I went to university." He sipped his coffee, then sat back, looking relieved. "Now it's your turn," he said, smiling.

"As I told you before, I was born and raised in Bradford. We had a nice house ... my Dad worked in the Town Hall and had a decent job. I have one brother, Brian, he's two years older than me." She paused, and looked thoughtful before continuing. "I did well at school, and went to Manchester University to study to study Law, but it didn't work out for me. I dropped out early last year, stressed out, I suppose, then later on I was asked to look after the house in Scarborough." She flopped back in her seat, then sat up and drained her coffee. "Like you I've had no serious relationships." She glanced at her watch. "We'd better go, George. I can't be too late." She looked around for her coat.

"Slow down, Liz, don't rush. Have another coffee." He filled her cup, as tears appeared in her eyes. He stretched out for her hand. "Don't get upset, love. I know there's a lot more that you haven't told me." She wiped her eyes, and reached for her coat.

"Oh George, I'm going to get upset. Let's get out of here." She stood up.

"Why don't you nip to the loo and freshen up while I pay the bill?" George suggested. "Alright?" She nodded and headed for the toilets in the corner. George picked up his jacket and went to the bar to settle the bill. Liz returned a few minutes later. "Better?" he asked.

"Yes, thanks, but I still want to leave. Will you take me home, then I'll tell you some more?"

George waited in a small lounge as Liz made some coffee. They had driven the few miles from the pub in silence, then George followed her car from the Safeway store. Liz had asked George to park his car in a nearby road. There was nobody around when they slipped into the darkness of the big house, and Liz led George to a small lounge, where she switched on a table lamp. He draped his jacket over a chair, then stood up as she returned to the room. She smiled briefly, nervously even, and put the tray on the table. "Help yourself. I'm fine." She sat down next to him. "I've been honest with you, George, but there is more." George nodded, and had a drink. "When I was at university, my brother Brian had got mixed up with some drug dealers in Leeds. The main guy is called Marshall, or at least that's the name

I know him by. I met him once or twice when I went to parties with Brian and some others." She paused and looked guiltily at George. "I did do drugs for a time, nothing heavy, but not now. Brian was hooked, however. He got his drugs from Marshall by doing deliveries for him. One day last summer, Brian was attacked by people from another gang, and they stole his drugs. Marshall threatened to take him out unless he worked for him for free and ..." another pause "... if I agreed to look after his house in Scarborough." She grabbed George. "I was so frightened and stressed out. I didn't know what to do. I couldn't tell my parents, so I dropped out after my second year and came to Scarborough. I told them I was taking a gap year, and planned to travel abroad, back-packing. It's a nightmare, George. How can I get out of it without my brother being killed and my parents finding out?" The tears were rolling down her cheeks. George stroked her hair and held her close to him, while he thought about what to say next. He moved her back slightly and kissed her face. She hugged him as another wave of tears arrived.

"Liz, you told me that Marshall phoned today. What did he say?"

"He just thanked me for looking after things last weekend, and told me that he's having another party a week on Friday. He said that he would contact me again with guest numbers and so on, and I have to make sure that the house is ready as usual." She looked terrified.

"Look, Liz, try not to be too worried. You need to know that we, the police that is, know about Marshall

183

and we're doing our best to bring him down. I can't say too much at the moment, but we hope that this will happen soon. For the time being, you have to carry on as normal, but I really believe that your nightmare will be over before too long."

"This sounds too good to be true, George," she gasped, clinging on to him. "Can't you give me any more details?"

"I'm sorry, Liz, but you have to trust me on this one. I really like you and I'll help you as much as I can, but that's all I can say just now. Believe me, there is some light at the end of the tunnel." He grinned, and they hugged each other. George eased her back and muttered, looking more serious: "Don't forget, Liz, try to act normally, especially when you're on the phone to Marshall or when he is here. It's vital that he thinks everything is just the same. OK?"

"Oh George, I'm so happy. Don't worry, I'll do as you say, trust me."

"I'll be there for you, Liz, and I'll help as much as I can." He smiled, and sat back on the settee. "When can we see each other again?"

"This evening isn't over yet, is it? Oh George, I'm so excited, but still worried and frightened. Please stay with me tonight." She held his hands, and looked longingly at him. He leaned over and kissed her.

"Of course, I'll stay, but I have to be at work early tomorrow."

"Shut up," she instructed, pulling him off the settee, and leading him up the stairs.

CHAPTER TWENTY-SIX
MANCHESTER

Sergei Rudnev took another drink of his beer, and glanced around the pub again. He shifted in his chair, looked at his watch, then surveyed the faces of the other customers. He was sitting at a small table on a raised section near the back of the room where he had a good view of everything that was going on, as well as who was entering and leaving the pub. A group of girls giggled their way out of the swing door as two men entered the pub, quickly followed by a young woman dressed almost entirely in black. She was tall, attractive with shoulder-length black hair, and was wearing a dark jacket, a knee-length black skirt and black high heels. She paused at the doorway to wipe her glasses, which had steamed up as she entered the pub, then she gazed around the room. Putting her glasses back on, she then spotted Rudnev at the back of the room and slowly made her way through the groups of drinkers to the bar, ordered and collected a vodka and coke, then walked elegantly to Rudnev's table.

"Anna!" he said gustily, getting up from his seat and kissing her on both cheeks, "it's good to see you again." He spoke in Russian, and she continued their conversation in the same language.

"It's good to see you again, Sergei. How are you?"

"Very well, thank you, and I am pleased to see you again. I was beginning to worry about you." His smile disappeared.

"I'm fine, Sergei, just fine."

"You're certainly looking well," he smiled again, "and very well-dressed, if I might say. Where are you staying?"

"A small hotel near Piccadilly, not too far from here."

"Good, and you will be in Manchester tomorrow?"

"Yes, I will."

"Very well. We can discuss everything in detail tomorrow. I can tell you that we now know where Orlov and the others are living. It is a flat in a city called York. There are many students living in that area, and the flat is on the first floor. He has chosen it well. He knows that we, or anyone else for that matter, will not go in with *all guns blazing,* as the Americans like to say. You will have to be discreet, Anna, and lure him away from there."

"I thought he would be living in a location with lots of people around him, not somewhere like a farm in the countryside. Have you brought the gun?"

"Yes, I have it, but not here, of course. I will bring it tomorrow, together with the address details and some maps."

"Good." She smiled at Sergei. "I'm starving. Where are you going to take me for a meal?"

CHAPTER TWENTY-SEVEN
SCARBOROUGH

George Ryan knocked on Bentley's door, waited for a muttered *Enter*, then shuffled into the office and sat down. He waited until the chubby-faced DI finished reading a sheet of paper. "Hmm," he said thoughtfully, rubbing his chin, then, looking up, "Morning, Ryan." He pushed the paper to one side. "What's on your mind?"

"It's about Liz Coward, Sir. I took her out for a meal last night and ... well, I have some new information." Bentley gestured for him to continue. "She's from Bradford originally, and has been to university, but her brother got into big trouble with Nathaniel White." Bentley raised his eyebrows.

"Big trouble ... how?"

"Her brother's a druggie, and got drugs by delivering for White, but then he got robbed by another gang. White's threatened to kill him unless he works off the debt, and part of the deal was that his sister, Liz, had to look after his new house in Scarborough. She's scared stiff, Sir, on the edge."

"In that case, you're going to have to be very careful, George, not just for her but for you as well. If White finds out that she's been seeing a policeman, well it could be curtains for both of you, as well as scuppering our entire operation against him." He paused for a minute. "Does anyone else know about your date with her?"

"No, of course not, Sir. We've been very careful."

"You might think that, but that evil bastard is capable of anything. If Liz Coward acts suspiciously, he'll get Orlov involved, and we both know how he operates. Tread very carefully, young man," he warned.

"Hopefully it won't be for much longer, Sir. Liz told me that White is having another party, or meeting, a week on Friday. She hasn't been told the details yet, but she has to make sure that the house is ready for his guests. He's going to phone again early next week."

"Does she know much about White?"

"Not really, except that he's involved in drugs. She still calls him Mr Marshall."

"OK, George, listen carefully. Don't tell anybody that you've seen Liz Coward. We'll tell the team that you've phoned her, and that she's let slip that White's having another do a week on Friday. I'll let Jefferson know in Leeds, then we can make some arrangements when it happens." He paused to search for a jelly baby in his pocket, and chewed on it thoughtfully. "In the meantime, keep Liz Coward at arm's length, George. I can see that you're fond of her, but there'll be plenty of time for romance when this is all over. Remember what that bloke from MI6 told us … we're dealing with some serious killers here. *Comprende?*"

"Don't worry, Sir. I'll watch my step."

***

Karl Griffin glanced at his watch, looked anxious then went into the store to grab his jacket. "I'll see you tomorrow," he shouted to one of the shop girls. "I'm off to meet Natasha," he called back as he dashed out of the shop, then hurried along Westborough as he made his way to the station. Dodging through a group of passengers leaving the station, he emerged on the platform and looked for a space to sit down. He looked up at the Arrivals board, double-checking the time the York train was due to return to Scarborough. Within minutes, the train glided into the station, and Karl stood up, scanning the passengers as they alighted from the train. He quickly spotted the tall, blonde figure carrying a small case, and moved towards her as she walked along the platform. Natasha hadn't seen him, and Karl hid behind a group of track-suited youths until she was very close.

"Heh, Snow Maiden!" he called, and jostled over to the surprised Russian.

"Karl" she grinned, accepting his lively hug and kissing him passionately. "You did not say that you would meet me. I was planning to leave my case at our flat, then to walk into town to see you at your shop. What a nice surprise!" she spluttered, as he kissed her again.

"I couldn't wait, Tash, I've missed you too much."

"Me too. It's only been a couple of days, but it seems much longer."

"Come on," he said, grabbing her case and putting his arm around her shoulders, "I've got the rest of the day off, so let's not waste it." They headed for the exit, laughing.

Further along the platform, Maggie Buxton scowled as they left the station, then she got up from her seat and followed them at a distance.

***

"That was fantastic, Natasha," Karl grinned as he collapsed back on a pillow. "It reminded me of those days when we first made love in Moscow." He eased her gently into his arms and kissed her softly, caressing her body as she nuzzled into him.

"Hmm, those days seem years ago, Karl. I think only of my life here now." They lay entwined for a few minutes, then Karl sat up.

"Just stay there for a minute or two, pet. I'll make some coffee, then you can tell me all about York." He disappeared into the kitchen, and returned a short time later carrying a tray. Natasha stood naked, near the window.

"I've almost forgotten how beautiful it is here," she muttered, without turning around. Karl put the tray on a table, then eased up behind her, and cupped her breasts in his hands. He kissed her neck softly, then guided her away from the window.

"Come on, you sexy beast, if you stay there for much longer, you'll have a crowd outside, watching you through binoculars!" They laughed, and she reached for a dressing-gown and put it on. She sat down, as Karl poured the coffee.

"I don't care, Karl, I feel so relaxed here with you. Anyway, who can see me, a seagull?" More laughter, as they sipped the coffee. Karl put his cup down.

"So, how was York? I want to know everything."

"Good," she said, draining her cup. "I stayed with my two friends, Ella and Tanya. They share a flat not too far from the centre of the city. We spent hours just talking. It was nice to speak Russian again." She smiled apologetically. "When they were studying, I just walked around the city for hours. It's so beautiful, Karl, so many interesting buildings and nice shops. I particularly enjoyed the large church, the cathedral?"

"Yes, it is like a cathedral, but we call it York Minster."

"Right, York Minster, well it was very quiet and peaceful inside, and there were so many interesting things to see. The people in York were so friendly, so helpful, Karl. I've had a great time."

"We'll have to spend a weekend there, Natasha. I know York well, and can show you some places that the tourists don't know."

"I'd like that. Anyway, while I was there, we phoned our other friend, Ludmilla, who is studying at Liverpool. We're going to spend a few days with her. Is it possible to travel to Liverpool by train?"

"Oh yes, no problem. You'll have to change trains at Manchester, but there'll be plenty of trains available. It should be an easy journey. Where will you all stay?"

"Ludmilla shares a flat with two other students, but she told us that they are away on a course just at the moment. It's probably a good time to visit her, so we might go after the weekend."

"On Monday! Jesus, I'm going to be stuck in the shop while you and your friends have a great time gadding about the country."

"Don't worry, darling. You have to work during the week, so at least we'll have the weekend together. You know I'll make it up to you." She cosied up to Karl and began kissing him.

***

George and Liz walked hand-in-hand along the harbourside at Whitby. It had been a chilly, overcast day and now, as the skies were darkening, the late weekend visitors were making for their cars and the road home. George watched people heading for the car parks and turned to Liz. "I suppose we'd better head back to Scarborough soon, Liz, just in case you receive a call from Marshall. He's planning a visit at the end of next week, isn't he?"

"Trust you to spoil a lovely afternoon," she scowled. "When I'm away from the house with you, I can switch off and forget all of my troubles, but now you've brought me back to earth with a nasty bump."

"Sorry, Liz, but let's hope that it won't be for much longer. I have a feeling that we're nearing the end of the road, and that soon your nightmare will be over."

He cuddled her into him, and they paused for a few minutes as other visitors passed by. "I've really enjoyed today, and we had a nice meal in that fish restaurant. My boss would have been jealous." They laughed softly as the skies continued to darken and drops of rain began to spot on the pavement. "Come on," he grabbed her hand and began walking briskly towards the car park, "let's go before we get soaked. It won't take long to get back to yours and get a fire going to keep us warm. I fancy an evening just watching telly." He broke into a run.

"Oh George," she gasped, trying to keep up with him, "you're such a romantic!"

***

In Chapeltown, near the centre of Leeds, a crowd began to gather and sirens could be heard in the distance as two skimpily-dressed girls opened the front door of a well-known brothel and staggered through the smoke. The rain began to lash down heavily, but it could not prevent the flames licking up around the upper windows. Screams could be heard coming from the bedrooms at the rear of the house, but no-one in the crowd made any effort to rescue the remaining occupants. A fire engine and an ambulance roared noisily up the street, but the crowd stood and watched in silence as the flames began to envelop the roof.

CHAPTER TWENTY-EIGHT
YORK

Anna Menshikova stepped off the train, glanced around the spacious station, put her case on the platform and ran her fingers through her black hair. She adjusted her glasses, placed a jacket over her case then picked it up and headed for the exit, looking for a vacant taxi. A queue was forming, and Anna waited patiently until the passengers in front of her had been driven away. She hopped in the back seat of the next taxi, gave the driver the name of her hotel and sat back, enjoying the journey as the driver passed by some of the city's impressive architecture. Twenty minutes later, her taxi arrived at the hotel and she got out quickly, tipping the driver and making her way elegantly for the Reception.

Half an hour later, Anna stepped out of the bathroom and dried herself with a large towel. She sat down naked on the bed and glanced at the contents of her case, which lay open at the base of the bed. Selecting a pair of jeans and a casual top, she dressed quickly then sat at the desk and looked for some writing paper. She spent a few minutes in thought before writing a short note in Russian.

> Борис Владимирович Орлов.
>
> Нам есть что обсудить. Встречайте меня в пабе Punch Bowl в Stonegate в 8 часов вечера. Я буду одинок и невооружен.

See Below

She scribbled a signature, sealed the note in an envelope, then put on her jacket and made her way through the streets of the old city, heading for the Bishopthorpe Road area. Anna had studied her maps again during her train journey but already knew exactly where she was going, as she had visited the street where Orlov and the others were living after meeting Sergei Rudnev in Manchester. She was familiar with the house, and the comings and goings of the students who lived in the area. By the time she arrived, it was late afternoon and beginning to get dark, and no-one took any notice of her as she mingled with other students making their way home after their studies. She had to wait for over twenty minutes until a student arrived at the house and was able to let her in. "Thanks," she muttered to him, "I'm just delivering a letter." He smiled as she walked up the stairs to the first-floor and looked for Orlov's flat. She knew from Rudnev's informers exactly where it was and she quickly walked along to the door and pushed the letter under it. Anna then rushed down the stairs and

---

1 Boris Vladimirovich Orlov.
We have much to discuss. Meet me in The Punch Bowl pub in Stonegate at 8 o'clock this evening. I will be alone and unarmed.

out of the front door, hurrying around the corner where she could not be seen by anyone looking out of Orlov's window. Breathing heavily, she walked in the direction of the Skeldergate Bridge and headed back to her hotel.

***

In Scarborough, Liz was tidying the kitchen when the phone rang. She picked it up nervously, and said a quiet *Hello*.

"Liz, hi it's me, George. Can you talk?"

"George, oh thank God. I thought it would be Marshall with the arrangements for the weekend. I'm so relieved to hear your voice."

"I don't have much time, Liz … we're really busy in the office, you know, getting ready for the weekend, but my boss has given me a day off tomorrow. He told me to have a good rest, because I'm going to have to put in some long shifts later in the week. Would you like me to come around tonight? We could perhaps go out somewhere for a drink, then watch a bit of telly and have an early night." A pause. "What do you think?"

"That would be great, George, but I'm not sure about going out for a drink, unless Marshall has already phoned me with the details for the weekend. Call round about seven, then we'll decide what to do."

"Fine. I'll bring a bottle of wine."

"George, I'm terrified about this weekend, you know, really worried."

"I know you are, Liz, but it's going to be over soon.

I can see some light at the end of the tunnel, so try to relax. It will finish soon, I promise." He could hear her crying softly at the other end, and waited until she had stopped. "Are you alright, Liz?"

"Yeah, I'll be fine. See you later." The phone went dead.

***

There were few tourists staying in York in March, before the season became busy with the Easter holidays, but the city always enjoyed a busy social life in the evenings throughout the year. Most of the pubs and restaurants in the centre had a good following, whether it be locals meeting friends, families celebrating a birthday or anniversary, or groups of students making the most of their time at the university. Boris Orlov carefully studied faces as he made his way through the darkened streets to Stonegate. He was looking for potential danger, and arrived at the pub just after seven-thirty, buying a pint and selecting a small table near the exit to the toilets. He also had a good view of everybody who entered the pub. Orlov was disguised as usual and was armed, and as he drank, he kept caressing the gun in his pocket as if it were a small dog.

He glanced up as Anna opened the door and, without looking around, headed for the bar. She was still wearing the jeans she had worn that afternoon, but had changed her trainers for high heels and was wearing a dark blue jumper and a jacket. She thanked the barman and paid for her drink, then turned around and caught sight of Orlov. She continued sipping her drink and surveyed the rest of the pub, noting the other customers who were drinking in the pub. Picking up her jacket and drink, she walked elegantly over to Orlov's table and sat down, studying the bulky figure across the table.

"I knew they would come looking for me," he said softly in Russian, "but I did not think they would send somebody so young ... or so beautiful."

"Thank you," she replied in Russian, then smiled briefly, and took another sip. "I expect that you know what I am going to say to you?" she asked quizzically. "As I said in the message, I have come here to talk to you, to discuss ... possibilities. You can relax, Boris," another brief smile, "I have no gun and, as you can see, I am alone. I have no wish to create a disturbance here, whereas you seem to have created several during the time you have lived in the north of England." She took another sip, as he remained silent. "My name is Anna."

"Very well, young lady," Boris muttered as he sat back in his seat, "I'd better listen to what you have to say."

"They think highly of you in Moscow, Boris. You have always been a trusted agent, very reliable, so your actions have surprised everyone. I am sure you understand that your activities cannot be made public, as it would cause so much embarrassment for Russia, for the Secret Service. At the moment, most people here do not know that a Russian agent, and a Pole, have been involved in these gang wars in Leeds and elsewhere in Yorkshire. If you return to Russia now, you will be forgiven for your ... indiscretions, shall we say, and can be of service to us in another country. Your experience can still be valuable in other operations, or in training future agents." Anna relaxed in her seat, and glanced around the room, as Orlov began laughing softly.

"Is that really what they asked to say, Anna? Come back to Russia, have your arse smacked, and then we will find you another country to spy in?" He grinned at the young woman across the table. "Surely you are not that stupid, Anna? If I return to Russia I will be tortured, then shot in the back of my head in *Lubyanka*. That's what will happen, young lady."

"You've been watching too many James Bond films, Boris. Good agents are hard to find these days. Your cover is blown here in England, but you can easily be given a new identity in another country or, as I have said, be used to train new agents in Moscow." Boris thought for a few minutes, as Anna drained her glass. He stood up.

"Another?"

"Please, a small beer." She watched him go to the bar, and nodded as he returned with more drinks. He drained half of his pint, then leaned across the table.

"Your offer is tempting, Anna, but my situation here is complicated."

"Stephanie Garrett?"

"Exactly. Everything I have done is for our ... her future. We have almost reached the point where we control all of the prostitution in Leeds and this part of Yorkshire. I cannot give her up, I've risked everything for her. I love her, Anna." She nodded slowly, then offered another possibility.

"I understand that you have deep feelings for her." She smiled briefly. "It might be possible to arrange for her to join you in Russia, or wherever you settle after leaving England."

"And Jan Tobolski?"

"I think you may have to forget about him, Boris." He looked thoughtful again.

"I need some time to think about this, and to discuss matters with Stephanie." Anna nodded. "I would also need some guarantees from Moscow, Anna."

"Sergei Rudnev is in England. I could arrange for you to see him. He has shown support for you in Moscow."

"He is a good man, but it is very difficult to know who can be trusted these days." He drained some more beer. "Stephanie and I are going to meet a man called Nathaniel White later this week. We intend to discuss the future with him, and to decide who controls what. This meeting is very important to us, Anna, and I hope it will be the last time we have to see him."

"So, White is the man you have been working for, providing the muscle, to control drugs, prostitution, all of that?"

"Yes, everything. White is a dangerous man, but whatever I decide to do, I must make sure that everything is secured for Stephanie. Have you a contact number for Rudnev?" Anna rummaged for pen and paper in her handbag, noted down the details and passed them over to Orlov.

"My number is there too. While we are exchanging information, Boris, I need the details for your meeting with Nathaniel White." She passed over the pen, and waited until Orlov finished writing.

"Thank you. I need to know if anything changes." She put the paper into her handbag, then looked across the table at Orlov. "You have a lot of thinking to do, Boris, but I think that's all for tonight." She finished her drink and reached for her jacket.

"Just one more thing, Anna. If I refuse to return to Moscow, or just move to another secret location … what then?"

"I've been ordered to kill you, Boris," she replied impassively, then she stood up and, without looking back, brushed past a group of students and left the pub.

***

Returning to the flat, Orlov found Tobolski watching a football match, and gestured for Stephanie to join him in the kitchen. "Do you need a beer?" he shouted through to Tobolski.

"No, I'm fine," came the reply. Orlov poured two drinks for himself and Stephanie.

"I've been worried," she said, dragging her fingers through her hair. "I assumed you were going to the local shop." Orlov drained half of his bottle.

"Earlier today, I received a note. The Russians have found us, Stephanie." She looked horrified, and glanced quickly around the room. "Don't worry," he said, touching her arm, "they're not going to shoot their way into here. I've been expecting this, Steph. They sent a young woman."

"A woman!"

"Yes, I was surprised. She told me that I'm finished here, in Britain, but that they still value me in Moscow. I might be able to work somewhere else, or train new agents in Russia."

"That sounds a load of crap, Boris," Stephanie replied angrily. "How can you trust her, or believe what she told you? They're just trying to lure you to somewhere quiet where they can get rid of you."

"Rudnev, my old handler, is in England. Anna, the woman I saw, has given me his mobile number, so that I can verify the information she gave me."

"This has got to be a trap, Boris."

"I'm not so sure, after all, they know where we live and could probably have shot us by now. Anna was not armed. She told me that you could come to Russia with me, and that we can start a new life there, or somewhere else in Europe. If I don't agree to return to Moscow, she has orders to kill me."

"What a fucking mess, Boris. We're so close to getting what we want in Leeds … so close."

"We can still do that, Steph. If we can get rid of Nathaniel White, I can make sure that you're set up here for life. Jan will stay and provide any protection you need, but I have to go."

"Look, Boris, we can move somewhere else, find a new base, another secret location." She had a look of desperation in her eyes. "We can do it again."

"I can't run forever, Steph." A brief smile. "They'd find me again, only next time there won't be any beautiful young agents with tempting offers, just a bullet when I'm off guard somewhere. We don't have a lot of choice, but I'm determined to see things through for you, for your future."

"My future is with you. We stick together. You sacrificed everything for me, so we'll do whatever is necessary to finish this thing. They have shops in Moscow, don't they?" They both laughed.

"OK, then I think we need to phone White tonight and arrange an emergency meeting at Scarborough tomorrow. We need to keep ahead of him and sort things out, before he finds out that the Russians know where we are living." He looked at her seriously. "We deal with him first, then decide what to do about the Russians."

"I'm frightened, Boris, but you are probably right. We can't just stay here and do nothing. Come on," she said, standing up, "Jan will be wondering what we are talking about. Let's tell him what's happened, then you can make that call to White."

***

Anna paused after describing the evening's events to Rudnev. "I think that's everything." She could almost hear Rudnev thinking.

"You cannot wait to see what Orlov does now, Anna. You must be ready for his next move. Here is the number of one of our contacts in York, and her address." She wrote it down. "I will phone her when we have finished talking, and tell her to bring her car to your hotel. Get packed and be ready, then drive to Orlov's house, and wait to see what he does next. I think he will move quickly. Keep me informed of everything, OK?"

"Of course. I'll speak to you later."

***

Liz Coward sat up and stretched over to the bedside table, pouring the remnants of a bottle of wine into the two glasses. She passed one to George Ryan and smiled.

"Feeling better now?" he grinned.

"Ah, men, you think sex is the answer to everything, don't you?" The grin widened, and she laughed. "Don't worry, George, I enjoyed it as well. I certainly feel more relaxed now, but I wish that Marshall had phoned earlier. I hate hanging on for his call."

"Let's forget about Marshall tonight, and tomorrow. I'm as anxious as you to get this week out of the way, then we can take you out of this hell-hole and get on with our lives." He drained his glass, and turned to her. "Now, where were we?"

***

Maggie Buxton woke up suddenly, and glanced around the darkened room. Her parents' house was quiet, but she had struggled to get to sleep. Wide awake again, she slipped out of bed and went downstairs to the kitchen, switching on a dimmed light and the kettle. She made a mug of tea, returned quietly to her bedroom and thought again about the day's events. Keeping vigil across the street from Karl's flat in the morning, she had watched him leave for the town centre, followed about thirty minutes later by Natasha, who was carrying a small case. Maggie kept her distance as the tall blonde made her way to the railway station, and queued at the ticket counter. Maggie heard her ask for a return to Manchester, and watched her walk to one of the waiting coaches. She ordered the same, and found a seat at the back of the coach, where she had a good view of Natasha, who was reading a magazine. After about thirty minutes' travelling, Maggie watched her walk along the coach to the toilet. Every time the train slowed to a halt at a station, Maggie tried to keep a careful watch of all of the passengers who got off the train and those who got on. The train was busy, but at some point after the train had left York, Maggie was shocked to see that Natasha was not in her seat. Puzzled, Maggie stood up and walked nearer the toilet, waiting for just a minute or so until a different passenger came out of the door. Maggie glanced quickly at Natasha's seat. The magazine was still there, but she had gone.

How did the bitch get off the train? Where did she go? Maggie re-wound the morning's events again and again in her head, but could not find an answer. *Fuck it!* A fruitless day on her mission to get rid of Karl's girlfriend. *All the way to Manchester and back for nothing,* she scowled. *Something doesn't add up,* the thought hammered inside her head. *I will find out ... soon, then I'll deal with the bitch!* Wrestling with her thoughts, Maggie turned over and eventually fell into a deep sleep.

CHAPTER TWENTY-NINE

SCARBOROUGH

Liz glanced at the alarm clock, then across the bed where George was sleeping soundly. *It was quite a night! My shy little PC Plod is becoming quite a little tiger!* She smiled to herself, then carefully slipped out of bed, put on her dressing-gown and made her way quietly downstairs to the kitchen. She filled a tray with coffee, orange juice and toast before heading back upstairs to her attic bedroom. George roused and smiled as she placed the tray on a table.

"Room service!" she announced, as he laughed.

"I wasn't expecting this."

"Don't get used to it, George. This might be a one-off, but in any case, it's your turn next time."

"Fair enough," he muttered, sitting up in bed, "I'll have the juice first."

"Cheeky bugger!" she grinned, passing him the glass and sitting on the edge of the bed. He took a sip, slid out of bed and parted the curtains slightly.

"Dark and miserable, raining, and looks like it will be all day." He closed the curtains and placed the tray on the bed. They both helped themselves to coffee and toast. "This is the life," he muttered through a mouthful of toast, before reaching for his cup again. He was about to take a sip when the front door slammed, and voices could be heard downstairs.

"Fucking hell!" Liz gasped, "hide behind the bed or somewhere, and don't move." She shoved the tray under the bed, then made for the door.

"Liz," George whispered, "my jacket is downstairs, and my phone's in one of the pockets."

"Stay put," she whispered, a terrified look on her face. "I'll try to get back as soon as I can." She left the room, closing the door behind her, and shouted *Hello* as she moved down the first flight of stairs. "Who is it?" she called nervously, as she carried on to the next flight.

"Who do you think it is?" Nathaniel White answered gruffly. "The Ghostbusters, or the fucking Jehovah's Witnesses?" The other men with him laughed loudly, as Liz walked down the final flight to the hallway. "Well, well!" White muttered, glancing at her dressing gown, "if it isn't Florence Nightingale, the Lady with the Lamp." More laughter.

"You gave me a shock, Mr Marshall," Liz half-smiled, thinking furiously. "It's so early in the morning, and I wasn't expecting you until later in the week."

"A change of plans, dear," White continued, "and it isn't early in the morning." He glanced at his watch. "It's gone ten o'clock, for Christ's sake. Why are so late in getting up, Liz? Have you got company?"

"Been shagging all night?" one of the others asked,

as the rest laughed again. Liz looked apologetically at White, then answered angrily.

"I had a late night … watching TV, that's all." She glared at them.

"Right, enough about last night, we haven't got much time. Make us a brew, Liz, then get dressed quickly and I'll tell you what's happening today." She looked puzzled. "Come on, for fuck's sake, get a move on, woman."

***

Anna opened her side window slightly and stretched across to do the same with the passenger window, before wiping off the condensation on the front screen of the car. She pushed her blankets onto the passenger seat and yawned widely before rummaging in a carrier bag for a bottle of water, then had a drink and searched for a Twix bar. Chewing in between yawns, she glanced up at Orlov's flat. A couple of students had emerged from the house half an hour ago, but the curtains were still closed on the first floor. *How much longer?* she asked herself, finishing the chocolate bar and crumpling the wrapper into the side pocket. She thought back to her conversation with Rudnev the night before, when he convinced her that Orlov would make a move quickly and stressed the need for an all-night watch outside his house, using the red Mondeo the Russian student had left for her. After that, she had a shower and used the toilet, checked out of her hotel, and bought a few things at a late-night supermarket before finding a parking space near Orlov's flat.

Anna glanced around the street junction, thinking for the first time that she would have to find a toilet soon. The cafes would soon be open on Bishopthorpe Road, but could she risk leaving her watch on the house? A couple of minutes later, the front door opened and Orlov, Garrett and Tobolski emerged, glancing around them and heading for a nearby street. Anna started her car, and drove off slowly in the direction the trio had walked. A few minutes later, she saw them outside a white-painted garage and she stopped the car, glancing in her mirrors and watching the garage. Tobolski waited outside until Orlov drove out of the garage in an old grey Renault, then he closed the garage door, got into the car and it sped off towards Bishopthorpe Road. Anna followed at a sensible distance, having made a mental note of the Renault's registration details. The traffic was light, and Anna kept Orlov's car in view, making sure that she would not arouse suspicion. As they reached the outskirts of the city, the Renault took the main A64 road, heading in the direction of Scarborough. Anna smiled and relaxed in her seat. She knew where they were going now.

***

"Liz! Where the fuck are you?" White's voice boomed up the stairs. She cast a frightened glance at George Ryan, who was partly dressed but still hiding behind the bed.

"Don't leave the room, for God's sake," she whispered. "I'll try to get your phone, but stay put. If they find you, we're both dead." She pulled on a jumper, then left the bedroom and headed downstairs.

"About time," grunted White, standing in the hallway. The other three men were sitting in the lounge, and the conversation ceased as Liz entered the room. "Get a move on, woman, and make us some coffee. We need something to eat ... biscuits, toast, whatever." Masterman nodded.

"I'm bloody starving. Can you do us a full English?"

"I'm not sure what we have in the fridge," Liz stammered. "I'm sorry," she looked at White, "but I planned to shop later today for the weekend. You've taken me by surprise."

"Alright, message received, Liz." White waggled his thumb in the direction of the kitchen and turned to sit down, as Liz left the room. White waited until she was out of earshot of the lounge, then spoke quietly to the others. "Right, Orlov and Co should be on their way now. The more I think about it, they must be wanting to negotiate a split, otherwise why ask for this earlier meeting?"

"To discuss the next move?" Masterman suggested.

"It can't be that, Jim, we've more or less sewn up the prostitution scene in Leeds, and that's what Stephanie and the others are really interested in. They were never bothered about drugs. We just needed each other's muscle and contacts, but now *we* don't ... and neither do they. No, I'm convinced they're ready to go it alone, but I can't risk having Orlov and that baboon Tobolski running around loose and threatening us if things go wrong. They're too dangerous. We can do without them now, and we need to make the first move." He paused and sat back in his chair, glancing across at the other men. "You two know what to do, yes?" They both nodded. "We don't need to discuss it again?"

"No, we're fine," answered Adam Thompson, the bigger of the two men. "Just give us a nod when you're ready." At that point Liz returned to the lounge, carrying a tray.

"That smells good," White smiled at her, as she put the tray down on the coffee table.

"I've done some more bacon and sausage sandwiches," she muttered, turning to return to the kitchen.

"Great!" Jack Dickinson, the youngest of the four men, grinned. "Bring some sauce," he shouted, reaching for a sandwich.

"Please," snapped White. "Where are your fucking manners, Dickinson?" The others helped themselves to coffee and the plates of toast and sandwiches. Liz arrived with more food and some ketchup.

"We're expecting company, Liz … soon. Have we still got plenty of food and drink for the others when they arrive?" White asked her. Liz thought for a minute.

"There's plenty of alcohol, but not much food. We'll need more milk if you want tea or coffee. I can go to the supermarket while you have your breakfast."

"No, you're alright, I want you here. Tell Jack where it is and he can go and buy a few things."

"Would you like me to write out a shopping list, Jacky boy?" Thompson teased.

"Piss off," Dickinson spluttered through a mouthful of bacon.

***

Boris Orlov edged out past a slow-moving tractor and checked that the road was clear before overtaking it. It was raining more heavily now, a murky day, and he squinted ahead as he pushed hard on the accelerator. The Renault breezed past the farm vehicle, then Orlov relaxed with a clear road ahead. Tobolski had dozed off on the back seat.

"Not far to go now, Boris," Stephanie muttered, a little nervously. "We're going to be OK, aren't we?"

"Look, Steph, we've discussed this many times before. White will not try anything in his great house. He cannot risk letting his neighbours hear something, he is so proud of that house. We are at more risk in Leeds. We know what we want. We have helped him to become strong in Leeds, but we all agreed that eventually he would control the drugs trade, and that we would have the sex trade. This is the right time to move on. We can tell him that we will still provide protection or remove trouble-makers if he needs us, but that he will have to pay for our services now. We tell them nothing about Anna, and that the Russians now know where we live. We can decide what to do with them later when we have finished with White."

Stephanie brushed her long, brown hair into a ponytail and checked herself in the mirror. "I still think that we should find a new base and forget about the Russians.

We've worked hard to set up our business here, and should fight hard to keep it. You're no danger to the Russians now, so when that woman contacts you again, tell her to forget about you and go back to Moscow. They surely won't keep trying to find us, once they realise that we're not a threat to them?"

Orlov laughed. "If only life was so simple, Steph. The Russians will *never* forget about me. We can keep moving, keep hiding, but sooner or later they *will* find us again. I'm more concerned about White. I want him out of our lives, so that if I do have to leave England, you will have this business and will be safe. Jan will protect you, and he will soon find others who will help. It might be possible for you to join me in Russia or somewhere else in Europe, but you belong here." He stared ahead for a few moments, then turned to look at her. "You're so beautiful, Steph, and I love you. I want you to be safe and successful, so let's deal with White first, then we can discuss and decide what to do next. Agreed?"

Stephanie nodded slowly, but didn't look convinced. Orlov kept his eyes on the road ahead, thinking back to the conversation he had with Jan Tobolski after Stephanie had gone to bed - how the Russians had found out where they were living, about the need to break away from Nathaniel White, the possibility that he would have to return to Moscow, the need for Tobolski to stay and protect Stephanie's interests. The loyal Pole had listened carefully to everything he said, appreciating the logic behind all of Orlov's arguments, and at the end Tobolski had promised to carry out his friend's wishes.

Orlov glanced in the rear-view mirror, saw that Tobolski was still fast asleep on the back seat, and realised that he would miss the lumbering Pole as well.

The conversation with Stephanie and thoughts buzzing around in his head had lowered Orlov's usual alertness, and he gave little thought to the red Mondeo which occasionally appeared in the distance, far behind him. Other vehicles closed behind and overtook him, but as Orlov neared the outskirts of Scarborough the red Mondeo maintained its distant contact with the Renault, like a parasite fish swimming alongside a great whale.

***

Liz was nearly crying with fear as she washed the coffee cups in the sink. *How could she get George out of the house without alerting the others?* Perhaps when the other guests arrived there would be an opportunity for him, but then she realised that the other two men with Marshall were there just as guards, as lookouts. She glanced along the hallway where George's jacket was hanging up. *The phone!* She had to find an excuse to get to the attic bedroom and give George the phone. One of the men came out of the lounge and leered at her.

"Alright, love?" he asked. She nodded, turned away and washed the cups again.

***

Mid-week in March, an overcast and drizzly day, few people shopping in Scarborough. Karl came out of the store in the family gift shop in Westborough. His mother was carefully re-arranging one of the window displays as he walked behind the counter.

"Finally," he muttered, "I think I've sorted out of all of the old stock … odds and ends mainly … in the store. When the girls are in next week they can get things on display in a "sale" area. God, I'm parched. Are you ready for a drink, Mam?"

"I'm always ready for a drink," she grinned, emerging from the window. "Tea, please, and don't forget the two sweeteners." Karl headed back into the store, filled a kettle and sat down behind one of the counters. His mother glanced over. "You haven't said much about Natasha recently. Is everything alright?"

"Yeah, fine, we're good. She's gone to Liverpool with a couple of her friends from York. They know another Russian girl who's studying there. I think she might be back tomorrow night."

"Wasn't she away for a few days last week?"

"Yes, that's when she was at York. After that business with Maggie, Natasha wanted to travel a bit and look up some of her university friends. I'm busy during the week at the moment, so it made sense for her to visit them mid-week." A middle-aged lady entered the shop, shook her umbrella outside and propped it up by the door.

"Is it OK if I leave my brolly here?" she asked, smiling. "I'm looking for a present for a friend's birthday."

"That's fine," Karl returned the smile, "go ahead. Just shout if you need any help." The lady nodded and began browsing. Karl went and stood next to his mother. "So, we have our weekends together, and it will be Easter soon, with better weather hopefully. We'll see more of each other then, and do more travelling. Things are really fine, Mam, I love her to bits and can't wait to take her to other parts of the country. The girls will be in for the holiday season, so it will be easy for me to spend more time with Natasha." He grinned at his mother. "Apart from that little episode with Maggie, things have gone really well, much better than I could have hoped."

"That's good, Karl. When she returns, you must bring her round for a meal, or we'll have a meal out somewhere. It's your Dad's birthday soon. Let's arrange something for then. At least it will get your father away from the golf course!" They both laughed.

***

"Debbie, have you got a moment?" Bentley called across the incident room, where she was busy at her computer. She looked up, saw Bentley waiting by his office door and grimaced.

"Can you give me a few minutes, Sir? I'm just in the middle of searching for something." He scowled. "Ten minutes tops." Bentley nodded, stepped inside his office and closed the door. Chapman winked at Sharpe. "He's like putty in my hands, Sharpie." He just shrugged. "Honestly, though," she continued, "he expects everyone to jump on his command."

"He is the boss, Debbie."

"Yes, I know, but I bet it's not important." She turned back to the computer, and continued with her search.

A few minutes later, Sharpe left the room, returning with hot drinks shortly afterwards. "Cheers," she smiled. She sipped her coffee as she continued with her work. "Done!" she exclaimed, "now I'll see what the old grump wants. I bet he'll want me to go and buy some jelly babies, as George isn't here." Sharpe grinned.

"Cheeky bitch! Go and put him out of his misery." Debbie swivelled on her seat, and stood up.

"I just can't be arsed today. This had better be something important." She headed for Bentley's door, dropping her paper cup in a bin before knocking and entering. He looked up, and gestured to a chair.

"Ah, Debbie, sorry to have dragged you away from your important work, whatever it is, but I'm getting jumpy through lack of news. It's this weekend's meeting between White, Orlov and the rest. I was hoping for a call from George this morning. He's got today off, but wasn't he seeing that girl last night?"

"I think he was planning to see Liz, Sir, but it is only Wednesday today. Perhaps he'll phone later."

"I bloody hope so, Debbie. I've got Jefferson on my back, plus that bloke from London, then that neighbour is forever on the phone."

"Mrs Mills, you mean?"

"Yes, her, she thinks she's Mrs Marple or someone like that." He looked exasperated. "Have you got George's number?" Debbie took out her notebook, checked a couple of pages and nodded.

"Good, then give him a ring, please."

"What if he's busy, Sir, you know, with her?"

"Sod that, it's after lunch, isn't it? Anyway, make some apology, but see if he knows anything." Debbie keyed in the number, and lifted the phone to her ear.

"No reply, sorry. He must be busy," she said, grinning.

"Shit!" Bentley stood up and took a couple of paces. "Our most important week for ages, and we're sat around like spare parts. Come on, George Ryan. Pick up your bloody phone!"

***

Across the town, near Peasholm Park, Orlov's car slowed to a halt outside White's house and Tobolski got out of the back door to activate the secured doorway. Within a minute, the car was inside and parked near the wall on the driveway. The three passengers got out of the car and headed for the front door, where Nathaniel White was waiting. There was a brief flurry of handshakes, then the door closed.

At the end of the road, Anna watched as the gateway closed, then glanced at her watch. *At last!* She desperately needed to use a toilet, and to freshen up. She had a short time, at the very least, to do what was necessary, so she put the car into gear and drove off slowly, heading for the old town. Having parked, she brushed her dark hair, checked her appearance, then walked up the steep alleys and narrow streets until she neared the town centre. She paused for a few minutes at the gift shop, studying the window displays and noting who was inside the shop.

After that, she hurried more quickly, glancing around her, as she made her way back down Eastborough towards the old town and Karl's flat. Anna paused for a minute or two outside the old buildings, then quickly opened the front door and headed upstairs.

Once inside the flat, she rushed to the bathroom, used the toilet and freshened up. She decided it was too risky to have a shower, so she filled a small carrier with a few clothes then searched behind the chest of drawers for a small package, which she placed at the bottom of the carrier. Glancing around, she made her way downstairs, paused at the main door, then walked slowly back to her car.

Sheltering in a corner doorway, Maggie Buxton had waited in vain for Karl to return to his flat for lunch and was finishing her sandwich when she noticed Anna leaving the building. She studied the tall, dark-haired young woman, noting her black glasses, dark coat and jeans, then pushed back against the door, puzzled. *Where has she been? All of the holiday flats are always empty at this time of year.* She looked again at the woman as she walked slowly down the street. Something about her was familiar, but where had she seen her before? *The train!* That day when Natasha had disappeared from the train, and another woman had walked out of the toilet. *It had to be her!* Maggie threw the rest of her sandwich onto the pavement, and rushed down the street after the dark-haired woman.

***

"What would you like to drink, Stephanie? Wine, vodka, you name it." Nathaniel White smiled, towering above her with a bottle of red wine in his hand.

"I'll have a gin-and-tonic, thanks, but can I have a coffee as well? I feel jaded today." She slumped back in her seat, then looked around the room for Orlov.

"Boris, Jan, just help yourself to a drink," White said, pointing to the wide selection of alcohol on the table. "Adam, go and check in the kitchen. Tell Liz to get a move on with the sandwiches." He watched Thompson leave the room, then turned to the others and apologised. "I'm sorry about the delay with the food. I don't know what's wrong with her today. I'll have to get rid of her if she doesn't buck up her ideas." He smiled at Stephanie, moved to the table and poured himself a whisky, as Liz appeared carrying a tray of sandwiches, crisps and cakes. "About bloody time," White barked, glaring at her. "Leave that lot on the table, then go and make a pot of coffee." He turned to face Orlov. "We'll wait until Liz has brought the coffee, then we can get started, OK Boris?" The Russian nodded, as White continued organising everyone. "Jack, tell Masterman to get in here and check on Liz in the kitchen. You and Thompson can keep an eye on her, and make sure that she keeps the refreshments coming through." A few seconds later, Masterman entered the room, followed by Liz carrying the coffee and once she had set it down he quickly ushered her out of the lounge. White finally sat down and relaxed. "At last," he beamed around the room, "now we can get down to business." He poured himself a coffee, took a sip and grinned across at Orlov. "You've caught me with my pants down, Boris, I was getting things ready for the weekend so … what's the big rush?" Orlov opened his mouth to reply, but Stephanie continued the conversation.

"Some of Boris' Eastern European contacts are arriving in England this weekend, and they want a meeting in London, so we contacted you to bring this meeting forward." She paused, looking very serious, before moving on. "The people we're going to meet are very important for our future," she said, gesturing at Orlov and Tobolski, "so we want to get a few things clear before we meet them. When we teamed up with you last year, Nathaniel, we agreed to provide the muscle you needed to get a grip on the drugs and sex market in Leeds." White nodded. "After that, if you remember, we said that we would agree areas of control and discuss our future relationship. OK so far?" White pursed his lips, smiled at her and nodded. "I think you would agree with us that we have secured things in Leeds and can now move on. Boris and I are happy to give you control of the drugs market there, but we now want sole control over the sex scene. We have plans for the future … plans which involve some of Boris' contacts. Things have gone very well so far, and we have all worked together to become successful. Boris and I want our friendship to continue, and we are willing to provide you support if you ever need it in the future. There will be a cost, of course," the others laughed softly, "but we are sure that we can come to an agreement … as we have done so far."

Stephanie reached for her coffee, drained the cup and sat back in her seat. She glanced nervously at Orlov, who just smiled. White stood up and walked slowly to the window, before turning to face the others.

"I've been expecting this conversation, Steph, ever since we began eliminating our rivals in the sex market. So, let me guess, Boris' contacts will supply prostitutes from Eastern Europe … right?"

"Yes, that's part of our plans."

"What else, open one or two clubs in the city, strip clubs and so on?"

"Possibly, Nathaniel, we have a few ideas. We think there's some potential for expansion, as there is in the drugs market. That's why we think the time is right to split, to divide our interests and to go our separate ways. You can concentrate on branching out into other areas near to Leeds and like I said before, if you need any help in getting rid of any rivals, we'd be willing to help if we can. In any case, there's bound to be some overlap for a while, isn't there? A lot of prostitutes take drugs, don't they?" More polite laughter. "So, what do you think?" White glanced at Masterman, gestured for him to stand up, then replied to Stephanie.

"Just give us a few minutes, Steph." The two men left the room, and spoke quietly in the hallway for a few minutes. When they returned, White poured himself a coffee and placed a cheese sandwich and some crisps on a plate. "Help yourself, everyone," he muttered, before taking a bite of the sandwich and settling down in a seat. The others waited as he swallowed some coffee and ate some of the crisps. "As I said before, Steph, I have been expecting this conversation. We've all worked well together, but I knew that at some point you and Boris would want to go your own way. I think you're being a little premature, a little hasty, as I don't feel that we've got a complete hold of the drugs market yet, with those bastards in Bradford still posing a threat, and as for the sex market … well, there's some way to go, I feel."

"We understand what you mean, Nathaniel, but this is why we're talking to Boris' friends at the weekend. We want to plan the next phase and it will involve them, or at least, their money. I am sure that you appreciate why we need their help?"

"Yeah, that's not a problem, but they're Boris' friends. How can I trust them? How can I be sure that they won't move against me sometime in the future? I've got enough potential rivals without having to worry about them as well." He noticed that Masterman and Tobolski were working their way through the sandwiches, and stood up to take another one before they all vanished. He moved to the door and opened it. "Liz! More coffee," he ordered. Within seconds she came into the lounge and took the coffee pot. "Bring some more sandwiches too." She half smiled and scurried out of the lounge. White looked at Stephanie and raised his eyebrows. "Well?"

"Look, Nathaniel, we can assure you that you have nothing to fear … has he, Boris?"

"No," Boris stood up and moved nearer White.

"Stephanie is right," he continued. "My contacts are only interested in the sex market. They provide women and protection. They're not interested in drugs - unless they have a headache!" The tension eased as the others laughed at the Russian's joke. Orlov waited for a moment before continuing. "Stephanie and I have never been interested in drugs. We wanted to help you get established, then for you to help us get hold of the sex market. That's always been our real interest. The drugs scene is too complicated in my opinion ... Scousers, Asians, students, the police ... too many people wanting a share, a "piece of the action", I think you say? Well, we are not interested, and neither are my friends from the East. This is the right time to split, my friend." He put his arm around White's shoulder, and grinned. "Now, pour some vodka, and let us drink to our future!" Masterman reached for the bottle of *Stalichnaya,* and settled a few glasses on a tray. As he did so, Liz came in with two more plates of sandwiches and a bowl of salad.

"Good!" White exclaimed, nodding at her and watching her leave for the kitchen. "You're right, Boris. This is the right time to go our separate ways." He poured several shots of vodka. "Let us drink to our future." He pushed the glasses towards the others.

"The future!" they toasted in unison.

In the kitchen, Liz pondered her next move. Thompson and Dickinson had gone outside, perhaps for a smoke. Had she enough time to rush upstairs with George's mobile?

Mrs Mills got up from the settee and glanced sternly at her husband. "I don't like it, Arthur. I'm sure something's going on next door. It's just so difficult to see in this weather."

"Leave it, Joyce. That policeman told you that he would contact you again when they had news of the next meeting. He hasn't phoned, so just settle yourself. They'll think you're a nuisance, a fussy, nosey old woman. Just be patient, dear."

"I can't settle, Arthur. I'll just have another look from upstairs, then I'm going to phone him. It can't do any harm." She left the room and walked up the stairs.

Next door, Orlov, Stephanie and Tobolski were preparing to leave. White stood up and escorted them to the front door. "Are you sure?" he said, looking first at Stephanie, then at Orlov. "Should we sleep on it tonight, or do you want to see your contacts at the weekend before making a final decision? I'm quite happy to wait," he smiled.

"No, we've given it a lot of thought, Nathaniel," Stephanie answered, "and know what we want to do, but I will contact you after the weekend to tell you how our meeting in London has gone." She smiled briefly. "Ready?" she asked the others. They all shook hands and White opened the door, watching them walk to their car which was parked by the wall. He pressed the button to open the secured gate, and waved as they drove slowly out of the drive. Slamming the door shut, he returned to the lounge and looked seriously at Thompson and Dickinson. "Two minutes," he instructed, "and don't lose them." They both stood up and grabbed their coats.

Joyce Mills almost lost her footing as she hurried downstairs. "A car's leaving," she shouted through to her husband. "I'm phoning George Ryan." She picked up his card, dialled the number and waited for a reply.

At the end of the road, Anna glanced in her rear-view mirror then ducked down as Orlov's car passed by and halted just beyond her at the junction. She peered carefully as it turned right, then started her car and was about to move off when she noticed another car leaving White's house. She looked at the two occupants as they too passed by and paused at the junction, then she drove off once they were out of sight. Anna switched on the screen wipe and made sure that she kept touch with the second car, noticing that Orlov's car was slowing for a traffic light. *Perfect!* She thought to herself. She knew that Orlov could not see her in his mirror, but she was ideally placed to watch both cars, trying to understand why the other car was following Orlov. Whatever the reason, Orlov was her main priority. She needed to conclude matters with him quickly, preferably today. She peered through the heavy rain on the windscreen, glancing from one car to the other.

A short distance behind her, Maggie Buxton kept her father's car within sight of the rest of the strange motorcade.

***

White watched as Adam left the driveway and closed the door behind him. He was about to enter the lounge when he heard the muffled sound of a phone ringing, hesitated, listening for the source of the noise, then turned and saw Liz hovering near the kitchen.

"What's that?" he asked angrily.

"It must be my phone, in my jacket," she muttered quickly, pointing upstairs, "sorry."

"Get it switched off," he barked, "them make us some more coffee." Liz paused. "Get a move on, lass," he ordered, as he moved towards the lounge. Liz scurried up the stairs to the first landing, located the mobile in George's jacket and brought it out gingerly, the ringing tone getting louder. "Switch that fucking thing off!" White shouted from the lounge, "and get back down here." Liz glanced upstairs, then silenced the phone and rushed down again, heading for the kitchen. She could hear the sound of drinks being poured. Glancing upstairs again, Liz went into the kitchen and closed the door behind her.

In the lounge, White and Masterman clinked their glasses together, and drained the whisky. "Not long now," White grinned at his friend, "not long now."

***

The rain lashed on the screen as Orlov drove the car slowly through the mid-afternoon traffic, passing through the town centre and heading for the outskirts of Scarborough. He glanced at Stephanie beside him in the front, then looked in the mirror as Tobolski made himself comfortable on the back seat. The wiper blades flicked back and forth as the rain rushed down the windscreen.

"Well?" he glanced again at Stephanie. "That seemed to go as planned, Steph."

"Yeah, easier than I thought. I expected White to put up more of a fight, though, thinking about it, he didn't really have much choice. He knew that we planned to break away at some point, but he just seemed to accept it so easily." She bunched her hair behind her head, shook her head lightly then let her hair tumble over her shoulders. "We have to hope that he has accepted it, Boris," she sighed. "We have other things to think about, remember?"

"Hmm," Orlov muttered, watching again in his mirror as Tobolski eased himself into the corner of the seat and began to go to sleep. Looking beyond the car, Orlov noticed that the traffic was building up behind them. "It's getting busy," he remarked, peering through the screen and braking gently as the cars slowed in front of him, "but I'll lose some of this traffic when we reach the main road. This Yorkshire weather is foul," he laughed at Stephanie, glancing around then peering again through the rain.

"Just be careful, Boris," Stephanie warned, "we're in no hurry. I want to get back to York in one piece." In the back, Tobolski began to snore gently.

Some way behind their car, Anna kept a distance from the car in front of her, disliking driving in such heavy rain, but she made sure that she could still see both Orlov's car and the other car which had followed soon afterwards from White's house. Two cars behind her, Maggie concentrated on keeping touch with the red Mondeo swishing ahead, the traffic easing slightly as they neared a large roundabout.

"We need the A570, Boris," Stephanie muttered, peering at the road sign, "that one," pointing, "the second exit."

"I know, Steph, stop making a fuss," he snapped, reaching the roundabout and looking concerned as the brakes seemed to respond slowly. He slammed the gear lever noisily into second, then lurched onto the outside lane. "Fucking brakes," he shouted, "useless in this weather. If only this was a Russian car."

"Well, it isn't," Stephanie replied, touching his leg, "just be careful, Boris. Don't take any chances, right?" He eased the car further around the roundabout and signalled to take the dual carriageway.

"At last, a decent road." He changed up a gear, and powered past the car in front.

"Easy, tiger, there's no rush, remember?" The car roared on through the driving rain, and the traffic gradually thinned out along the A570. Boris relaxed, looked across at Stephanie and grinned.

***

George Ryan crept down the upper flight of stairs, lay on his stomach and peered round the bannister. There was no-one in sight. He paused for a minute or two, listening to the distant hum of voices far below him, trying to work out how many people were left and who was speaking. Earlier he had heard the noise of car engines, and from the tiny attic window had managed to catch sight of cars leaving the house, but the view was too obscure to recognise who was in them.

A door opened downstairs and footsteps could be heard in the hall. "Make us some more coffee, Liz," White barked in the distance, "I'm going to the bog, Jim. I won't be a minute. Wait till I get back if there's a call. I wish to fuck they'd get a move on." George backtracked quickly and crept back to the attic room.

***

Orlov accelerated again to overtake another slow-moving vehicle and sped on into the driving rain. "You're going too fast, Boris," Stephanie tapped him on his arm, a concerned look on her face.

"Stop making a fuss," he grinned at her, "we've left most of the traffic behind us. Look," he said, peering in his mirror, "Jan isn't worried. He's sleeping like a baby!" Stephanie turned to the back seat, and Orlov looked again in his mirror. "Snoring like a Polish pig!" He laughed again at Stephanie, then cursed softly as a wagon suddenly loomed ahead of them in the murky weather. Orlov jammed on the brakes and swerved as the two vehicles began to ease around a tight bend, then he cast a worried look at his frightened passenger. "No brakes!" he shouted, as he changed down quickly and swerved more to avoid the slowing wagon. The old

Renault swung into the centre of the road, just missing the wagon but heading straight for the lights of an oncoming vehicle. "Shit!" Stephanie held her head as the two cars skidded, then collided and glanced off each other. Orlov lost control as the Renault left the road, turning over as the car tumbled down a slight slope, bounced along a hedge and finally came to rest, upside-down, after hitting a tree. The driver's door swung open as steam rose slowly from the battered car.

Back on the road, Thompson and Dickinson instinctively ducked as a car lurched across their path and careered off the side of the road. Thompson slammed on his brakes, glancing behind him then trying to see what had happened in front of him. He could just make out a wagon making slow progress in the distance, then Dickinson stared across the road. "I think they might have crashed, Adam," he muttered, looking back as their car slowed around the bend and eased along the road. Both men looked ahead, trying to spot the old Renault. "Turn around, Adam, they've fucking crashed. We need to see if anyone's left alive."

"Give me a minute, for Christ's sake, I can't see a bloody thing in this rain. Fucking weather!" he cursed, driving along slowly, looking for a lay-by or a flat verge.

Orlov eased himself out of the wrecked car, then looked back at Stephanie. She had a deep gash on her forehead, and her body, still secured by the seat belt, was contorted like a rag doll, her head twisted grotesquely and hanging down towards the roof of the car. Grimacing, Orlov staggered forward on his knees and peered in the back, where Tobolski was lying almost upside-down on the parcel shelf, moaning softly and trying to touch his head. "Jan!" Orlov shouted, moving towards the back door, but his friend did not respond. A figure appeared suddenly in the rain, glancing quickly at the occupants of the car.

"Boris," Anna shouted in Russian, "you must come with me." Orlov looked back inside the car. "Hurry," she shouted again, shaking his shoulder. "You can't do anything for them, but you can save yourself. White's men are following you. They'll be here any minute. Come on!" She helped him to his feet and guided him to her red Mondeo, before moving off in the direction of York.

Maggie Buxton halted her car fifty yards before the bend, looking in horror at the two vehicles that had crashed on either side of the road. The car which had been travelling towards Scarborough suddenly burst into flames, but Maggie kept peering at the other car, trying to see what was happening. She couldn't see Anna's red Mondeo parked further along the road, but noticed someone helping one of the passengers away from the wreck. Within minutes another car arrived, parking just off the road, and Maggie gasped as she watched two men dragging one of the injured passengers out of the back door and towards their own car. The car reversed, turned around and moved off in the direction of Scarborough. Maggie glanced at the wrecked Renault before turning her car around and heading for Scarborough. She could hear sirens in the distance and watched as first a police car, then an ambulance sped towards the crash scene. Glancing in her mirror, she concentrated on keeping touch with the other car heading for Scarborough. The rain continued to pour down relentlessly as the cars drove slowly towards the darkened skies above the seaside town.

***

Nathaniel White put the phone down angrily and stormed back into the lounge. "What a fuck up!" he glared at Masterman. "The car crashed as planned, but Orlov's managed to get away. Adam thinks that another car gave him a lift."

"Another car, how?" White shrugged. "What about the other two?" the bulky figure asked.

"Stephanie Garrett's dead, but they've got Tobolski. He's badly injured, but they're bringing him back to the house."

"What for? It's Orlov that we want."

"Don't be a fucking dope. Get the basement ready. When they arrive, we'll drag Tobolski down there, then you can turn your *charms* on him. He knows where they've been living, and Orlov must be on his way back there. He'll have another car hidden somewhere, so speed is the essence, Jim. We need to make Tobolski talk as quickly as possible. But listen," White held up his finger, "don't fucking kill him, at least not until he's talked. If he dies, we'll never find Orlov and remember, he's seeing his mates at the weekend. The last thing I

233

want is a gang of Russian mafia running loose around Leeds or here, looking for us. Be nice to Tobolski, just use the gentler techniques, then we can get rid of him once we know where Orlov is hiding." He heard a noise and spun round. "What do you want?" he barked at Liz.

"I just wondered if you needed anything else, Mr Marshall?" she answered meekly.

"No, piss off back to the kitchen, and stay in there. I'll fetch you if we need anything." Liz hurried out of the room. White listened for a few seconds to the sound of a car arriving. "They're back. Get downstairs and make sure everything's ready." Masterman pulled a bunch of keys from his coat pocket, then unlocked the cellar door. White watched him switch on the light and make his way down the steps, then he headed for the front door. Car doors slammed, then Thompson and Dickinson appeared through the rain, half-dragging Tobolski with them.

"Questions later," White grunted, "just get him down in the cellar as quickly as you can. What state is he in?"

"Not too good," muttered Thompson. "Looks as if he's broken an arm, probably some other damage. He's been moaning a lot on the way back."

"OK, keep him in one piece," White moved out of their way and closed the front door. "Masterman's down there. He knows what to do. Tell him I'll be down soon. Adam, come back up here when you've got Tobolski down to the cellar." He walked into the lounge and poured himself a drink. A few minutes later, Thompson came into the lounge. "Help yourself to a drink, then tell me exactly what happened." Thompson sunk back into one of the seats.

"I'll get a drink later, Boss," he said. "Everything went to plan at first. The weather was foul, but that meant that Orlov couldn't see us following him. We got out of town, then he put his foot down when we reached the dual carriageway. The rain was really heavy, and he left us behind, but then he must have collided with another car, took a bend too quickly. The cars were on opposite sides of the road, Orlov's car was upside-down. I'd driven past it before Jack realised that there'd been an accident, so I turned around when it was safe and parked near Orlov's car. A red car was disappearing when we arrived, so he must have got a lift in it. Stephanie Garrett was crumpled up dead in the front seat, and Tobolski was trying to get out when we got there. We managed to drag him out before the cops arrived. That's all really." He stood up and poured himself a drink.

"I wish to Hell that the crash had taken them all out, but it's too late now. We need to make Tobolski tell us where they've been living, because that's where Orlov will be heading right now. As soon as we know, I want you and Jack to drive to their hideout and check it out. Give me a bell what you've got some info, then Masterman and I will join you later." He stood up. "I'll go and see how they're getting on downstairs. You keep an eye on Liz and make sure she stays in the kitchen. OK?" Adam nodded, and White made his way down the rough and uneven cellar steps, making sure that he didn't lose his footing as he descended into the gloomy room. Part of the cellar was full of unwanted furniture, cardboard boxes, two old chest freezers and a variety of odds and ends, but one area had been left clear, with just a table and a few chairs. Some tools and pieces of wood lay on a cloth on the table. When White reached the rough floor, he could see the back of Tobolski, his body slumped in one of the chairs, stripped to the waist with his hands tied behind his back. His body jerked back and he shouted as Masterman aimed another blow into his stomach. Tobolski slumped forward again.

"Talk, you Polish bastard. Where have you been living?" Silence. Masterman prepared to punch again as White walked over, holding up his hand for him to stop. He reached for one of the chairs and sat in front of the giant Pole.

"Look, Jan," White smiled as Tobolski partly opened his eyes, "we don't want to cause you any more pain. We can see that you've been injured, and if you help us we can dress your wounds and give you some painkillers. We don't want to hurt you, we want to find Boris. All you have to do is tell us where to find him, then all of this will stop. It's as easy as that. Tell us where you have been living and we'll untie you and take you to hospital. Help us, Jan. Just a few words and then you will be free. All of this blood and pain is unnecessary." He paused, before leaning forward and speaking more softly. "Where can we find Boris?" Silence. White stood up and gestured for Masterman to walk with him towards the corner of the room, while Jack sat on the edge of the table, staring at the injured man. "You can't go on beating him, Jim, he's going to die on us, then we're sunk. We've got to keep him alive and get him to talk. Beating him isn't going to work. Put yourself in his shoes. He's been badly injured in the crash, Steph has died, and Orlov has disappeared. He probably thinks he's going to die anyway, so he's going to stay loyal to Orlov and tell us nothing. We haven't much time, but there is someone else who might be able to persuade him." He turned to Dickinson. "Fetch Liz from the kitchen, quickly!" Jack hurried across the room and up the steps, returning a few minutes later with Thompson and the frightened young woman. "Go back and close the door." White put his arm around Liz's shoulders, and spoke quietly to her. "Listen, Liz, we haven't much time. There's been a car crash, and Boris Orlov has disappeared. Tobolski is the only person who knows where he is. He won't talk to us, but he likes you and might tell you where to find Orlov. Go over there, look sad and sympathetic, and ask Tobolski where he and the others have been living. We need an address, and quickly." He smiled at her. "I'm relying on you, Liz. Give us the information we need, and after this is all over you can go back to a normal life. I'll forget about your brother's debt. You'll be free. OK?"

"I'll try," she whispered, glancing over to the injured man, "but he looks awful. He's badly injured." She began to cry.

"You can do it, Liz, I know you can. Remember, I'm relying on you. Go on." He pushed her gently towards Tobolski. She walked over and sat on the chair in front of him.

"Mr Tobolski," she said quietly, glancing quickly over to White. *Jan,* he mouthed. "Jan, I'm so sorry to see you like this. You've got some horrible injuries." Tears trickled down her cheeks. "Please help us, and help yourself by telling us where we can find Mr Orlov. If you do that, we can set you free, take you to hospital, make you safe. Please, Jan, I beg you, please tell us where to find your friend Mr Orlov." Tobolski raised his head slowly, smiled at the young woman in front of him, then shook his head.

"He is my friend," he muttered slowly through bloody lips, "and I will not betray him. They can kill me if they want." His head slumped forward again.

"Please, Jan, don't punish yourself," Liz pleaded with him. "You can save yourself. Just tell us where he is." She held his great hands, squeezing them gently. "Please, Jan." She glanced to the four men standing in the corner, then cried out as Masterman moved suddenly towards her, pushing her to one side then thumping Tobolski again and again on his body and on his injured arm.

"Tell us, you bastard, tell us!" White strode over quickly and shoved Masterman out of the way and back towards the corner.

"I told you that thumping him won't work," he seethed, grabbing his throat, "just fucking listen, will you? A dead man is no use to us, for Christ's sake." He loosened his grip, and looked across at the tortured man and the frightened woman. "Adam, Jack, get over there and tie Liz to that other chair." They both looked puzzled. "Now!" he shouted. They walked over and grabbed Liz, who began struggling and screaming loudly. Thompson forced her onto the chair and Dickinson taped her hands behind her back. "Blindfold her," White ordered. He pointed at some cloth on the table, waited as his instructions were carried out, then walked over behind Tobolski and held his head up. "Liz is over there, Jan, and we know you like her and we don't want to hurt her, but we need to know where to find Boris. Where is he?" Silence again, as the Pole shook his head slowly. White glanced at Masterman, and held up his little finger. Masterman moved over to Liz's chair, untied her left hand and with a quick movement, broke her little finger. She shrieked loudly, struggled violently and began to cry. Tobolski came to life, trying to free his hands and to stand up. White forced him back onto the chair, and waited until he had calmed down. "Just a few words, Jan, then we can free you and the girl. Where is Boris?" The Pole opened his mouth to speak, then his head dropped again. White pointed to a knife on the table, tugged at his shirt then pointed to Liz. "Adam, do the honours," he ordered softly. Thompson picked up the knife, took hold of Liz's jumper and sliced it up the front, pushing the two sides behind her. He glanced at White, who nodded, then he held Liz and cut the straps of her bra until it tumbled to the floor. Her large breasts moved from side to side as she struggled with her captors. White lit a cigarette and nudged Masterman, who was staring at Liz's breasts. He pointed to her arms, then moved over to Tobolski, raising his head again. "Look, Jan, she's beautiful, isn't she? You can stop her pain right now. Just tell us where to find Boris and we will release both of you. If you refuse, we will have to cause more pain for her. I am sure that you don't want us to harm her again?" Once again, Tobolski moved to speak, but remained silent. He stared at the young woman as Masterman touched the cigarette onto her right arm, and she shouted out and screamed as she struggled once more with the men who held her.

"Tell us where he is," Masterman bellowed at Tobolski. "Tell us." He placed his right arm across her breasts, then touched the cigarette onto Liz's left arm, waiting to see if the Pole would react to her screams. They were all waiting for the Pole to break, and again he made to speak, but shook his head instead. White gestured to Masterman, and the two walked a few paces away from the rest.

"We're nearly there, Jim. I'm sure he's going to break. We're running out of time, so let's up the ante." He pointed to a baseball bat lying near the table. "Right leg," he instructed, returning to Tobolski and holding up his head again. Liz was crying constantly, and was starting to shiver in the cold, damp room. She was sitting still as Masterman swung the bat forcefully at her right leg, striking it just below the knee. Everyone heard the *crack!* as the bat struck home. Liz screamed loudly, then fainted. Tobolski stood up in horror, tried to shake loose his bonds, until Masterman and White forced him to sit down again. "This is crazy, Jan. You like the girl, so why hurt her, why let her die? Just tell us where to find Boris, then we will stop and treat your injuries, and the girl's. Please, for Liz's sake." Tobolski leaned forward, and looked across at Liz.

"He's … at 58 Macadam Terrace … the middle flat," Tobolski spoke slowly, gasping for breath, staring at the injured young woman.

"Macadam Terrace … where?" White asked quietly.

"York."

"York, so that's where you were hiding." He looked across at the other men. "Did you hear that?" He gestured for them to move closer. "York, 58 Macadam Terrace, the middle flat. Adam, Jack, drive there as quickly as you can, stake the place out, let me know when you've got there and if there's any sign of Orlov. Masterman and I will follow when we've tidied up here."

"What if he's lying, Boss?" Adam asked.

"Look at him, he's a broken man. It's sickened him watching us torture Liz, don't worry, he's told us the truth. Now get a move on."

***

Anna had just driven a short distance towards York before halting and parking in a lay-by, making sure that she was not being followed. She switched the engine off and turned to Orlov. "Are you injured?" she asked in Russian.

"Nothing serious. Stephanie was killed in that crash, but Tobolski was still alive, I think, probably injured." He looked close to tears. "Did you say that White's men were following me?"

"Definitely. I was watching the house, and saw them leave soon after you. That's when I followed behind."

"The bastards!" he growled angrily. "There was something wrong with the brakes. They must have tampered with them, otherwise, why did they follow me?"

"Forget them, Boris. We need to return to your flat, then to decide what to do. You still have the choice to return to Russia."

"No," he said thoughtfully. "I'm not finished here. White's men will have taken Jan back to Scarborough to torture him, to find out where I am living." He looked across at Anna. "I need to settle things here, for Stephanie's sake. I loved her, Anna … I owe her. I want to return to the house, to see if I can save Jan, then to deal with White and his men."

"That's taking a big risk, Boris. There must be at least three of them in the house."

"Four, all armed."

"Four then, and how are we going to get into the house?"

"I know the code to the gateway. If we can get inside the house, we can deal with them. I won't decide about Russia until I've finished things here. Will you help me, Anna?"

"I don't seem to have a choice," she muttered, starting the car and turning it around before heading back to Scarborough. The rain was easing slightly, but Anna drove carefully on the saturated roads, reaching the junction of the road near Peasholm Park in good time. She parked just past the corner, and Boris walked a few paces to check if any of the cars were outside White's house. He returned in a few minutes.

"Have you an umbrella?" Anna looked in the door pockets and found one. "Good. There's no time to lose. We'll walk down to the house and get inside the grounds. If the front door's locked, we'll have to blast our way in." Anna looked concerned. "Don't worry. My gun has a silencer, and we'll have the element of surprise. Come on, let's go." They scrambled out of the car, and walked under the umbrella towards White's house.

Maggie Buxton had followed the other car back to Scarborough, and had parked, trying to work out what exactly was going on. Soon afterwards, Anna's Mondeo returned and parked close to the junction, and now she mulled over her options. Maggie decided to say where she was, to find out more about Karl's girlfriend, but to contact her parents. She phoned home, and her mother answered.

"Mum, it's me."

"Margaret, we've been so worried, and your father is going mad here because he wanted the car this afternoon. We had to catch a bus to the centre to go shopping … and in all of this rain. It was most inconvenient. Where are you?"

"Never mind that for now, Mum. Listen, I still need the car for a bit longer, so I'll be home later. I'll tell you about everything tomorrow."

"Margaret, we're worried about you. Can't you come home now?"

"I'll get back as soon as possible, Mum. Oh, I need you to write down a car registration for me." She read out Anna's number slowly. "Got it? Good. I'll see you later. Bye." She sat back and smiled. Now, *what next?*

Anna and Orlov were only twenty or so yards away from White's house on the opposite side of the road when the gateway began to open. "Keep walking past the house to the end of the road," he instructed. A car emerged from the driveway and sped along the road.

"They're the two men who followed you, Boris," Anna spoke in his ear.

"Good," Orlov grinned. "That means there's just two left, Masterman and White." They walked quickly across the road and Boris peered through a gap in the gateway to see if anyone was at the front door, then he turned to Anna. "Let's go," he whispered, and they hurried towards the house. "They've left the gateway open, so they must be planning to follow the others. The front door may be open as well. Before we go in, Anna, I want White alive if possible, wounded perhaps, but alive. OK?" He stepped forward onto the porch, took out his Makarov pistol and gently pushed the door. It moved a little, and Orlov gestured for Anna to follow. She drew a gun from her handbag, and followed Orlov gingerly into the hallway. Empty. Orlov looked towards the lounge, then upstairs before pointing towards the cellar door, where a narrow shaft of light showed that the door was open. The front door rattled.

"Go and shut that fucking door, Jim," White's muffled

voice resonated from below. Orlov and Anna froze, then they heard Masterman on the steps. He walked up three, four steps, then Orlov moved like a snake, kicking the door open and his gun coughed twice. Masterman flew back down the steps in a flurry of arms and legs and crashed to the floor, one small hole bleeding from his forehead. Anna followed as Orlov moved onto the steps, and she crouched, looking for White in the gloom below. *To your right!* she shouted in Russian, pointing at White as he moved behind the table, pulling a gun from his jacket and preparing to fire. Orlov fired again, neatly wounding White in his gun hand, then again in his left thigh. White shouted in pain as the two Russians rushed down the steps, and Orlov moved close and struck him on the forehead with his pistol. The huge black man dropped to the floor. Orlov looked around at Tobolski and Liz, who was still blindfolded and unconscious, then at the table. He grabbed the roll of tape.

"Bind his hands and cover his mouth," Orlov ordered, pointing at White, "and cover the girl. Use Masterman's clothes if necessary." He moved to the chair where his friend Tobolski was still tied and cut the tape, catching him as he almost fell off the chair. "Jan," he said quietly, lifting the Pole's head, "Jan, you're safe now." Tobolski moved his head very slowly, looked at Orlov and tried to smile.

"I'm finished, Boris," he whispered, tears appearing on his face, "and I had to tell them about York." Anna moved close to the chair.

"Forget all of that, my friend, you were always loyal to me. I can see what has happened here, and how …" He broke off as Tobolski collapsed into his arms, then Orlov lowered him gently to the floor. He looked up at Anna. "He was my best friend, Anna, and now I have to finish things for him." He glanced across the room at the prone body of White.

"Just shoot him, Boris, then we can go."

"No, Anna, not here, that's too easy. I want him somewhere where I can watch him die slowly." He looked at the assortment of tools on the table. "I need your help, Anna. White's a big man, but I want to get him away from here. Go and bring the car to the front door, then I want you to help me move him into it." She hesitated for a few seconds. "Hurry! The neighbours may have heard or seen something. It can't end here. Be quick!" She stood up and dashed up the steps, as Orlov began binding White's wounds.

Five minutes later, Anna returned to the house to find that Orlov had managed to drag White halfway up the steps. "Quickly, Anna, get to his feet and help me drag him out of here. We need to do this before he regains consciousness." They both heaved and sweated to haul the big man to the top of the cellar steps and along the hallway. "Now," Orlov sat back, sweating profusely and exhausted, "open the back door of your car. We need to get him in there as quickly as possible." He stood up again and waited until Anna returned, then they continued to drag White into the lobby and out of the house. A few minutes later he was lying on the back seat of Anna's car. She got into the front seat and started the engine.

"What about the girl?" she asked.

"When we've got well away from here you can phone the police if you like." Then he thought for a few seconds. "Just a minute, Anna. I need a few things from the house." He rushed inside and returned five minutes later with two carrier bags, which he threw onto the floor by the back seat. "OK, go!" The car roared along the road.

George Ryan glanced nervously downstairs from the landing, and wondered for the umpteenth time if it was safe to make a move. He had listened to the various comings and goings, and to some muffled screams in the cellar, but now all seemed to be quiet. He gripped a lump of wood that he had found upstairs, crept down to the hallway and fumbled in his jacket for his mobile phone. Switching it on, he scurried quickly back up two flights of stairs before phoning the station. A sleepy voice answered. "Listen carefully," he whispered, "this is DC George Ryan. Get a message to DI Bentley. I'm trapped in Nathaniel White's house near Peasholm Park, and need urgent assistance, armed assistance. There's no time to lose." He crept downstairs again and listened carefully for a couple of minutes. Nothing. Ryan returned to the hall and glanced quickly in the lounge, then noticed the light coming from the cellar. Peering around the door, he saw Masterman's body lying contorted near the foot of the steps, then he moved onto the steps and saw

Tobolski's body on the floor, with Liz sitting close by. "Liz!" he shouted, forgetting about any potential danger, and rushed headlong down the steps. He removed the tape and blindfold, checked her pulse then phoned the station again. "It's me again, George Ryan. White's house, we need an ambulance here - urgently!" The reply was slow. "Get a move on, man! Armed police and an ambulance, right now!"

***

Anna pulled into a lay-by on the edge of Scarborough, and switched off the engine. It was dark now, and still raining. She turned to Orlov, who seemed lost in his thoughts.

"Boris, we need to talk. I need to know what you intend to do, firstly with him," she jerked her head towards the back seat, "and then afterwards. Are you returning to Moscow with me and Rudnev?"

"I'll speak about White later, he's not important. As for returning to Russia, I'm sorry, Anna," he spoke slowly, smiling, "but that was never an option for me. You are young, new to this game, you do not understand how the system works. Yes, I have been a good agent. Yes, I could train more agents for Russia. But I have been disloyal, I have betrayed my country, I have lost my way. They would never forgive me for that, Anna. I took a gamble, I pursued my happiness, and thanks to this bastard," he glanced behind him at White's prone figure, "I have lost everything. My loyalty to Russia, my friendship with Tobolski, above all my love for Stephanie ... all of that has gone, and I cannot turn back the clock. They will not forgive me in Moscow. Yes, they have asked you to persuade me to return, but that is only so that I can tell them all that I know, all of my contacts, try to help them understand why I chose a different life, and I can tell you this, Anna … they will torture me until they have every detail, and they will take pleasure in doing that, then they will take me to a yard behind *Lubyanka* and shoot me in the back of my head." He smiled at Anna again. "That is what waits for me in Moscow."

"And Nathaniel White?"

"Everything ends *here* for me, Anna. Fate has driven me to this place, and now it is nearly over. All that remains is for me to take revenge on White for Stephanie, for Jan, for the many others he has wronged, and for me. After I have finished, my fate is then in your hands. When we spoke in York, you told me what would happen to me if I refused to return to Moscow. So be it. When White is dead, you can dispose of me. I am ready, I will look forward to death, and I will be happy that you have completed your mission successfully." He looked relaxed, and smiled again at Anna. "I still need your help, young lady, so tell me … where is there a secluded place near here, a place with plenty of trees, perhaps somewhere not too far from the sea?" Anna thought for a moment.

"There is a place called Oliver's Mount, Boris, a high place, a sort of park on the outskirts of town which overlooks the sea. I have run through the park a couple of times. It will only take a few minutes to drive there, and it should be quiet now. It is dark and the weather is still awful, so the usual runners and people walking their dogs will not be there in the evening. What do you think?"

"It sounds perfect, Anna, let's go." Anna started the car and headed for the south of the town, checking the road signs as she drove around Scarborough. Behind her, keeping a distance, Maggie Buxton continued to stalk her rival.

***

George Ryan waited by the front door for the cavalry to arrive. The police got there first, and Ryan held up his hands as two black-suited and heavily armed policemen jumped out of a van and shouted at him to lay down.

"It's alright," Ryan called to them, "they've gone." He glanced up from the doorway and saw Jim Bentley emerging from a patrol car. "It's safe, Sir. They're dead." Bentley had a word with the armed officers and strolled over to Ryan, helping him back onto his feet. Debbie Chapman and Tim Sharpe joined them at the front door.

"I'll get them to double-check, just in case," Bentley muttered, ushering the armed men past them. "Make sure that it's all clear," he shouted as they rushed by. "Are you alright, George?" An ambulance pulled into the driveway, its sirens blaring.

"I'm OK, Sir, but Liz Coward is injured badly. She's in the cellar." They waited until the men returned and nodded that all was well, then Bentley pushed Ryan into the hallway.

"Show us, Ryan," he ordered. Ryan quickly headed for the cellar steps, followed by the police team and two paramedics.

"Liz is over there, covered by blankets," Ryan pointed, calling to the paramedics and moving aside to let them past him. They knelt down and began examining Liz's injuries. Ryan followed them, listening to their findings.

"Who have we got here?" Bentley quizzed the team.

"I think that's the Polish guy, Tobolski," Debbie pointed to the figure laying on the floor near the chair. "Looks like he's been tortured."

"Well, he's definitely not been sunbathing," Sharpe looked at Chapman, laughing softly.

"Shut up, Sharpie, you dickhead," she retorted angrily. Bentley studied the other corpse.

"This brute looks like one of White's men, Monster-something."

"Masterman, I think he's called, Sir," Ryan corrected him, as he re-joined the others. "Liz has been beaten, Sir, they think she has a broken or fractured leg."

"You can't stay down here, George, you can see her later. Listen everyone, get upstairs so that the SOC team can do their work. Where are they, Debbie?"

"Just arriving, Sir."

"Right then, let's get out of their way, into the lounge, I think, then young Ryan can tell us what's been happening here." He led them through to the lounge and they settled into the comfortable seats. Bentley glanced across at Ryan. "A brief explanation will do for now, George. What happened to the so-called weekend meeting?"

"I can't tell you that, Sir. I was here last night with Liz," Sharpe raised his eyebrows and grinned briefly until he saw Chapman's disapproval, "and we were just having breakfast around ten this morning when White and some of his people arrived unexpectedly."

"That goes without saying, George, otherwise you would have had breakfast ready for them, wouldn't you?" Sharpe grinned again.

"Shut up, for fuck's sake. If you can't say something useful, just shut the fuck up!" Debbie Chapman was seething.

"OK, Debbie, calm down. Sharpe … button it," Bentley said sternly, glaring at him. "Carry on, George."

"We were in the attic, and White shouted for Liz to go down and prepare some refreshments. I laid low. My mobile was on the lower landing, in my jacket pocket. I was worried for Liz, but I thought it would be worse for her if they caught me and found out who I was." Bentley nodded.

"Go on."

"Liz made them something, then they forced her to stay downstairs. More people arrived, Orlov and Co, I guess, then it was quiet. They must have all been in the lounge." He thought for a minute. "No, at one point, one or two of them went outside by the kitchen door." He looked apologetically at Bentley. "I'm sorry, Sir, but it was really difficult to see anything out of the attic window, and the voices were muffled."

"It's OK, George." The door opened and one of the

paramedics entered the room.

"We've got the girl on a stretcher." George stood up. "She's got a break or a fracture just below her knee, and one or two minor injuries. She's in a lot of pain and very upset. We're going to get her to the hospital, so if you need to speak to her you'll have to wait. She needs urgent medical attention."

"That's fine," Bentley said. "Sharpe, make yourself useful. Go with them to the hospital and make sure no-one has any contact with her. Stay with her as much as possible, and take a note of anything she says." Sharpe moved away to wait for the stretcher.

"Sir ...," Ryan started to speak.

"You're staying here, Ryan. I know you're worried about Liz Coward, but she's in good hands. You can see her later, but right now, I need you here." Ryan sat down. "Now, where were we?"

"I was in the attic room, Sir. There was always someone in the house, so I didn't have an opportunity to go down to the lower landing to collect my mobile. After the meeting, there seemed to be a lot of coming and going. I heard two cars leave the house, then sometime later another arrived. I sneaked down a landing at one point and thought I heard someone going into the cellar. There was some more commotion, then it all went very quiet. That's when I plucked up the courage to dash down to retrieve my mobile and to phone for help." Ryan collapsed back into his seat. "I'm sorry, Sir, I've been pretty useless, haven't I?"

"Don't knock yourself down, George," Bentley consoled him. "Don't forget, we were told that these people were dangerous, and advised not to go solo." Debbie nodded in agreement. "You acted sensibly, George, so don't worry."

"I feel bad for Liz, Sir. She trusted me and I've let her down, let her get badly injured."

"She'll be fine, George, in time. Her injuries can be healed. These others have had it." He gestured below, towards the cellar. "Now, let's fill in some of the blanks." He glanced at Chapman.

"What you don't know, George, is that there was a car smash, on the A570 outside Scarborough. A couple of cars were involved, including Orlov's, and Stephanie Garrett was killed."

"I see, so White's men must have been following," Ryan mused, "and they grabbed Tobolski." He continued thinking. "That means that Orlov must have escaped the crash, but where is he now ... and where is Nathaniel White?"

"Until we get some more information when Liz recovers," Bentley continued, "we have to assume that Orlov somehow got back here to the house, killed Masterman, captured White and made off with him."

"If that's true, Sir," Debbie took up the thread of thought, "someone must have helped Orlov, but who?"

"Yes, Debbie, and where are they all now?" Bentley looked at both faces in turn.

***

Anna drove her car along the narrow road which twisted around much of Oliver's Mount, parked by the war memorial at the summit and switched off the engine. She glanced back at White, who was still unconscious, and looked at Orlov. "Come with me," she ordered, and walked around the memorial to a viewpoint, where the twinkling lights in Scarborough harbour could be seen far away in the distance.

"Beautiful," Orlov enthused, "this is an excellent place for an execution." He descended a few steps below the viewpoint and looked around the bushes that covered the hill, then returned to Anna. "We need to find somewhere to park the car, away from the road." They returned to the car, and Anna drove slowly away from the memorial until she reached a turn-off. She drove into a clearing a short distance away from the road that ran through the park, got out of the car and walked a little way, checking that they could not be seen from any cars passing through. Soaked, she got back into the car and switched off the engine. "This seems safe enough, Boris. We're parked away from the road, and the ground is still quite firm here. Now will you tell me what you plan to do here?" Orlov got out of the car and walked around for a few minutes, before getting back in.

"Just drive a little further, in that direction," he pointed as Anna started the engine, and crept along a few more yards, halting behind some large bushes which surrounded a clearing. "Perfect," he said, peering through the rain at the nearby trees. "I just need a little assistance from you, Anna, a little help in dragging

White to that large tree over there." He pointed again, and she could just make out the features of a large tree through the side window. "When I've finished, Anna, you can deal with me." He got out of the car, opened the back door, shook White firmly to wake him and then took the two carrier bags over to the tree. White stirred slowly, looking very groggy, blood matted on his forehead, then with widening frightened eyes as he took in his predicament. He began struggling to break the taped bonds. Orlov returned and began dragging White out of the back of the car. "Give me a hand," he shouted to Anna. She got out of the car, and they hauled the big man onto the ground and slowly dragged him, kicking and stumbling, towards the tree. When they reached the tree, Orlov leaned over and smashed his fist into White's face, knocking him unconscious once again. He and Anna continued moving their victim until he was sat against the base of the tree. They both stood up and took a breath, drenched and exhausted by the ordeal. Orlov was the first to recover, then he rummaged in one of the bags and brought out a hammer. "We need to get him onto his feet, Anna," he shouted, "and you must hold him against the tree for me." She looked puzzled. "Just do it, quickly." They slowly eased White up the trunk, and Anna pushed hard against him to make sure that he stayed upright. Orlov searched the bags again, brought out a knife and sliced through the tapes that bound White's hands. Anna glanced to the side and looked quizzingly again, as Orlov stretched White's left arm onto a thick branch, then brought a heavy six-inch nail out of his pocket, positioned it on White's left wrist and gave it an almighty thump with the hammer. White's body jerked fiercely with the pain and his eyes opened widely, terrified as Orlov continued thumping the nail, bending it over before it almost disappeared. White's free hand clawed at Anna, but Orlov moved behind her, grabbing the wrist and forcing it onto another branch on the other side of the tree. The weakened White could only offer token resistance and kicked at Orlov as he swung the hammer again and pinned him to the tree with a second nail. The giant black man's head shook in agony and blood was pouring onto his face as Orlov hammered home. The Russian nodded to White's legs and Anna took a grip as Orlov found another nail and began banging it through one of his ankles. The crucifixion was finally completed as Orlov secured the remaining leg onto a large root with another nail driven through White's right ankle. Anna stepped back quickly, her hair soaking, her head cradled in her hands in horror at the punishment meted out by the demonic Russian agent. He, on the other hand, appeared to be glowing in satisfaction at the work that had been done, and began mocking his tortured enemy. "That's for Stephanie," he bellowed in the darkness. "And for Tobolski, and for betraying me, you bastard." He stepped forward and grasped White's head, slapping it and trying to wake him up. "Wake up, you bastard! See what your betrayal has achieved! Wake up before you rot in Hell". Orlov was shaking his enemy now, and Anna moved forward and dragged him away.

"Enough, Boris, enough! Stop it, stop it! He was already wounded, and now, with what you have done, he's as good as dead. Leave him alone, for God's sake." Orlov stared at her, looked down at White's blood on his hands, then he rummaged in his pocket for his loose change and threw it violently at the pinned man.

"Traitor! You betrayed us all, you bastard!" In shock, Anna scrambled back into the car, and watched as Orlov, soaked to the skin, continued to stand in front of White, shouting and haranguing his helpless victim. Minutes passed before Orlov collapsed to his knees, finally worn out by the day's ordeal.

Thirty yards away, hidden by the bushes near the turn-off, Maggie Buxton stood, a hooded figure, with her hand over her mouth, shocked and horrified by the events she had just witnessed. She decided that she had seen enough, and turned to sneak back to her car, which was parked back down the road. As she moved away from the bushes, she lost her footing in the rough ground, tried to regain her balance but only succeeded in skidding on the wet grass, crying out as she half-fell to the ground.

Orlov heard her soft cry, got to his feet quickly and pulled out his pistol from his jacket pocket. Anna crouched down in terror as he ran towards her car, then looked through the back window as he passed by. She opened the door, rushing after him and shouting "Boris!" A few seconds later, she saw him halt and steady himself before sending a single bullet at the fleeing figure. Maggie Buxton collapsed to the ground and lay still, as both Orlov and Anna rushed towards her. Orlov turned the body over and pushed the hood back, revealing Maggie's face. "It's a woman!" he exclaimed, turning to look at Anna, then reaching forward to find a pulse. Seconds later, he shook his head. "She's dead," he muttered. Anna stared at the dead woman, and put her hand over her mouth.

"Oh my God," she gasped, "she looks familiar, Boris. I think I have met this woman before." She knelt down and rummaged in the jacket pockets, finding a purse, a mobile phone and some car keys. She returned to her car, Orlov trailing behind her, and switched on the interior light. A quick glance at a couple of the cards confirmed her fears. "Margaret Buxton. Oh God, it is her."

"Who is she?"

"It's a long story, Boris, but she lives here in Scarborough. Well, *lived here.* The man I am living with, Karl ... she used to be his girlfriend, and since I moved here she has been very jealous. She once tried to attack me and to get me arrested."

"If that is correct, then the police know that she is linked to you. That's not good, Anna. We need to get rid of the body." Anna continued to look through Maggie's purse, holding up a small piece of lined paper, and showing it to Orlov.

"Look at this, Boris. This is the registration number of my car. She must have been following me, perhaps for days and, oh God, she must know that I am Karl's girlfriend, in disguise. I'm finished, Boris," she muttered, looking terrified.

"Be calm, Anna, let's think about this logically. This woman may have seen through your disguise, but she hasn't told the police that she knows who you really are. They would have arrested you by now if that were the case. My guess is that she's been following you, but hasn't told anyone else who you are. You're still safe, Anna, and remember that I killed her, not you." Anna started to cry, then started beating Orlov on his arms and shoulders, angry and very upset. He grabbed her arms and waited until she had calmed down.

"Oh Boris, why did she have to get involved and to get killed? My God, I love Karl and I want to stay here and, one day, to get married to him. I told all of this to Rudnev, and he agreed that I could remain in England and still work for Russia - like a mole, gathering information, perhaps the occasional assignment. I had trained for that, Boris, but now my dreams are shattered."

"I don't understand, Anna. We can easily get rid of the car and her body. If the police do find her, they will only find my bullet. They will think that she found me by accident, after I had dealt with White, and that I killed her to stop her from going to the police."

"I wish that were true, but the police are not stupid. When the police know that she is missing, they will link everything together. A Russian at White's house, this bloodbath here in the woods, and they will remember that she was involved with me, another Russian. No,

260

Boris, the police will understand everything. I may not have killed her, but I'm still finished here. I have to leave, and quickly. We need to finish everything here, then I will phone Rudnev. I have to get out of England as soon as possible." She turned and stared at Orlov. "This is your last chance, Boris. You still have time to return to Moscow with me." Boris thought for a short time.

"Nothing has changed for me, Anna. There's no future for me in Russia, and I have finished everything here. My dreams have been ruined, just like yours, but at least I have taken revenge on those who betrayed me and killed Stephanie and Tobolski. We have to decide what to do with the body and the car, then," he glanced at Anna, "do you remember what you told me in York if I refused to return to Russia with you?"

"I told you that I have been ordered to kill you."

"Exactly. We will decide what to with her," he pointed back at the body, "then you can complete your assignment. You have done well, Anna. A jealous woman will always complicate matters, but at least you will have carried out your main task to Moscow's satisfaction." He smiled. "Now, the most important thing to you is time. We have to work out how best to keep you ahead of the police." He looked towards the tree, where White's blood-soaked head had dropped and his body was hanging limply. "He's finished, Anna," he grinned at her, "now let's finish your business. Go to her car and drive it here, then we can get her body into the boot. After that, you are on your own. You need to dispose of me, making it look as if I have committed suicide after killing White.

Next, you need to drive that woman's car and park it in a street, somewhere not too far away because you have to walk back here. Throw her keys, purse and mobile into some rubbish bins, into the sea, whatever ... but get rid of them! After that you can phone Rudnev and drive to Manchester. He will arrange the flights."

Anna held her head in her hands, and looked totally shocked and exhausted. "I can't believe that all of this has happened. Just a short time ago, I was so happy and really looking forward to my life here with Karl. Now, all of that has gone." Suddenly she was calm. "You are right, Boris. I do not have a choice. I will do everything that you have explained, but before I leave here I must return to Karl's flat."

"You can't risk that, Anna, and there's no time to lose. You have to leave here as quickly as possible!"

"Don't worry, I have enough time. I will wait until Karl has left for work, then I will collect all of my belongings from the flat." She looked across at Orlov. "I can't say goodbye to him, but I'm determined not to leave any evidence in the flat for the police to find." She took a deep breath. "OK, Boris, I'm ready."

***

Early morning, dark clouds over Scarborough and still raining, though lighter than the grim evening before. Frank Porter eased his car to halt on Oliver's Mount, and turned to look at his pet Labrador sitting patiently on an old blanket on the back seat. "Five minutes, Jess old girl, that's all you're going to get. Run around a bit, then

I'll rub you dry and we'll get home for our breakfast." He smiled at the old dog, pausing as if he expected the animal to reply. "It might have stopped raining tonight, then we can have a good, long walk." He got out of the car, opened the back door and watched as the dog jumped out of the car and splashed towards a path between some bushes. He closed the door and got back quickly into the front, peering into the semi-darkness and waiting for his dog to return. The minutes passed, then he thought he could hear a noise. He wound down the window slightly and grimaced as he realised that it was Jess who was making all of the noise. "Shit!" he exclaimed, reaching for his coat from the other seat. "Bloody dog! Probably found a dead rat." *True, but not the kind he was expecting.* Porter pulled his hood over his head, closed his car door and trudged along the path towards the barking.

***

The phone in Don Bentley's lounge began ringing. "Bloody Hell!" he muttered through a slice of toast and marmalade, "can't get my breakfast in peace."

"Finish your breakfast, Don," his wife Jean smiled at him, putting down her mug on the kitchen table, "I'll get it." She walked through to the lounge, picked up the phone and listened for a few seconds. "You'd better listen to this quickly, Don!" she shouted, "it's Debbie Chapman." He hurried to the phone, chewing the last remnants of the toast.

"Debbie?"

"Sir, you need to get to Oliver's Mount as quickly as

263

you can. There's been a right bloodbath up there, looks like Nathaniel White and that Russian bloke."

"Orlov, you mean?" He could sense her nodding her head. "Have you contacted anyone else? No? OK, ring the team, and make sure that the uniforms keep the public well away from the scene. The rain will have washed away most of the evidence as it is."

"Alright, Sir, but hurry. They say it's horrendous. Looks like White's been fucking crucified."

"Crucified? What have we got now, the bloody Romans? I'm on my way, Debbie."

Ten minutes later, Bentley arrived at Oliver's Mount, and was guided into a parking area by one of the yellow-jacketed constables. He could see that a large area behind the cars had been taped off, with several other police vehicles parked nearby, and as Bentley watched a few onlookers and joggers were being politely turned away from the area by other constables. Bentley caught sight of Debbie Chapman and made his way towards the murder scene. It was getting lighter now, and the full horror of the events of the previous evening could be easily seen by all present.

"Christ, it's like a tableau from Madame Tussauds!" Sharpe quipped, but the others remained silent, staring from the edge of the clearing at the two corpses in the woods. White's body, totally sodden, covered in blood, sagged limply from the tree, whereas Orlov's body lay on the ground in a widening pool of blood, his pistol still clutched in his right hand.

Bentley spoke quietly to members of the SOC team, who were still setting up an awning to cover much of the crime scene, then he gathered his murder team around him. "I've told everyone that we're going back to the station. There's too many people here, the ground's bloody soaked right through, and we're going to lose valuable evidence if we're not careful. You don't need to be Poirot to work out what's happened here, so let's get back to town and start piecing everything together, to make sure that we've tied up all of the loose ends. I need a strong coffee." The others nodded silently, and they made their way back to their cars.

At the station, coffees had been passed around and there was a shell-shocked atmosphere in the incident room. The white-boards were half-empty, with room for photos and information from the latest killings on Oliver's Mount still to be displayed. Bentley waited until everyone was settled before opening the briefing.

"I can't remember two days like this," he said, pointing towards the white-boards, "and we've still more to add. It's been more like Chicago in Al Capone's time than sleepy old Scarborough." One or two brief smiles. "I know it's still early days, but I want to check through the events of the past couple of days and to see if we can make sense of it all … to make sure that we haven't missed anything obvious. I've been in touch with Jefferson in Leeds, and he's like a dog with two dicks at the moment." More smiles. "All of his top criminals wiped out in a couple of days, with no loss of life to the city population - he's a happy man."

"Just wait, it won't be long before another White or that one found in Whitby harbour …" Slater started to comment.

"Alan Murrell?" Ryan suggested.

"Yes, that's him," Slater continued, "well it won't be too long before another one steps forward to take White's place."

"Jefferson's well aware of that," Bentley took up the threads of the briefing again, "but at least he's ahead of the game for now. I've also been in touch with Maynard-Smith, that fellow from MI6. He was surprised that the Russians hadn't dealt with Boris Orlov, but he wasn't interested in the rest, just domestic crimes he reckoned. Still, he's coming to Scarborough tomorrow or the day after." He paused for thought. "We haven't been able to question Liz Coward yet, and I'm sure that in time she will be able to add a few pieces to the puzzle, but here is where I think we are. The weekend meeting at White's house is shelved. They have a mid-week emergency meeting instead, probably requested by Garrett and Orlov. My guess is that they felt confident and strong enough to go it alone, at least on the sex scene. Perhaps Orlov had contacts in Eastern Europe to develop the sex trade in Leeds. Whatever the reason, the meeting breaks up amicably, but on the way home Orlov's car crashes on a bend on the A570. Initial examination of the wrecked Renault suggests that the brakes were tampered with."

"White must have believed that he was strong enough to do without Orlov's muscle, and he tried to take them all out in one go." Sharpe looked for Bentley's approval.

"Exactly, but it failed. Ryan heard two cars leaving the house, so the second must have been White's men, following the Renault to make sure that everyone was killed. They must have grabbed Tobolski, who was badly injured, and took him back to the house to persuade him to tell them where Orlov was hiding. So far so good," Bentley paused for breath, "but the next bit doesn't make sense to me. Orlov survives the crash, gets himself back to the house, kills Masterman, kidnaps White and takes him to Oliver's Mount, where he crucifies him then shoots himself. All of that with no fucking car."

"Scarborough has a great bus service," Sharpe chipped in with a grin, but immediately turned away when the look on Bentley's face suggested that he was next in line for crucifixion.

"Back on planet Earth," Bentley continued slowly, "Orlov was a mixture of Superman and James Bond or …"

"He had an accomplice," Debbie Chapman concluded the sentence.

"Now we have to find out who," Bentley drained his coffee, pulled a face because it had gone cold, and rummaged in his pocket for a consoling jelly baby.

***

Anna rubbed her eyes, yawned again, and pushed back into the corner of the doorway. She shook her umbrella, hid underneath it again, then turned briefly as Karl emerged from the house they had shared. He pulled on a baseball hat, and headed for the town centre. Anna watched tearfully until he had disappeared from her view, paused for a few minutes to regain her composure, then moved quickly along and across the street, opened the front door and hurried upstairs. She entered the flat, paused and looked around, tears forming again in her eyes. *I was so happy here,* she thought to herself, *so happy.* She walked slowly through the flat, opening drawers, touching Karl's clothes, sitting on his side of the bed. She shuddered into floods of tears, took several deep breaths, then went into the bathroom and washed her face. Now she was settled. She had allowed herself about thirty minutes to shower, get changed and to pack all of her belongings in her large case. She didn't want to leave any trace of "Natasha" in the flat. When she had finished, she dressed in the same smart clothes she had worn when she met Rudnev in Manchester, then she double-checked everywhere in the flat, gazed at the harbour through the tiny window, took a last look at the bed, picked up her case and left the flat. A few minutes later, she was back at her car, which she had parked close to the harbour.

***

Bentley was busy in the incident room, assigning a variety of tasks to his team - setting up the whiteboards, interviewing possible witnesses, liaising with the forensics people, and so on. His phone rang, and he snatched at the handset. "Bentley."

"It's the desk, Sir. We have a lady down here who wishes to report a missing daughter."

"*That's the last thing I fucking need*," Bentley thought to himself, then "I'll send someone down," he spoke loudly into the phone. "Ryan, go downstairs and see to a Missing Person query." Ryan tidied the papers on his desk, then headed downstairs. He was back within ten minutes, and spoke urgently to Bentley.

"Listen up everyone," Bentley ordered. "There's been a new development. Ryan." He gestured him to speak to the team.

"I've just spoken to a lady downstairs, reporting her daughter missing. She told me that her daughter borrowed her father's car yesterday morning, and hasn't returned to the house. She did phone her mother in the evening, saying that she would be returning soon, but as yet she hasn't turned up."

Sharpe supplied the obvious answer. "She's got lucky, shagging a bloke somewhere."

"Sharpe, you're getting worse," warned Bentley. "Who is this woman?" Ryan looked at his notes.

"Margaret Buxton."

"Maggie Buxton," Chapman stood up suddenly, "she's that woman who assaulted that Russian girl on the promenade." She looked at Slater for confirmation, then around at the others. "Remember? She tried to claim that the Russian assaulted her, but it was the other way around." One or two heads nodded. "Her ex-boyfriend had dumped her after he met the Russian in Moscow, and now she's living over here."

"Russians again," fumed Bentley.

"There's more, Sir. Maggie Buxton told her mother to note down a car registration." He passed Bentley a piece of paper. "Debbie, Slater, get on the blowers and find out who owns this car," he passed over the piece of paper, "and get a general message out to look out for Maggie Buxton's car. It's a blue Ford Focus, and it's probably in town or nearby. Make it quick."

Within the hour, Debbie Chapman had some news for the team. "We've traced the owner of that car to a student in York ... a *Russian* student. The local plods have been in touch with her and she told them that the car was stolen a few days ago." She glanced at Bentley. "No news as yet about Buxton's car."

"I've just thought, Sir," Sharpe half-raised his hand, "could Buxton's car have been used by Orlov?"

"It must be one or the other," Bentley raged. "I don't like it, we seem to be having another Russian Revolution on my doorstep. Sharpe, get out a general alert for that student's car, a red Mondeo, wasn't it? Contact other forces in the North. Debbie, take Slater and Ryan and go and see that Russian girl in town, the one who was assaulted. Pick up her boyfriend before you go to her flat. Doesn't he work at a gift shop or something like that?"

"Yes, his family owns it."

"Right, then get a move on."

***

Karl was busy in the stockroom when the police arrived at the gift shop on Westborough. His mother opened the store door. "Karl, it's the police," she said anxiously. He furrowed his brows, put down the clipboard he had been using and followed through to the main shop.

"Morning," he said, smiling at Debbie Chapman. "We've met before, haven't we?" The shop was empty of customers, so Chapman started with her questions.

"Is your girlfriend here today, Mr Griffin?"

"Natasha, no, she's visiting some friends in Liverpool. She'll be back later this afternoon though. Why do you ask?" he dropped the smile.

"We've had a number of incidents in town during the past two days, you may have heard?" Karl shook his head, and looked across at his mother, who just shrugged her shoulders. "I won't go into details, Mr Griffin, but there appears to be a Russian link between them." Karl looked puzzled. "Has Natasha been to York recently?"

"Yes, she has as a matter of fact, last week sometime."

"The other thing, Mr Griffin, is that Margaret Buxton has been reported missing. Her father's car is missing as well."

"Maggie? Well I can tell you that we've had no contact at all with her since she tried to accuse Natasha of assaulting her. We've not seen her," he added angrily.

"Would you mind if we have a look around your flat, Mr Griffin? There just might be something that will help us with our enquiries."

"Not a problem. We've got nothing to hide." He looked for his jacket. "Hold the fort, Mam. I won't be long." He turned to the police officers. "It's only a short walk away."

Within ten minutes, they had reached Karl's house. "I can't see that you'll find anything here," he said, unlocking the front door, "but of course you're welcome to look. Anything to help. My flat is on the top floor, the other flats are empty, just holiday lets." He led the way upstairs. "Here we go," he said, opening the door to his flat. "There aren't many rooms, the bathroom's over there and the bedroom is through that door," he said, pointing in various directions. "Would any of you like a drink?"

"We're fine, thank you," Chapman answered. "Where does Natasha keep her clothes, Mr Griffin?" He led them to a wardrobe.

"In here, and she has some things in those drawers. There's a large suitcase somewhere." He began searching for the case, as Chapman peered in the wardrobe.

"Has she taken everything with her, Mr Griffin?"

"What do you mean?" Karl asked looking puzzled, and checking the wardrobe, then the drawers. "Where …?" He looked in the bathroom. "I can't understand it," he muttered, looking at the three officers in turn, "there's nothing here, nothing at all. Natasha's gone," he said, walking slowly over to the window and staring out at the harbour. "My Snow Maiden has vanished," he whispered softly.

***

There was a buzz around the incident room as Debbie

Chapman spoke quietly to Don Bentley. He nodded occasionally as she outlined the police visit to Karl Griffin's flat, then stood up to address the team. "More developments, everybody, this is a fast-moving case. Debbie and Co have seen Karl Griffin and checked his flat, and there is no trace of Natasha Petrova, or whoever she really is. No trace at all. He last saw her two days ago, when she told him that she was going by train to visit friends in Liverpool. That, we now know, is a load of bollocks. My guess is that she was involved in some way in the murders of the past couple of days, probably using that red Mondeo which was "stolen" or otherwise from that Russian student in York. There seems to have been some kind of Russian conspiracy at work right under our bloody feet! Anyway, I've sent over some forensics to check Griffin's flat for this Natasha's fingerprints, then we'll be able to see if she left any in White's house or on Oliver's Mount. In the meantime, we're still waiting for sightings of the red Mondeo … Sharpie?"

"Nothing as yet, Sir. I've contacted all of the northern forces so far."

"What about the airports, Sir?" Ryan added.

"What do we tell them?" Debbie Chapman asked. "That Russian girl is sure to have changed her appearance, and we don't know her real name."

"True, but they can still look out for that car. If we turn up hard evidence that she was at one or both of the murder scenes, then we can release a nationwide alert for her – wanted for murder!" Bentley glanced back down at his notes. "What about the other car, and Margaret Buxton?" A few shakes of the head. "Nothing? I'm convinced that the car must be hidden around here. Get back to the plods, Sharpe, and tell them to check every blue car in town, and to look in a few garages."

"I'll get onto it right now," Sharpe reached for his phone.

"Any news from the murder scenes?"

"They're still doing tests," a voice answered from the back, "but preliminary results suggest that the same gun was used to kill Jim Masterman, to wound White and to kill Orlov."

"Orlov's gun?"

"We presume it was. We've accounted for five bullets, but six were used. There were only two bullets left in the cartridge."

"He might have practised on a seagull," Chapman joked.

"Let's hope that's all it was," Bentley muttered, looking down again at his notes. "Any news from the hospital?" he said, looking at George Ryan."

"I visited Liz last night, but she's still heavily sedated. She may be up to a few questions tomorrow."

"OK, that's all for now. Let's hope we get a lead on one of the cars soon."

***

Mid-afternoon. The incident room was quiet, everyone going about their various tasks quietly, concentrating hard. A phone rang, and Sharpe answered it, listening for just a few seconds. "They've found Maggie Buxton's car, in Weaponness, and are on their way to her father's house to collect a spare key." Ryan looked puzzled. "Weaponness, George, is an area of town close to Oliver's Mount." Ryan nodded *thanks*.

"Sharpe, Slater, stay here. Give me a call *immediately* if there's any news about that other car, and get forensics over to Buxton's car as quickly as possible. The rest of you, with me!"

Bentley arrived to find a patrol car parked near Maggie Buxton's car, with two yellow-coated constables keeping watch. One of the over-stretched SOC team arrived from Oliver's Mount and parked behind Bentley's car. Bentley glanced at him as he got out of the car, and said: "At least it's stopped raining. You can do the honours, Brodie. Who's got the key?" One of the constables waited until Brodie had donned new gloves, then passed him the key. He walked around the Ford Focus, opening each of the four doors carefully, then moved around the back of the car to open the boot. The lid sprung back, revealing Maggie Buxton's sodden and blood-soaked body.

"Jesus Christ!" Chapman exclaimed as Bentley edged forward for a closer look. Ryan joined him and peered down at Maggie Buxton's back.

"There's our sixth bullet, Ryan. Now all we have to do is to find out who fired it. Call the SOC squad over at Oliver's Mount, Debbie, and tell them where to come next." Bentley's mobile sounded, and he listened intently. "No rest for the wicked," he sighed, turning to the two constables. "Stay here until the SOC team arrive, OK? Get some tape around the car, and keep all nosey bastards well clear … understand?" He looked at Chapman, Ryan and the others. "You lot, let's get back to the station. They've found the red Mondeo, somewhere in Manchester."

"They found it in a car park in the city centre," Sharpe announced, as the team re-assembled back in the incident room. "Empty, of course, and they're looking for any decent prints."

"Manchester," George Ryan thought for a minute, "it can only be the airport, Sir."

"You're probably right, Ryan, and our bird has flown. I'd hazard a guess that she's not on her own. These bloody Russians are everywhere, it seems." He sat down at his desk, exhausted and disappointed when he realised that his pockets were empty. He beckoned Ryan as the team drifted away. "You must be worried about Liz, George, so how is she really?"

"As I said before, Sir, she's still sedated, but I manged to have a few words with her. The doctors told me that she'll mend."

"She's the lucky one, George." He paused for a few seconds. "Would you like to come around to my house for tea? Jean's making stew and dumplings."

"That would be lovely, Sir, thank you," Ryan replied, smiling.

"Six o'clock on the dot, lad, don't be late."

CHAPTER THIRTY
SCARBOROUGH

Karl was serving a customer when the phone rang. The assistant was in the store, so Karl picked up the receiver and heard DI Bentley's distinctive voice.

"Sorry to disturb you, Mr Griffin, but I wondered if you would come to the station, just to tie up a few loose ends?"

"When, Inspector?"

"Today, if possible, anytime that's convenient for you."

"I'll phone my mother and see if she can cover for me, then I'll drop in."

"Thank you very much. I'll look forward to seeing you later." Click.

Loose ends? The papers had been full of the multiple murders for the past few days. Karl wondered what else there could be.

Karl arrived at the station just after lunch, and was shepherded to a downstairs interview room. A few minutes later, Don Bentley and DC Slater joined him.

"Thanks for sparing us some of your time, Mr Griffin."

"Karl, please. I'm happy to help, but how?"

"I'm sure that you've seen all of the gory headlines in

the papers and on the news over this past week? You may have noticed that we've kept "Natasha", we'll call her, out of the headlines, partly out of respect for your privacy, but also because we don't really know who she is and will probably never know fully what part she played in the recent events here and elsewhere." Bentley took a moment to gather his thoughts. "As I told you this morning, Karl, we're trying to tie up some loose ends. We found the car that Natasha was using in a Manchester car park last Thursday afternoon. There's been no sighting of her since then, and we assume that she's left the country. We asked the security people at Manchester Airport to send us any footage they had from Thursday afternoon and evening, to see if there is any trace of her. We know that there is no "Natasha Petrova" on any of the passenger lists, but if she did fly out of the country then, she'd be using another name. We have got some details of possible Russian or Eastern European passengers on that day, but it would be a great help if you could scan some of the footage and see if you can recognise her. Would that be OK?"

"Of course, no problem."

"This could take some time, but DC Slater will flick through the tapes with you and pause if you spot a passenger who looks familiar. I think he can enlarge the picture for you … right, Slater?"

"Yes, Sir, I can do that."

"Excellent, so I'll leave you with DC Slater. I don't want to breathe down your neck, so please take your time, and he will call me if you think you've found something. OK?" Karl nodded, and watched as Slater loaded the first tape.

"There are a few tapes to view, Karl, but I'll fast-forward when necessary to save some of your time. Ready?"

The time passed slowly, and Karl began to get bleary-eyed with staring at a huge mixture of humanity. "God!" he muttered at one point, "I hadn't realised that so many people used the airport!" He rubbed his eyes.

"I'll order some coffee," Slater said. "Relax and have a break." He left the room, returning after a couple of minutes, and soon afterwards a WPC arrived carrying a tray with drinks and biscuits.

"Thanks, Anne," Slater smiled at her. All was quiet for a few minutes as the two men drank their coffee. "How are you after last week's events, Karl?" Slater asked.

"Getting over it now, I suppose," Karl smiled briefly. "It was a hell of a shock at the time. You think you know the person you're living with, but not this time. I still find it hard to believe. It's like a dream, but I don't mind admitting that I miss Natasha terribly. I thought we were going to spend the rest of our lives together." Slater gave him a sympathetic smile.

"With my job, you get used to shattered dreams, you know, people not being what they appear to be." He finished his coffee. "Are you ready for the next tape?"

"Yes, let's crack on." Slater switched on the machine. Minutes passed, half an hour or more, then Karl sat up suddenly and gestured for Slater to pause the tape.

A couple could be seen clearly on the screen, an older man and a younger woman, dressed elegantly in black, with black hair and dark glasses. As they approached the desk, the woman removed her glasses and looked up at the camera, smiling. Karl gasped, as the woman appeared to be smiling directly at him. "Can you focus on the woman, please?" he asked Slater. The policeman enlarged that part of the screen, and Karl peered closely at the smiling woman. He sat back, clearly shocked. "That's Natasha," he said dejectedly. Slater phoned for Bentley to return to the room. He looked at the screen, then at Karl.

"Are you sure, Karl?"

"Definitely, Inspector. Natasha is blonde, but she's wearing a dark wig here."

"How certain are you that it's her?"

"Absolutely certain. Do you see the pendant she's wearing? It's a rare Whitby jet sunburst pendant, and I bought it for her last Christmas. That's definitely Natasha."

"Which tape is that, Slater?" The DC looked at the information on the tape.

"These were the passengers for the KLM afternoon flight to Amsterdam, Sir."

"The Netherlands, eh? We have a full passenger list for that flight, but there's no rush to check. You can bet your bottom dollar that they were travelling on false passports, perhaps not even Russian ones. OK, Slater?" He turned to address Karl. "Many thanks again, Mr Griffin, for taking the time to help us with our enquiries. I think that should be all for now." He smiled at Karl, who was still sitting down, staring at the screen.

Was it just his imagination, or was Natasha looking up at him, smiling as she always did, saying a final goodbye? Karl continued staring at the screen until Bentley touched his shoulder gently, and ushered him out of the room.

PART TWO
MARCH 2012

CHAPTER THIRTY-ONE

MOSCOW

Karl returned to the table with two more glasses of orange juice, and pushed one of them across to the attractive blonde woman sitting opposite him.

"Thanks," she smiled, taking a sip. "So, what's on the agenda today, my wonderful guide?" She looked thoughtful. "Let me guess - a visit to an even bigger monastery, or is it a trip on the Trans-Siberian Express, or perhaps even a flight on Sputnik to the Moon!"

"Very funny, Rosie, very drole," Karl smiled thinly. "Look, it was your choice to spend our honeymoon in Russia, but if you remember correctly, I did suggest Egypt."

"True, so I could have spent the past four days being dragged around lots of ancient monuments in the heat, instead of the cold?" They both laughed. "I'm only joking, Karl, but I'm knackered. It's our last day in Moscow before moving on to St Petersburg tonight, and I'm really looking forward to seeing everything there, but can we just have a little bit of a rest today … please?" she pouted pleadingly. Karl pretended to give the idea some thought, then he grinned.

"No need to worry, flower, because I've already planned

a different day - we're going shopping!"

"Oh great, not for more of those bloody nesting dolls?"

"No, proper shopping, your kind of shopping. I had a word yesterday with one of the girls on Reception, and today I'm taking you to the huge shopping centre at the Alexander Gardens. It's sounds like a fabulous underground version of the Trafford Centre, and it's only a short walk from our hotel! I think we can spend a couple of hours in there before coming back and relaxing in the hotel, don't you?"

"Fantastic! What a lovely surprise," she said, draining her orange juice and looking across the table. "Have you finished?" Karl nodded, smiling at her newly-found energy and enthusiasm. "Good, because I need to polish my credit card!"

**

Three hours later, Karl was beginning to regret his suggestion to take Rosie on a shopping trip. Outside, it was a lovely spring day in Moscow, with light cloud cover, some blue sky and warmer temperatures. Groups of people were wandering around the Alexander Gardens, visiting the Tomb of the Unknown Soldier or simply enjoying the sight of the winter snow beginning to melt away, revealing the green shoots of the brief Moscow spring. Inside the Manezhnaya Shopping Centre, however, Karl had long ceased to admire the beauty of its construction, with its marbled floors and stained-glass panels, but was struggling with the heat and stifling atmosphere everywhere they walked. Rosie, a hardened shopaholic, seemed oblivious to Karl's discomfort and managed to keep flitting from one international branded shop to the next, occasionally dumping another colourful carrier bag into his arms and smiling sweetly.

"I'm flagging," he explained as she slotted yet another package onto his right hand, "really flagging. It's so bloody hot in here. Can we have a break?" Rosie paused, looking as if she had noticed his presence for the first time, then glanced along the corridor.

"I'll just finish along here," she announced with a flourish of her left arm, "then we'll go and have a drink in the Food Hall that we passed before."

"About an hour ago," he said defeatedly. He peered towards the end of the corridor, and his face brightened up. "I think there's a bench at the end of this section, Rosie, so I'll wait for you there." He turned for her approval, but she had already entered the next shop. Karl staggered towards the bench and flopped down, steadying his various bags carefully. He looked around, and a corner store caught his eye.

VARYKINO

Varykino? Karl thought for a moment, *wasn't that the winter palace in "Dr Zhivago"?* He placed his collection of carrier bags carefully on the floor, and walked slowly to the store, looking at a wide range of traditional crafts and gifts neatly displayed in the window, then gazing beyond into the store. It was like an Aladdin's Cave of riches. *At last, an interesting shop!* A few customers were wandering around inside the store, and Karl could see two assistants, dressed brightly in regional costumes. There was no sign of Rosie, so he retrieved his carrier bags and entered the store. One of the assistants, an older blonde woman, dressed in blue and white, smiled at him and said "Hello". Karl nodded, and began looking around at the myriad of goods for sale. A large glass cabinet caught his attention, and he moved over to gaze at an impressive display of Russian lacquered boxes. They were priced in US dollars and looked expensive, but of excellent quality. Karl studied the collection carefully, thinking to himself: *One of these would make a nice souvenir of our honeymoon.* He focused on two of the boxes – a large square box depicting the *Firebird* tale, and an oblong box showing the *Snow Maiden,* dressed in a vivid blue costume. Karl looked around, and saw a dark-haired assistant at the counter. She was wearing a long dress in red, gold and white, with a cap to match. He walked towards her, smiled and asked: "May I see two of your lacquered boxes?"

"Of course," she replied, smiling and opened a drawer for the cabinet key. She followed Karl back to the cabinet and asked: "Which boxes would you like to see, Sir?" Karl glanced at her, noticing her attractive face, and pointed in the cabinet.

"Er, the *Firebird* box, and that one with the *Snow Maiden* design, please." He studied the woman as she unlocked the cabinet and reached carefully for the two boxes. *There's something about her, something familiar,* he thought, as they returned to the counter. She moved to the back of the counter and placed both boxes down, so that Karl could study them more closely.

"Please," she smiled briefly, and gestured to the two boxes. Karl stared at her for a few seconds, until she looked away, then he picked up each box in turn, placing them back down on the counter. The assistant was still smiling, and he looked at her again – tall, slim, attractive, but with dark hair. The store door opened suddenly, and a beautiful blonde-haired teenage girl stepped out and began talking quickly to the assistant in Russian. Karl gasped, hearing the word *Mama,* and he stepped back a pace and felt faint.

He looked down again at the boxes. "I'll take the *Snow Maiden* box, please," he muttered, wiping his brow and handing his credit card to the dark-haired woman wearing the colourful costume. He scribbled his signature on the receipt and looked up as the young girl turned, smiled straight at him and gently touched the Whitby jet starburst pendant hanging around her neck. Her mother smiled as she returned his card, and Karl swayed for a second or two. "Wrap it, please, while I go and look for my wife." He picked up the carrier bags and staggered to the door, looking back at Natasha and her daughter, who were both still smiling *beautifully* at him. He managed to make it back to the bench, where he collapsed, clinging onto the bags, opening his coat and wiping the sweat off his brow once more. A few minutes passed before Rosie arrived, clutching yet another purchase.

"Jesus, Karl, what's the matter with you? You look as if you've just seen a ghost. Are you alright?"

"It's just so hot in here. I feel a little faint, need a drink."

"Come on then, we'll find that Food Hall."

"Just a minute, Rosie," Karl muttered, standing up. "I bought something in that souvenir store, it's getting wrapped. I won't be a minute."

"I'll come with you," she said, looking concerned, "you look as if you might collapse at any time." She helped him walk slowly back to the store, and they headed for the counter. The blonde-haired assistant, dressed in blue and white, was standing behind the counter.

"Ah, you have returned for your box, Sir," she said, smiling. "Here it is." She held up a brightly-wrapped parcel.

Karl glanced back at Rosie, who was looking around some of the displays, then at the woman behind the counter. "The dark-haired lady, and the blonde girl, are …?"

"I'm sorry, Sir, there's only me here today."

"But when I was in before, they were here, behind the counter," he stammered, looking worried. "My *Snow Maiden* …"

"Your *Snow Maiden* box is in here, Sir," she smiled, pointing at the parcel, and handing it to him. "Look outside, Sir, it is spring and the Snow Maiden has melted away." She continued smiling as Rosie arrived at the counter and stared at her husband.

"Close your mouth, Karl, before you catch a fly!" she said laughing. "Sorry," she apologised to the assistant, "he's not used to shopping," and she helped him out of the store.

CHAPTER THIRTY-TWO
SOUTHPORT

"Almost the end of the Easter holidays, Karl, and back to work on Monday," Rosie sighed. "It's hard to believe that we've been on a magical honeymoon to Russia, and that in a couple of days we're back to our daily routine, just as if nothing has happened." She glanced over to her husband, who hadn't seemed to listen to a word she had said. "I'm nipping out for an hour or so. I need one or two new blouses for work, and some other bits and pieces. I want to get everything sorted today, so that we can enjoy the weekend before we get back to work. OK?" Karl at last responded.

"Oh, that's fine, Rosie. You carry on, I've got a lot of paperwork to check before Monday, so I want to get on with it. I don't need anything in town, but I wouldn't mind a meal out somewhere tonight."

"Are you fed up of my cooking already?" she joked, and Karl laughed.

"No, of course not, it's just like you said before, let's enjoy our last couple of days before we return to reality on Monday."

"Alright," she said, putting on her coat, "I'll catch you later. Book somewhere for a meal, will you?" Karl waved, and looked for the phone book.

Return to reality? he thought, as soon as she had closed the front door. *What reality?* For the past fifteen years Karl had tried to put his relationship with Natasha to the back of his mind, to convince himself that it had never happened, that the Snow Maiden was just a Russian fairy tale. He had moved on. He decided to follow a career in teaching, had attended a teacher training college in Manchester for a year, and had taught Geography in schools in Manchester, Liverpool and Southport. He was now Deputy Head of a large comprehensive school in Southport, and was enjoying the challenges of the job. His parents had been disappointed when he told them that he was leaving the family business, but they had supported his decision to follow a career in teaching and had sold their shops. Karl's father had died four years ago and he had tried to persuade his mother to move to the Lancashire coast, but she still enjoyed good health and was reluctant to leave her friends in Scarborough. She now lived in a comfortable bungalow in the town, and Karl and Rosie visited her every two or three weeks. Karl's mother still owned the holiday lets in Scarborough, but he had not been inside them since leaving his flat in 1997. He planned to sell the properties when his mother died.

Karl and Rosie had met in Southport two years ago. She was enjoying a weekend break with friends in the town, and Karl spotted her in a local pub. She was a primary school teacher in Widnes, so they lived fairly close to each other and their romance had blossomed.

Karl had avoided steady relationships after his experience with Maggie Buxton and his romance with Natasha, and indeed his Snow Maiden had become a very distant memory until Rosie had suggested that they honeymoon in Russia. She knew that he had visited Moscow before, but had been told virtually nothing about the events of 1996-7.

The chance meeting with Natasha and her daughter, *his daughter,* continued to sadden and to haunt him, and Karl found it difficult to concentrate on his paperwork for school. He was looking forward to returning to school on the following Monday, and to keeping busy to take his mind off Moscow, to make Natasha a distant memory once more. After spending the best part of an hour on his paperwork, Karl went through his wardrobe, making sure that he sufficient work clothes for the following week or so. His hands brushed against the heavy fleece-lined coat he had worn in Russian and touched something solid in the inside zipped pocket. The parcel! The Snow Maiden box! He had forgotten all about the purchase he had made, but he now unzipped the pocket and took out the colourful parcel. He carefully unwrapped it and gazed at the beauty of the workmanship of the lacquer artist. The Snow Maiden smiled at him and she even had blonde hair. He opened the lid to examine the typical dark red interior, and a small piece of paper fell onto the carpet. He unfolded it, and read the juvenile handwriting:

> Papa
> One day I will come to
> England and find you.
>   Lara x

Karl took a deep breath, thinking furiously. Lara! His beautiful daughter! When he first met Natasha in that Russian village, he had told her that his favourite Russian name was Lara, and she had remembered! Karl sat down on the edge of the bed, stared at the piece of paper again, then slowly grinned from ear to ear.

THE END

Bentley and Ryan will return ... soon!

THE SNOW MAIDEN TALE

The tale of the Snow Maiden (or *Snegurushka*) may have its roots in Slavic mythology or in the general European oral tradition, but the first written version of the tale appeared in 1869. Alexander Afanasyev described how a childless peasant couple, Ivan and Maria, made a doll out of snow and she grew into a beautiful girl and made friends with the other girls in the village. One day, whilst jumping through a fire in the forest, the Snow Maiden evaporated into a cloud.

Another version of the tale has her as the daughter of Ded Moroz (or Father Frost, a kind of Santa figure) and as she grows up she meets a shepherd called Lel, but doesn't know how to fall in love with him. Her mother gives her the gift of love, but when she falls in love with Lel, her heart melts and she dies.

The Snow Maiden tale was developed into a play in 1873, with music by Pyotr Tchaikovsky, and into an opera in 1880-1 by Rimsky-Korsakov.

In more recent times, the Snow Maiden has become associated with Christmas, where she is seen as the granddaughter and helper of Father Frost, and wooden ornaments of the Snow Maiden, in a variety of colours, have become popular Christmas decorations.

I have taken some liberties with traditional versions of the tale, but essentially, my Snow Maiden appears with the first snows of the year, falls in love, and melts away in the spring!

ACKNOWLEDGEMENTS

Some of the inspiration for this book came from my many visits to Russia between 1986 and 2005, and I have to thank Ludmila, Sergei, Taissiya and many others for the friendship and generosity they showed me, particularly when I stayed in their homes. I have dedicated this novel to my friends in Russia.

My thanks also go to my cousin Phil, for his advice on nautical matters; to Steve Johnston, for providing invaluable information on police matters; to Chloe Morris, for agreeing to be the lovely Snow Maiden on the front cover; and to Russ Holden, for once again making a great job of putting this book together.

Finally, I wish to give members of my family and many of my friends a big pat on the back for continuing to support my quest to get all of this nonsense out of my head!

Naomi Hudson is married with two daughters and four grandchildren. She lives in south Cumbria. Following a varied career in teaching and other pursuits, she began writing only five years ago. She has written several Lakeland topographical books, and her first novel, "Bluebell", a romantic quest, was published towards the end of 2015. Another, "Aphrodite's Curse", a tale of seduction and murder, was published in 2016. "Snow Maiden" is her third novel. All are set in Yorkshire.

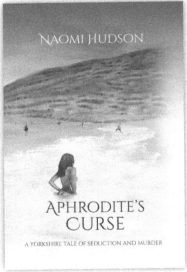

The author may be contacted at <u>bluebellnovel1@gmail.com</u>, or on Facebook under Naomi Hudson (Bluebell author). Her books are available on Amazon and on Kindle. (2015)

Milton Keynes UK
Ingram Content Group UK Ltd.
UKHW021157271124
3180UKWH00044B/435

9 780995 619098